Nineteen-year-old Lucas Burke prefers being alone. He likes the silence, and he loves not having to care about anyone else's problems: the less he's forced to feel, the better. But after a year of college-induced isolation from everyone he used to know, the wedding of a former classmate sends Lucas back home, and that means reconciling with a group of friends that now might as well be strangers.

His sister hardly knows him, his "genius" best friend is nothing more than an addict, and his ex-boyfriend is still in a coma. All the while, wedding preparations send Lucas head first into a relationship with the groom's best man—a recently cancer-free ex-Olympian who can't stop talking.

Lucas knows that if he wants to survive the summer, he'll have to learn to be a friend again, but it doesn't come easy, and it might already be too late.

PERMANENT JET LAG

A.N. Casey

Copyright 2017 by A.N. Casey

Published by
NineStar Press
PO Box 91792
Albuquerque, New Mexico, 87199
www.ninestarpress.com

Warning: This book contains a character death and mention of cancer and alcoholism.

Print ISBN # 978-1-947139-11-4
Cover by Natasha Snow
Edited by Sam Lamb

To Kathy, Elly, and my family who always believed in me,
and to Hanf who taught me to believe in myself.
To Lisa and Kirsten, for without their feedback and dedication,
this story never would have existed.

One

96 DAYS BEFORE

On the last day of my freshman year of college, my parents—dressed head to toe in the obnoxious green and gold colors of my school—arrived on the threshold of my dorm room with five extra-large boxes for packing, a tin of mom-baked chocolate chip cookies to cure my assumed "home sick blues," and two snippets of hometown gossip for my ears only. When you leave home for college, there's a certain assumption that says you will learn to be independent. You do your own laundry, you buy your own meals, and your parents never come knocking on your door to ask if you've done your homework or to ground you for coming home past curfew. You're alone—blissfully independent and free.

My mother had other ideas. Ideas that filled the voicemail on my cell phone until I could no longer receive friends' missed calls. Ideas that left a pile of cookie tins in the corner of the room and a dozen more care packages under the bed. Even now, as I finished the bulk of my packing, a poorly knit mom-made sweater hung limp over the side of the latest care package, threads unraveling and fraying in every direction with a note pinned to its sleeve with words I could not remember—words I likely never read.

My roommate sat on the other side of the room upon his stripped-down bed, munching away at the first cookie handed to him. He wore a thick pair of headphones that flattened his usually unruly brown hair. Though the cord was not connected to anything, my mother seemed pleased with this sense of security and began her "top secret" gossip. As though my roommate would care at all about the small-town news of Franklin Creek, California.

"Rylie Graham is getting married!" she squealed. Despite her rising age, my mother's face still lit up with all the excitement and energy of the young woman I could just barely remember from the photographs on the walls at home. Today, my mother was plump and nearly always flushed in her cheeks. The freckles on her nose were faded underneath a splotchy tan that extended only to the bottom of her neck, and her clothes, though neatly pressed, still appeared crumpled by her slouch and the endless movement of her limbs. She went on and on about the wedding, the beautiful invitations, and the color schemes she hoped they'd use, how she could still remember Rylie as a baby, crawling around at the neighborhood block parties.

I was already aware of this news, of course. The invitation had arrived in the mail two days ago, vividly pink with a handful of red hearts and almost a dozen purple and green flowers decorating the edges. Unless the groom was a botanist, there was no inkling of his presence in the design. To top it off, at the very bottom of the paper, beneath the RSVP notification, was a dried crimson lipstick mark. Nine months since I'd seen her, and I could still vividly imagine Rylie prepping her mouth with that darkened color she had so adored in high school and kissing each invitation one by one.

The invitation was now crumpled up in my suitcase with the rest of my belongings, but the image of it had not left my mind for a second.

"Isn't it great, Lucas?" my mother asked, and I nodded. "She'll look so beautiful as a bride." Another nod. "Just wait until you meet the groom. What a charming young man." At this, I fidgeted with the zipper on my luggage and forced a smile.

My father, lounging lazily upon my still-sheeted bed, gave me a knowing smile over the top of his third cookie. My mother promptly smacked it out of his hand.

"That's enough, Tim. Didn't you hear a word the doctors said? I think one heart attack is quite enough for one year, don't you?"

"I thought two would make a more interesting story at this year's Christmas party," my father replied, grinning.

And so began an argument that lasted through the remainder of my packing, the long trek downstairs, and into the oversized van waiting for us in the parking lot. It continued as my father stabbed the key into the ignition, as my mother pulled on her seat belt, and as I peered through the window and watched San Francisco—all its big buildings and bustling bridges—disappear into the night.

By the time we pulled into the driveway of my childhood home, my parents were just progressing toward the makeup phase of their disagreement, or, as I'd dubbed it over the years, the honeymoon period. They sat, arms tangled in the front seat, kissing and whispering loving platitudes into each other's mouths with such nauseating enthusiasm that sitting through it was quite like staring at the sun: tolerance came in small doses. I left the car and dragged my luggage up the porch steps alone.

I had come home exactly twice since leaving for college, once for spring break and once after my father's heart attack, and I was greeted the same each time. Homecoming generally went like this: my oldest sister, now sixteen, would nod her head in my direction over the top of her cell phone, give me a hug if I came close enough, and then resume her texting. My brothers, identical in all but their clothing, would rush in for the tackle. And my youngest sister would wave from the couch—a simple twist of her hand—and then return to her TV show. Today it was an old rerun about a teenage spy, and because the theme song was particularly catchy, the wave was even shorter than normal, barely a twitch of her fingertips.

I disappeared into my room.

FROM THE WINDOW of my dorm room in the mornings, I could see the wide expanse of the San Francisco landscape for miles, a hundred buildings huddled together against the fading fog, life bustling below. From the window of my hometown bedroom, I could see the neighbor's pool. A thoroughly unexciting, lifeless pool. As summer had not technically begun, the water that would soon promise endless good times and relief from the heat was still currently abandoned. A heavy pile of leaves covered much of the surface, but through the spaces between, I could make out a glimpse of the water—a murky, untouched green.

Rylie called at half past eleven while I was cleaning the windowsill for the second time. Her voice was shrill and rushed as she screamed into my ear, "Why didn't you tell me you were home? I had to hear it from my mom, who heard it from your mom, and I feel like I'm in a weird stupid sitcom, because I'm not supposed to be hearing gossip from your mother, Lucas. You're supposed to tell your friends when you come home. Clay is pissed."

As she spoke, I tucked the phone between my shoulder and ear. Downstairs, my mom was yelling at the twins, and Dad was swearing about the score of a baseball game. I retreated farther into my room and closed the door.

"Sorry," I said.

"Sorry?" Rylie let out a long, exasperated sigh, and I thought I could hear her nails tapping against the back of her phone. "Will you meet me somewhere? I haven't seen you in ages, and everyone misses you. Please?"

"Okay."

"Is this how this is going to be now? One-worded conversations?"

"Probably."

Rylie laughed, a deep, chest-rattling sort of sound that in no way matched the high, squeaky pitch of her voice. It was for reasons like this I'd stopped trying to understand her in the third grade.

"You're an ass, Lucas. Meet me at the flower shop across from the grocery store, okay? Ten minutes, don't be late. Oh, and Todney is going to be there. I can't wait for you to meet him. Don't be late."

"We have a grocery store?"

"Goodbye, Lucas."

THE FLOWER SHOP across from the grocery store was a hole in the wall sort of place, stuffed between a liquor store and a dress boutique. There was just one small sign above the cramped door in an almost illegible cursive.

Rylie stood inside, the picture-perfect image of everything I'd always remembered her to be. Rylie was the sort of girl who was unfairly in tune with her body, so whether she was standing, sitting, or falling—drunk—down a flight of stairs at high school graduation, she always managed to come across as prim and proper. She stood now, back straight and her head up with the sort of modelesque posture that looked just natural enough that you knew it was forced. She wore sweats, her hair was tied up in a messy bun, and apart from the crimson red lipstick that was her signature mark, she did not wear a drop of makeup.

Beside Rylie stood a man I could only assume was the new fiancé, as he held her hand and stared at her with the love-struck gaze of a dating show contestant. He had dark brown skin and light brown eyes and wore a shirt so blue it seemed out of place next to all the pink flowers. Like Rylie, his back was straight as a pole, but less naturally so; every few seconds, he looked her over from head to toe and then readjusted his stance.

"You're late," Rylie said as I approached, but she was smiling. As I drew close, she threw her arms around my neck and hugged the breath right out of my lungs. "I missed you," she whispered. She pressed a kiss to my temple and then pulled away.

"I'm Todney," offered her fiancé. He thrust out his hand, and I was immediately introduced to the tightest and yet most enthusiastic handshake of my life. "Rylie has told me all about you. The big-city man. The one who got away."

"Literally," Rylie said. "He got out of the prison that is this beautiful, beautiful town." With each word, she picked out a different flower from around the shop and then gathered them all together like a bouquet. "What do you think?" she asked, holding them close to her chest.

I tried to imagine her walking down the aisle with the flowers in hand, maybe in some elaborate, flowing dress, but all I could see was a red carpet at her feet. "They're great."

Todney nodded his agreement. "Perfect." His small eyes widened in puppylike excitement, and he kissed Rylie with all the vigor and desperation of a soldier leaving for war. She returned the gesture immediately, her surprisingly large hands rushing to grasp at his chest and dig her fingertips into his T-shirt.

I had just enough time to wonder, briefly, what sort of chemical malfunction occurred in the minds of lovers that made them exchange spit quite so eagerly, before the door to the back room flew open and the most beautiful man I'd ever seen staggered out.

Now, I was in no habit of calling men beautiful, and in fact, the word was hardly part of my vocabulary at all. But there was no other way to describe him. Deep brown eyes, a jaw better than Superman, and a T-shirt on just the right side of too-small; he was completely, pant-tightening-ly beautiful. So I did what any normal, casual observer would do; I stared.

Clothes wrinkled and ripped, his dark brown hair sticking up in every direction, the new arrival was probably three inches, at least, shorter than I was, and yet he stood with a heightened presence that left me dwarfed in comparison. Like he owned the shop or the town or the whole damn world for that matter.

"So the florist says no tulips, and there are none in the back. I checked myself," he said, each word tumbling over the last in quick succession, his hands fluttering around as though to conduct an orchestra with each syllable. He gestured in my direction, treating me to the show.

"This the jailbird?" he asked. "Landon? Lillipher? What? It could be the masculine version of Lilly." Our eyes locked, and he smiled a great toothy smile.

Because I'm no romantic and not nearly pathetic enough to care, I did not imagine the look to mean anything. I told myself that strangers always smiled at strangers like that, and it was absurd to think otherwise. As would be thinking he was actually talking to me. I quickly closed my mouth, two syllables toward a reply, when he turned to Rylie instead.

"Lucas. And yes, that's him." Rylie rolled her eyes. Somewhere in my distraction, she'd swept up a new bouquet and was walking in long strips down the store aisle. Her fiancé stood before her, a grin on his face, like it was everything he'd ever dreamed of. Like standing in a crowded shop that smelled too strongly of perfume with a girl only a year out of high school was the end all to end all.

"Lucas, meet Christopher, Todney's best man. Christopher, meet Lucas, one of my friends from high school." Rylie gestured between the strange new man and myself twice before returning to her far more important duties of sorting pink lilies from white ones.

"Chris," the man corrected. "I see she's had time to mark you." He reached out a callused, long-fingered hand and wiped what must have been a lipstick kiss off my cheek. "Didn't your mom ever teach you that it's rude to stare? Unless it's because I'm pretty. Then stare. Stare away. Todney always stares because I'm pretty." He winked in Todney's direction.

Todney squeezed the bridge of his nose. "He thinks he's funny. He's not."

"Don't mind him. Us freaks of the Midwest are easily distressed," Chris said. "Your strange, diverse California mindset is revolutionizing our worlds. The gays and the people of color all out in the open! We don't have to hide anymore! What has this world come to?" Chris smiled. "So what *are* you staring at, the beautiful face or my lovely walking habits?

And I thought I was hiding it so well." He thrust out his left foot and tapped his fingers against his kneecap. "All metal. Just call me Bionic Man because I'm at least a hundredth of the way to being a robot. Tough part is you can't see it. I mean, I wanted a prosthetic just to look a little cooler. Todney here thought I should bedazzle it, wouldn't have to hide it that way. Board shorts every day. But I was thinking graffiti. Skull and crossbones all the way down. Or, and hear me out here, high school cast style: everyone can sign 'HAGS' on it."

He spoke too fast and too much, a tornado of words, and I was caught up in the endless swirl of it all.

"Sorry," I said.

"He only speaks in one-word sentences," Rylie said to Chris. She had roses in her hands now. "It's his way of expressing his locked-up hatred for us all."

Chris frowned. "You hate us all?"

Before I could even think to reply, Rylie had answered again. "Not you. Me. His friends. All of us who stayed here when he went off to college. What did you call it, Lucas? 'A life-sucking world of no opportunity'?" She looked back at Chris, exchanging a red rose for a white one while a wry smile played at the corners of her mouth. "He yelled that at me on the phone when I asked why he wouldn't come home for Christmas. Longest sentence he's said to me in months."

I stared down at the floor. From my peripheral vision, I could see Chris staring at me with what I assumed was a look of judgment. It was only after I'd raised my head and dared to meet his gaze that I realized it was actually curiosity. Despite all Rylie had said—all of it the truth—he was still waiting to hear my side.

I shrugged. "I don't like to waste words."

Chris cocked an eyebrow. "You can't waste words. Their only purpose is to be used. I, for one, love words."

"We know," Rylie and Todney said in unison. Chris threw his head back and laughed. It was the most beautiful thing I'd ever seen, and so, naturally, I felt nothing but jealousy.

JUDGING BY RYLIE'S reactions, you'd think choosing wedding flowers was as difficult as choosing a pet. Every flower had a "pro"—beauty, color, the sweet smell under her nose as she held the bouquet to her chest. But nothing was too beautiful not to have thorns or to attract bees or to clash with the table settings. One by one, the cons added up until it was quite clear we'd be getting nothing done today. Todney never flinched, never snapped, never gave in to the inevitable annoyance, but stood, soldier straight by her side, rubbing her back about these damned flowers.

This went on for an unbelievably long time until Rylie squeaked, suddenly, and ran to the window to stare out at another man.

"What is he doing here? Lucas, did you invite him?"

I glanced out the window. "No." I moved to stand next to her. "I thought you were still friends."

"We are. But I don't want him anywhere near the wedding planning."

"Well, he's coming this way."

"You are so helpful. Go get him out of here."

Chris pushed his way between us and pressed his nose against the glass. "Who are we staring at? Brother? Cousin? Cute ex-boyfriend?" Beside us, Rylie tensed.

Chris made a sound like a siren and knocked my shoulder with his own. "I was right, wasn't I?"

"Yes, you were right. Now, Lucas, go get rid of him," Rylie answered.

"I believe I was asking Lucas," Chris said, and though he spoke to Rylie, his eyes were all on me—two heavy searchlights that were impossible to turn away from.

So I gave up trying. I narrowed my eyes and stared back, squinting against the light in hopes that I had my own, that maybe I could blind him before he could blind me. I sort of doubted it.

It was Rylie's hand on my shoulder that inevitably pulled me away, that pulled me back to the flower shop with the wilting roses in the doorway and the morning dew on the window, pulled me back to the boy outside the window playing dress up as a man.

Well-pressed pants and an ironed dress shirt sauntered up to the shop. With heavy bags under his eyes, Clayton Ortiz caught my gaze through the wet and worn shop window and smiled. It was a smile so well crafted, so constructed, it could rival the natural world around me down to the very stem, down to the cell.

I was outside, crossing the distance between us, before I knew quite what I was doing.

Clayton threw his hands up into the air, his smile faltering slightly—but only for a second. In an instant, the corners of his mouth flickered upward where they had begun to droop, and he produced a pair of sunglasses from his jacket pocket to cover up the darkness in his eyes. The black shades contrasted glaringly against his pale skin.

"Lucas Burke, in the flesh," he said and grasped my shoulders with his well-manicured fingers. "He lives. So you *didn't* fall off a cliff somewhere. If you answered my calls once in a while, I might have known that."

I didn't say anything, but I did hug him, and it made him relax some, I think. The tension drained from his shoulders anyway as he sort of slumped against me, more warm noodle and less rigid telephone pole.

He said, almost breathless against my ear, "I've missed you, man."

I nodded and tried to say "I missed you too," but all that came out of my mouth was a mumbled "yeah." I thrust a thumb behind me instead and gestured at the flower shop. "Rylie doesn't want you around. She's freaking out."

Behind us, Chris pressed his face against the glass and stuck out his tongue, making one vulgar expression after another. Rylie stood beside him, cringing and trying to hide behind a bouquet of daffodils.

"He in there?" Clay asked, smile still in place. "Chris is here. That bastard Todney's got to be in there too, right?"

"Yeah. He didn't seem like a bastard," I said.

"He is. He's a stuck-up, rich bastard."

"Whatever you say."

"He is," Clay said.

"He definitely is."

"Thank you."

"You're a stuck-up, rich bastard too, you know," I said.

Clay laughed. "I definitely am. Want to get a drink?"

"Definitely."

We both waved in unison toward the flower shop window; Chris waved back, Rylie blushed, and then Clay and I headed next door into the small-town liquor shop. Clay pulled out a fake I.D. that was not even remotely close to the real thing and grabbed a bottle of scotch. Up at the counter, the shopkeeper stared at the fake, then at Clay's face, and then checked us out without a word.

"You have superpowers," I said. "I'll never take you for granted."

Clay's smile did that drooping thing again, like someone was pulling it down at the edges and he had to fight tooth and nail to hold it back up. "You already have."

If I was a better friend, I might have felt bad about that or at least found a way to lift that smile, a sort of pulley system or something to step in when the gravity of life took its toll. I could have at least apologized, I supposed. I could have said something to make up for it all—what, I don't know, but there's an awful lot of words out there, and one of them might have fit if I'd only tried.

But Clay had already started smiling again and was now rattling on about something else—something light, something easy—so we dropped it. As we walked to the parking lot of our old high school, Clay told me in great detail all about his plans, his inventions, and the colors he'd have on his business cards when he got his own company. Green because it promised a future of money with highlights of red to symbolize the blood he might literally have to sacrifice to ever get his ideas off the ground.

He was laughing—nearly hysterically—about some computer system he was working on when we finally reached the parking lot and settled down along the curb. It was late afternoon by then, and an unimpressive sunset of orange and pink hung low in the sky. This meant that cute suburban moms and cute suburban dads were sitting around on their porches, pointing out the cute colors and gushing about their cute, perfect lives. It meant that cute children were being called inside for cute around-the-table dinners. But mostly it meant that school was long over and the parking lot was abandoned. So when Clay pulled out the scotch and popped off the lid, no one questioned it. No cops came jumping out of the bushes, and, frankly, no one cared.

Clay took the first swig of scotch, gave a huge whole-body shake, and then handed the bottle over. I took it and did the same but with less theatrics; I sipped, I gulped, and I passed it back. This went on for a while—drink, pass, drink, repeat—and for several minutes, neither of us spoke but waited instead for that warm buzz that made loose lips pleasurable and social interaction easy.

It came to me like a punch in the gut, my crisp, dark world growing fuzzy and shining brighter, and that pressure around my jaw that always felt like a cage suddenly loosened, screws falling out at once.

Soon *I* was the one rattling on about nothing; *I* was the one babbling and apologizing, falling back flat on the pavement and yelling to the sky, "I'm sorry, I'm sorry, I'm sorry!" until I was sure God could hear me.

Clay clapped a hand over my mouth. Through my hazy scotch-soaked vision, I could see him smiling—a different smile this time, all loose and so damn frustrating that I almost punched it right off.

"No, you're not," he whispered through the darkness. "You're not sorry. And you don't have to pretend you are."

I sat up and rubbed my knuckles into my eyes. It did nothing but make my vision even blurrier. "That's not what everyone else says. Everyone looks at me like I abandoned them. Like... Like..." I paused and reached again for the bottle of scotch, but Clay tugged it away. I pouted and tried to grab it back, but soon forgot about whatever it was I wanted the scotch for in the first place.

I continued babbling instead. "The world is so much *better* out there, Clay. It's so much bigger. There's so much life. And there's nothing here. Nothing."

"There's people," Clay said.

I laughed. "People who don't care about anything. People who don't do anything." Flopping back onto the pavement, I raised my hands above my head and watched the stars twinkling through the spaces between my fingers. The stars were big and glowing and so shockingly clear that it was nothing at all like the city. In the city, the sky was dark and bright all at the same time—dark from the lack of natural lights and the lack of stars, bright from the streetlights and the building windows and the satellites.

"The people here aren't people," I said. "The people here are just empty shells." Empty shells that remembered everything I'd done in high school; empty shells that looked on with judgment in their squinty, little suburban eyes.

Clay lay down on the pavement beside me and turned his head so we were face-to-face. "And you're all filled up then, huh?"

"Yeah." I think I nodded, or maybe I just thought about nodding; my head was heavy and my brain was full even if the rest of me wasn't. "Yeah, at least I have a plan. Do you have a plan?"

Of course he had a plan. I knew he had a plan. He'd just told me all about it minutes ago—green and red and blood on business cards—and I was a terrible friend, and I just didn't care.

Clay nodded. "I have a lot of plans." He sat up and fumbled through his jacket pocket for a moment before pulling out a bottle of pills.

Full of that slitty-eyed confusion we call intoxication, I couldn't quite make out the name on the prescription, but it sure as hell didn't look like a "Clay" or anything resembling a C-name for that matter. Martha maybe. Or Mary.

Clay popped several pills into his mouth and then took another swig of scotch before he replied. "I'm going to prove my dad wrong, for one. I'm going to be a success. I'll be even bigger than he is. And then—" He twirled the bottle in his hands. "—I'm going to win Rylie back."

Todney's face popped into the back of my mind, full of a puppy-dog love and nauseating admiration that did nothing to settle my already churning stomach. "The wedding's only in a couple months," I said.

Clay shrugged. "She's not really going to marry him. We're just kids, Lucas. She's nineteen."

"Which is an adult," I said.

Clay shook his head. "Yeah, sure, but it's still a kid too. She's not going to settle down and have her happily ever after right now. That's just not how it works."

"Then why are you even going to bother? If she's too young to live happily ever after with him, how could she live happily ever after with you?"

"Because I'm not looking for happily ever after," Clay said. "I'm looking for a chance. You grow up and you find your way, and then you have that choice forever. We're still kids. Kids have a chance. That's what older people are always saying, you know: I missed my chance. When you're young, all you've got are chances. It's like you're standing in a room with a thousand doors, and you've got to pick the right one.

"That's why we're all crazy. We don't know which one to pick, and the pressure eats you alive. But then you finally pick one—because you have to, because society is screaming at you 'Pick one! Pick one! You're twenty-five; you're too old not to pick one! You're thirty; you're no good if you haven't picked a door by now'—and then you do, and it closes behind you, and you're stuck with that one choice forever. Rylie's not ready to close that door. I know her. And maybe she likes this guy. Hell, maybe he's even 'the one.'" Clay made quotation marks with his fingers. "But she's not ready to close that door. And I just want to open one."

I didn't answer, nor did it seem Clay wanted me to as, the second he finished, he lay back and stared up at the stars in silence. Between us, the bottle of scotch tumbled over, and the sounds of the glass rolling down the street and Clay's heavy breathing filled the air.

I closed my eyes and imagined myself in a room full of endless doors, each a different color, a different shape—different locks and different handles everywhere I turned. They were all open, all waiting, and then, all at once, every door slammed shut.

Two

95 DAYS BEFORE

When you live in a house with four other siblings, alone time is a rare occurrence. The morning after the Empty Parking Lot Scotch Party, I was considerably hungover—raging headache, allergy to bright lights, you name it—and my brothers and sisters were some of the least helpful people in all of the world. Granted, they weren't exactly *aware* of my situation, and I was in no rush to tell them, but the screaming down the hallway and the repeated slamming of their bedroom doors had me sort of homicidal.

Lying across my bed with my headphones on, a peaceful hippy band I'd learned about in college drifting through the speakers, I could still hear my sister—the younger one, Sharon—screaming about some Disney movie that was currently on TV. Sharon was seven years old, loved Disney, had fluffy, uncontrollable brown hair, and was a complete accident. The stories went that Mom and Dad had sworn off kids forever when the condom broke or Mom's birth control stopped working or God stepped in himself. I don't know. Point is: Sharon was loud, and my head was about to split open and spill my brains onto the new mattress my mom had just bought.

"Daniel! Anthony!" Sharon yelled, banging hard on the door right next to mine. It belonged to my twin brothers: twelve years old each.

The door swung open, old and creaky. "Sharon, I am not watching *The Princess Diaries* again," said Daniel or maybe Anthony. They sounded as identical as they looked.

"Please, pretty, pretty please?" said Sharon, and both of the twins sighed in unison.

"Fine. But this is the last time," said Anthony—I think.

The pattering of three pairs of footsteps disappeared down the stairs. I had all of about ten seconds of silence before my cell phone started to ring. I reached over the bedside table and picked up the call.

"Lucas," greeted a voice that was flying higher than my ceiling. The boy on the other end hiccupped loudly. "I was thinking about you last night. You still in town?"

Outside the window, the pool glistened in the early morning light. Two ducks had now settled in and swam circles around each other in some sort of bizarre mating ritual. I was in town; I was not in the city.

"I'm home for the summer," I said. "Guess you're going to need a new booty call."

"Don't want anybody else," said the boy, his words slurred. "What are you wearing?"

"It's ten in the morning. My mom is downstairs making French toast, and my little sister is running through the house dressed like the princess from *Beauty and the Beast*. I don't think what I'm wearing is going to help you to the finish line right now, do you?" I paused and looked to my bedroom door. From behind it, I could hear my oldest sister grumbling about "being woken up before noon" and Sharon still screaming from downstairs. I thought of the French toast and the mountain of syrup my mother always provided and then of the murky pool out the window and then of Chris's face and his whirlwind voice. "I'll call you tonight," I said and hung up.

MY MOM WAS the sort of mom that took cooking and cleaning very seriously. Our whole lives, she'd taught us that being a strong woman meant doing what you loved with determination—whether that meant being a lawyer, a doctor, or a stay-at-home mom. My mother was none of the above—an elementary school teacher by day and a family cook by night—but she excelled in both.

By 10:02 a.m. exactly, she had already finished grading her sixth-grade class's history tests, and a stack of French toast lay on the center of our table. It expelled steam in great clouds and was glistening with butter. It was probably unhealthy—probably a heart attack waiting to happen—but it was so damn good, it didn't matter. My father, who had indeed had a heart attack earlier that year, received a single piece of toast—not French, not sugared, and certainly not buttered—and several pieces of fruit.

"For your heart," explained my mother.

"For my death," countered my father.

Clay called as I was finishing my last piece of toast. I stuffed a final bite into my mouth and then excused myself from the table. My mother looked on with an expression of extreme disapproval but said nothing to bring me back—perhaps because I was an adult now, or maybe just because I'd finished her food before I left, and that, she conceded, was good enough.

My siblings—children as they were—stayed behind, picking at the last bits of their toast. The twins built theirs into a castle, Sharon serenaded her side of fruit, and my oldest sister, Frankie, glared her plate into surrender.

Clay's voice was nearly hysterical by the time I reached the peace and quiet of the living room. "Are you free? Tell me you're free today."

"I guess I'm free." The ducks had sort of worn out their entertainment value.

"Great! Are you ready to witness a complete and utter train wreck?" he asked.

"Naturally."

"Great! Because we're going on a road trip."

I scratched the bridge of my nose and tried not to think of Clay's expensive Mercedes plummeting off the side of a cliff somewhere. "Road trip?" I asked.

"Road trip," Clay repeated.

"To where?"

"To the reception venue that Rylie is thinking about renting out."

"Whose car?"

"Rylie's."

"And you're invited?" I asked.

"I invited myself. Trip to the beach. I'm not missing this."

"And that worked?"

"I did some convincing," Clay said.

"Who's coming?"

Clay took a deep breath as though to prepare himself. I sat on the living room couch and did the same. "Rylie, obviously," Clay began.

I nodded though he couldn't see it.

"And Todney. The rich bastard."

"Right," I agreed immediately.

Clay continued, "Chris."

My heart did a strange sort of jumping motion in my chest that I ignored.

"And Frankie."

"My sister?"

"That's the one."

I glanced into the kitchen to see Frankie still stabbing her pancakes. I hadn't noticed it when I sat down, but unlike the rest of my siblings—still in their pajamas and yawning—Frankie was dressed: makeup on, hair tied up, and even wearing a pair of earrings that looked as expensive as all of our kitchenware combined.

"Why is she coming?" I asked.

"She's a bridesmaid."

A frayed string on the edge of my T-shirt caught my attention, and I fiddled with the end while I imagined my sixteen-year-old sister dancing the tango at a five-star wedding. "And you're the track that derails us all?"

I thought I could hear Clay shrugging. "I want to be there."

"It's not your wedding. You *do* remember that, right?"

"I do remember the breakup with crystal clarity, yes. Are you coming, or are you really going to leave me alone with my ex and her royal entourage?"

There was another long beat of silence. I thought of the ducks—swimming in happy circles around one another, blissfully content with their pointless, hopeless duck lives—and wondered what one would do if the other flew away.

"So when do we leave?" I asked after a while.

"In an hour. I'll come pick you up. Bring a jacket."

AN HOUR LATER, I said goodbye to my family—my mom hugged Frankie and I and told us to be safe; the rest didn't notice—and waited outside for Clay's red Mercedes. I wore two jackets—a thin sweater underneath a heavily padded coat. If San Francisco had taught me anything—and it had taught me quite a lot—it was how to deal with the cold. As I waited, I settled down on the curb and crossed my arms over my chest. Frankie, dressed head to toe in sweater, scarf, and boots, stayed standing. We didn't speak.

Our house was the last on a pretty average suburban block—square front yards, square architecture, square sort of people. The sun was out, and the sidewalks shone with drying puddles and old chalk—a hopscotch game and a couple of pink and blue flowers drawn onto the neighbor's driveway.

The neighbor across the street stared at me above the top of her morning newspaper. I pretended not to notice.

CLAY PULLED UP to the curb five minutes after he'd said he would, lounging in the front seat. He wore a pair of driving gloves and dark glasses. He looked absolutely ridiculous, which I told him as I climbed into the passenger seat.

"I look rich," he corrected me.

"Rich and stupid," I said.

He laughed, and as Frankie—still glaring—sat in the back, we headed off to Rylie's house.

By the time we got there, a new car was already parked outside—an expensive-looking blue Cadillac I didn't recognize, Todney's, I assumed, next to Rylie's old yellow van. The whole gang sat outside, talking and drinking canned Diet Cokes.

"Take one," Rylie said as we joined the group. She thrust a Coke into Clay's hand, Frankie's, and then mine, and we popped them open without question. "My mom bought in bulk at Costco. Again. And then decided Diet Coke was bad for her health. So what did she do? She gave them to her children." Rylie grinned and took a sip.

Frankie took a seat next to Rylie. Tugging at her scarf—in the morning light, I recognized my mother's signature stitching—Frankie hardly looked her age: sixteen and nineteen sat side by side, and I couldn't tell the difference as they leaned in close, whispering and pointing at us boys.

As Clay and I approached, Todney waved, and Chris, working on his third Coke with the other two empty cans at his feet, beamed in my direction.

"You liar. You told me he wasn't coming," he said to Rylie.

She rolled her eyes. "I didn't want you peeing your pants in excitement, okay?"

I blushed, but Chris, miraculously, did not. "I have excellent bladder control," he informed me. I nodded and focused anywhere but on his face.

THE SUN WAS out and shining, so we wasted another ten minutes or so basking in the warmth before we all piled into Rylie's child-snatcher-looking van. "Where we are going, there won't be much sunshine," she said, "so everyone keep your jackets on."

The only problem with her theory was that there were six of us and four seats, so we all crammed together like the contents of one of my dad's sardine cans. Naturally, this meant it was hot—like sweat dripping down your back, heat rising in your chest, vomit-inducing, really, really hot. And whatever cold place we were going wouldn't change that.

Clay squeezed in next to Frankie. She gripped onto the lifeboat of his company and scooted closer to him and away from me—the two speaking of science and home and school as though they'd been doing it forever. Todney, naturally, got the comfort of the passenger seat. Rylie drove, and I ended up shoulder to shoulder with Chris, who rubbed his fake knee and announced the day, "the start of a grand adventure!"

I rolled my eyes. "We're all going to kill each other before we even get there," I reminded him.

"I know," he said. He clapped his hands together, his eyes seemingly lit up from the inside out. "It's going to be like *Lord of the Flies* up in here." His face broke into a wide, gleeful smile.

I laughed. "A grand adventure indeed."

I shifted slightly, overly aware of how my thigh rubbed against Chris's, and how Chris's thigh was warm and human, and I wondered if his knee was too. If it felt like flesh or like metal; would it be cold if I touched it? Our knees collided over a speed bump, and as my body flushed, I selfishly hoped he couldn't feel it.

Beside us, Frankie and Clay had moved on from the topic of best hamburgers in town and were now neck deep in a debate on particle acceleration. Rylie adjusted the radio and bounced around her seat to a Lady Gaga song while she drove us onto the main highway. Her hair flipped back and forth in front of her eyes, but she seemed to drive instinctively, taking the cross ramp and merging without anything more than a second's glance. If anyone besides me was worried, they didn't say.

Occasionally, her attention turned to the rearview mirror, and she stared back at Clay.

"You're pretty observant, aren't you?" Chris whispered in my ear.

I bit down the immediate instinct to jump out of my skin. Chris had that strange effect on people—it couldn't be just me—and whether it was good or bad was still up in the air. "Not really," I said.

Chris shifted in his seat. There wasn't a lot of room—a spare inch or so between our shoulder blades—but he managed to turn so we were face-to-face, his smile serious and mine terrified.

"Really?" he asked. "Because it sure looks like it. It's not a bad thing. It's actually kind of a great thing. If you always know what's going on, you never miss anything. I'm not like that. If I get in the zone, a parade of elephants could come running by, and I wouldn't even notice."

The image was vividly clear—all six of us, each with our own elephants, crusading around downtown Sacramento and crushing the city in our wake. "Get in the zone for what?" I asked.

Chris shrugged. "Could be anything. Could just be lost in my head. Thinking, you know. Or when the pain got bad. Used to be swimming." He shrugged again and rubbed a spot on the back of his neck that was growing pinker by the second. It occurred to me that it was the first time I'd seen him nervous. Back at school, everyone seemed nervous all the time—their first year alone and the first time anyone had to figure out their lives for themselves. I'd rarely met anyone so calm.

"Swimming?"

"Yeah. I used to a lot. BC."

"Before Christ?"

"Before Cancer." He leaned back, claiming the last couple of centimeters in his squished seat. "It was a good escape, you know. We didn't have a super lot of money, my family. But we weren't poor either. Suburb kid up in an okay area. But my uncle, he was loaded. Like designer clothes for all his kids, the best computers and phones—sometimes even before they came out—kind of rich. And he had this big sailboat. I was ten or eleven the first time he let me on it. Ten. Yeah, I was definitely ten. Anyway, I go out, and I fall into the water, and I can't swim. And my cousins tease me about it all day, but my uncle—Uncle Willy—he freaks out. Starts saying how swimming is this huge important thing, and I can't go my whole life not knowing how to swim because it's just not safe. It's not practical. So he signs me up for the best swim lessons in town, and I get addicted. And then I learn about the diving board and diving and tricks you can do and flips, and it's art. It's water, and it's freeing; it's an escape, but it's also art. So next thing you know, I'm diving on teams, and I'm learning new tricks. And I got good. Like really, really good."

"You're very modest," I said.

Chris laughed. "Sorry. No, you know what." He paused, and the hand that had been nervously gripping the back of his neck all this time now dropped to his side. "I'm not sorry. And I'm not going to be. No one in this life has time for modesty. I sure as hell don't. Do you? We got this one shot, and that's sort of the point, isn't it? To be good at it. I mean, it's my life, and I might as well do it well, and I'm not going to lie and say I didn't. I mean, you wouldn't go up to God when you die and say 'hey, thanks for the life and all; I didn't do anything special with it. Just a normal Joe with normal abilities.'"

I nodded. I supposed I'd never seen it that way before; then again, I'd never really cared. "So you were good?" I prompted.

"Right!" Chris's smile returned in full force. "So I was good. Senior year of high school, I graduate, and I'm all set to take my talents to the Olympics. Big life-long dream and all. So I'm eating Subway, because that's what Olympians do, and suddenly there's this pain in my leg, and I get up, and bang! Just like that, my leg breaks. I go to the hospital, and they find a tumor in my leg, in the bone, and they tell me it's cancer. Ewing's sarcoma, and I'm lucky—*lucky*—because it's *just* in my leg. It's 'localized,' and if I get started on the chemo, they can probably save it. My life and the leg. They say what I've got is rare—really rare. And cancer alone is pretty unusual, but this one? This one only makes up one percent of all childhood cancers. So I'm a winner. I'm already taking home gold, right? So, I do the chemo, and it shrinks the tumor, but it's not enough, and they have to remove the bone with the cancer in it so it doesn't spread." He rubbed at his knee and then a spot on his leg where I guessed his calf bone was hiding metal bits too. "And so I missed the Olympics. And well, that was that."

The whole time he was talking, his voice rose and fell like he was some sort of speech expert, like he'd practiced, and it came complete with pauses for inflection and the gesturing of his hands. Then his tone would rise up, up, up with that lingering note of desperation, that quivering, ringing, all-consuming note that said in just the simple tone of his voice "this is it, this is the moment, listen here because you're not going to want to miss this part." I had the feeling he'd told the story before—

dozens, maybe even hundreds of times. It must have gotten tiring being a statistic; "I had cancer" wearing itself out after the first confession. I probably would have told the long version too.

Funny part was, I didn't even mind that he did. For those short couple of minutes, I wasn't really hearing my sister all grown up with no warning, or watching Clay and Rylie exchange love-filled hate glances. I didn't even look at the road. I was a whole new type of observant, and this type meant seeing a whole lot less of the details of the world, and a lot more of the freckles on Chris's face.

"So are you cancer free now?" I asked.

He nodded and rubbed again at his knee. I wondered if he even knew he was doing it anymore. "Cancer free. In came the bionics, and out went the cancer."

"And there's no chance it can come back?"

"There's always a chance." Chris looked out at the road and then back to me. "But there's also a pretty good chance that this van will crash, isn't there? You still got in." He tried to smile, but it fell flat around the edges. Another overtold story, I guess.

To our left, Clay yawned, and Frankie squeaked.

"Ouch!" she cried. "That was my boob you elbowed. Watch what you're doing."

"Why is your boob so close to my elbow?" asked Clay.

"We're in a car! Where do you want me to put my boob?"

Clay sighed. "This is going to be a long trip."

It was. Between the debating of the science nerds in the back, Rylie and Clay's uncomfortable sideway glances, and Chris's leg continuously—and I was beginning to think purposefully—bumping mine, the trip seemed to last three times, at least, longer than it should have. By my count, Clay popped four pills and downed an airport bottle of whiskey in under an hour, so by the time we got there, he was babbling about electron generators and atom splitters with all the enthusiasm of a little boy discussing his favorite superheroes. Frankie went along with it, nodding where it seemed appropriate while Rylie seemed to have decided that ignoring Clay's general existence was the best plan of action for everyone involved.

When, finally, we'd come far enough to see the ocean glittering out the windows, we were all desperate to get out.

"I bet this is exactly the *opposite* of what sailors feel when they've found land," Chris said, nose pressed to the glass and scanning the sea ahead.

"Yeah, I would definitely rather drown at this point," Todney agreed. "If sailors get sea sickness, I think I have land sickness."

Frankie rolled her eyes. "You're all such drama queens. It's only been two hours."

"This could change the world," said Clay. He leaned his head against Frankie's shoulder and gave her a wide, toothy grin. "Don't you think it could change the world?"

"The atom thingy?" Frankie asked. "Yeah, sure, Clay, it could change the world."

"I could make it." Clay sat up, glanced quickly out at the ocean, and then turned back to Frankie. "I could do it. I could change the world."

"Sure you can, Clay." Frankie smiled. Maybe she thought that would work, that Clay would see the condescending sweetness in her eyes and in his booze- and drug-addled mind, he'd heel and be quiet. He didn't. If anything, it got him more riled up.

He rose onto his knees—a hard feat in the already squished interior of the van—and beamed at everyone around him. In the dark of the van and the foggy sunlight streaming in through the windows, Clay's smile almost looked real. Slurring and giggling, he told us all about his proposed scientific experiments and the future of the world.

"There's stages," I explained to Chris. "He gets like this first, and then he gets deep and introspective. Then he closes up and disappears."

Chris frowned. "Don't you ever get worried that he won't come back?"

I looked at Clay, who no one was listening to anymore. He slunk back into his seat and stared out the window with blank, dark eyes, his arms crossed over his chest. "I'm not sure he ever has," I said.

Chris sighed. "I like him."

"Yeah," I said.

RYLIE PARKED IN a lot fit for a queen's carriage. It was a basic parking lot, I suppose—a bunch of white lines marking the spaces, but it was more than that too, the road too fresh and the paint too white, and the buildings behind it too ornate to label anything about it ordinary. The streetlamps all around were tall and detailed, made of bronze, I think, and there was a statue of some explorer on a horse—craftily carved and artfully preserved—dumped in the middle of the lot. It seemed to me a whole lot of hard work to hold a bunch of old cars. All this skill so we could wait amongst beauty.

A man in a suit and expensive shoes came out to greet Rylie, and she flushed as she shook his hand. Todney clambered out of the car and came to stand beside her, introducing himself. For a while, the three of them talked and planned while the rest of us wandered around the lot.

"There's the beach," Clay said, pointing beyond the top of the ballroom.

Frankie sighed wistfully. "Can we go? They'll call us when they need us, right?"

The rest agreed, and we set off out of the parking lot and toward the sand.

"Awful lot of money," Chris said. He fell in step beside me but glanced over his shoulder at the ballroom.

"What?" I asked.

"This place. The wedding. All of it. Awful lot of money to spend on a promise. It's simple: Lucas, I promise you I will walk to this beach without falling on my face. See, promise made. Easy."

I shrugged. "I guess if you spend all that money, you're more inclined to keep it, aren't you? If you fall on your face, nothing is going to happen except that you fall on your face. There's no consequences. You spend all this money on a wedding, you sign the papers, you make it this big legal thing, and now if you break that promise—if you cheat or you stop being in love, well you're screwed. So you have to try not to cheat, and you have to try and stay in love. It's motivation. I get it."

"That was both logical and extremely cynical." Chris crossed his arms over his chest and shook his head. "And I refuse to believe we are a species so emotionally constipated that we need binding contracts to 'motivate' us to stay in love."

"Then what does motivate us?"

"Just love."

I rolled my eyes. "So you're a romantic, huh?"

Chris laughed. He pulled his leg along with him, struggling to move it through the thick sand. I thought of reaching out to help him but refrained, dropping my hands to my sides instead.

"I'm not a romantic," Chris said. His voice was firm—light and easy, happy even, but still determinedly firm. "I don't think people fall in love and become the center of each other's world. I don't think love conquers all. I don't think we have soul mates or that when you get together and you're together all your life and one of you dies as an old man, the other one is on their way out too. I don't think all marriages last forever. I don't even think they all should."

"So what do you believe?"

"I believe in human decency. I believe that when you make a promise to someone, you keep it. I believe that when you say 'I love you,' you should mean it. I believe that all of this—" He gestured around us—at the ocean ahead and the room behind, the chapel in the distance where the ceremony would take place, the elaborate parking lot and the statue: an angel and a man, hand in hand. "—this is all excess, and life is crappy and strange and too much most of the time. And it's hard. Hell, I *know* it's hard. But it's also really damn simple. You just live it, and you try not to treat people like crap while you do."

I rubbed my shoe against the sand and watched as it filled with ten thousand grains in under a millisecond. "Is that a promise?"

Chris smiled. "Yeah," he said. "You bet your ass that's a promise."

Three

RYLIE CAUGHT UP with us just before we reached the water. Her face was flushed, her smile wide, and her hands full of leaflets. "I have to take the tour," she said, brushing a stray bit of hair from her face. "Look around, meet with some people. Talk to all the important guys. It's boring bridal stuff. But Todney is going to hang with you all if that's okay."

Todney stood beside her, brushing sand off his pant leg. "Rylie—" he started, but she quieted him with a wave of her hand.

"It'll be fun. You all need a chance to get to know each other. I'll be back in an hour or less, I swear. Have fun, okay?" She started off, back across the sand and toward the chapel. She was only gone two steps before Clay ran after her.

"I'll keep you company," he said. The glare she shot him could have leveled a building but did nothing to lessen his determination. "What? I'm interested. This place is amazing, and you know how I am with architecture."

"It's true," I said. "He's an architecture nerd."

Rylie rolled her eyes. "Fine. You can come. Bye, sweetie." She blew a kiss to Todney, who returned the gesture, and then she and Clay disappeared up the beach.

The rest of us exchanged raised eyebrows, Todney stared down at his boots, and then we slowly made our way to the water—slowly because Chris kept tripping, and I kept stopping to help him, and Frankie kept complaining about the weather.

Truth be told, I wasn't really feeling it myself. You come to a beach on summer vacation, and I think it's a pretty unspoken expectation that it'll be warm, and if you're lucky—and into that sort of thing—you'll see something resembling a Girls Gone Wild film. "Chicks" in their bikinis, couples making out in the sand—despite the unsanitary retributions—someone playing a guitar, and, given that there's no killer sharks in the water, everyone swimming. And that might be the case if you live in

Hawaii or Cancún or something, or maybe even Southern California, but up North, the Golden State sort of loses its gold.

To say the beach reached fifty degrees that afternoon would have been a gracious overestimate. Cold and gloomy, the beach was filled with coarse sand, driftwood in every direction, and a storm rolling in from the north; we could see it gathering around the horizon—gray clouds for miles. As far as I could tell, we were the only ones out. Needless to say, there were no topless girls, no streaking guys, no bong, and certainly no ocean-side concert. There were a couple of pelicans fighting over an old sandwich and a shit-ton of shells, but that was it.

Frankie settled down on a patch of dry sand. At the places where her toes touched, it turned gray and wet. "You know, I'm starting to think Rylie is a pathological liar. I was promised a beach. She said there'd be sand, hot guys, and music. I didn't think she meant that crap music she plays in the car and Todney."

"You think I'm hot?" Todney asked.

Frankie nodded, and I did my best not to meet either of their gazes. I sat down next to my sister and blinked, dumb, as she pat my knee and said, "Don't worry, you're cute too. You're not hot, and I don't think I'd know what that looked like even if you were because it's sort of gross, but you're cute."

I shrugged. I guess I wasn't *bad* looking—the whole dark and handsome cliché could have been a whole lot worse—but my eyes were too close together, I had this one chaotic tuff of hair, and I had yet to hear hot and me in the same sentence. At least not on sober lips.

"Cute?" I repeated.

"Yeah, like in a dumb jock sort of way." Frankie licked her finger and attempted to calm my unruly rebel hair—the same way our mother always used to when we were young; when this didn't work, she ruffled my whole head instead. I tried not to flinch. "The girls in my class used to go on and on about you in your baseball uniform. It was gross. But the rest of the team..." She whistled and then grinned. "Baseball butt is God's gift to mankind. Or, womankind, I guess."

"And mankind." Chris fell onto the sand with all the grace of ten-car pileup. I suppose it had something to do with his knee, but I had a feeling it was more of him being too busy shooing away Todney's help to watch what he was doing.

Todney sat down beside him, a muscle twitching in his forehead.

"You played baseball?" Chris asked.

I shrugged. "Third base." I opened my mouth to finish the story the way I usually did, to say *I was all right* or *I only played for two seasons* or *it was just high school, no big deal*, but the words wouldn't come out. "I was pretty damn good," I said, and I was pleased to find that I believed it. The toxic syllables I had waited for never did come.

Chris's smile appeared to take up his whole face, making it brighter somehow and far harder to look away from. I thought about investing in sunglasses, but there were worst things in the world than getting burned.

"Love that modesty," he said. "You hiding any pictures? Because I'm going to need to see the butt."

Frankie cringed. Todney rolled his eyes. Chris scooted closer and bumped his knee against mine. "You are gay, right?" he asked.

I blinked. "What?"

"Gay. Or you know, somewhere on the spectrum. See, I don't want to invest all this time wooing you and potentially falling for you just to find out you're rigidly hetero."

With a statement like that, it was hard to know where to start. I'd thought a lot of things about Chris, but in the whole twenty-four hours I'd known him, the words "wooing" and "falling" hadn't really come to mind.

"You're planning to woo me?" I said once my mind had cleared enough to form a logical sequence of words.

"I am," Chris said.

"And you're planning to fall for me?"

"Potentially."

"Do you often woo and potentially fall for straight guys?"

Chris shrugged. "It's happened. But I'm trying to limit my personal character clichés down to just one. And 'bisexual dude that always falls for the straight boys and the gay girls' really wasn't doing it for me." Beside him, Todney rolled his eyes with all the pent-up annoyance of a man who had heard the same story a thousand times before. Every line of his body seemed to scream "here we go again."

I held back a laugh. "So which one did you pick?"

"Eternally happy and inspiring cancer kid." Chris puffed out his chest while Todney's eyes practically got stuck in the back of his head from his renewed and vigorous eye rolling.

"This is coming from the kid who broke every dish in my house the day he was diagnosed and then threatened to burn *the Bible*," Todney said.

Frankie's eyes went into jumbo disk mode. "You burned the Bible?"

"Threatened to," Chris corrected. He rubbed at the back of his flushed neck and then shrugged. "The plan was to be sucked into hell and then escape the whole chemo process because, you know, the hell fire would singe the cancer out of me."

"Solid plan," I said, and Chris treated me to a smile that was all in his eyes.

"I've been telling him for years, anger is good," Todney said. "Anger is healthy. It's very good for you to just let it out every once and a while. It adds years onto your life."

"You told me that right after I was informed that years were being scrapped *off* my life. Wasn't exactly in the mood for a 'lifestyles' pep talk, Todney Boy." Chris lay back in the sand, his hands shielding his eyes from the surprisingly bright but cloud-covered sun. What it lacked in orange radiance, it made up for in a blinding paper-white glare.

Say what you want about a cold beach, but when the sun goes out and the clouds start looking like a spiraling vortex of death, it works wonders in getting a group to open up. Hard not to when it appears your life might end any second.

"What was it like?" I asked Chris. The sand was creeping up my pants and sticking to the hairs on my legs. I shook as much off as I could before turning to look him in his eyes. It was the first time I had initiated the contact. "The cancer? I mean, it had to hurt, right?"

Todney sat up flagpole straight, that muscle in his brow twitching again. "Let's not—" he began, but Chris quieted him with a wave of his hand.

"It's okay," he assured him. He smiled for maybe half a second before the happiness drained out of his face. I thought of taking the question back, of retracting the whole stupid idea, but my own selfish curiosity kept my lips shut. Beside me, Frankie sat up a little more like a rabbit with ears at high alert.

"It's just crappy, you know?" Chris said. "It's not some big secret. And I'm not going to ignore it if you ask." He shot Todney a look. "But it's not exactly my favorite subject either. You get cancer, and suddenly you *are* cancer. All anyone asks you is how you're feeling. How it's going. So I'll tell you right now how it feels, and then that's it. You're not going to ask me how I'm feeling or if my knee is hurting or if I need help because I don't. Got it?"

We all nodded in unison.

Chris cleared his throat. "It's just like being sick. And if you pretend that's all it is, then you almost feel normal. And then sometimes you remember that it's rare, and you could have gotten famous or had superstrength or something, and it'd be just as weird, and if you knew that, you'd think about burning the Bible too. But then you think, well, it was rare enough for me to get this, if I got those kinds of odds on me, why shouldn't I be the percent that beats it? So you hold onto the Bible, and you use all that anger and you turn it on the cancer. It's like drowning, and you can see the surface, and maybe you'll reach it before your lungs give out, and maybe you won't; you just can't tell until one of them happens. Because you can kick and swim as hard as you want, and sometimes that's enough; sometimes your head breaks through and you breathe again, and sometimes you don't, and they find your body at the bottom of the ocean. And that's it. That's cancer."

Chris finished speaking and licked his lips as silence fell around the group.

You always think you'll know what to say when the worst hits, that you're prepared for the bad—that you want to know. But it's always better in the dark, always safer. Because when pain and suffering looks you straight in the eye, your tongue just wraps around itself and leaves you dumb.

What was I supposed to say when I didn't know? What do you say when you haven't the slightest idea what it's like to die, to drown, to feel pain like that? I'd always been above the water. And sure, I'd clung to a life raft before, felt the waves crash over my head, tasted the salt in the sea, but I'd never *drowned*. And I sure as hell wasn't hoping to trade places either. I liked my oxygen-filled life.

"Oh," Frankie said, fidgeting with the edge of her blouse. She looked out at the ocean. I could practically see it in her eyes—the fear, that choking feeling that she too was being pulled under the waves and couldn't reach the surface. She gulped and turned her attention to her hands instead. "Well."

I nodded. "Yeah." See what I mean? Dumb as hell. "I always wore floaties when I was in the water. Until I was twelve. My mom didn't trust me in the pool. She said when I was a baby, I always put my head under the water during bath time, and it was a sign of my future impending doom or something."

Chris stared at me, and for a moment, I thought I'd said the wrong thing, that I'd been tactless again. But then he burst out laughing so hard it brought tears to his eyes, and the tension sort of drained out of the whole group. Everyone laughed along.

"So we know a lot about Chris," Frankie said once we'd all gotten our breath back. "But we know nothing about you, Todney. You're marrying one of my brother's best friends—" She paused to clap me on the shoulder. "—and you're a stranger. We'll have to change that."

"Yeah, Todney, we'll have to change that," Chris said.

Todney scratched the bridge of his nose. "Uh, I'm from North Carolina. My dad is a preacher, and my mom is a surgeon." He pulled off his shoes one by one and set them aside—toes aligned and perfectly straight—and then buried his sock-covered feet in the sand. "Pretty normal life, I guess."

Chris snorted. "And unaccepting of the abnormal." He pointed two fingers at his own head. His smile was tight-lipped, the kind of smile you picked up when you learned that a lot of the world hated you, a lot didn't understand you, and nothing you could do could change their minds. I'd picked up mine when my pastor told me I was going to hell, as did the next one, and the next, until my mom found a church that didn't care who I might love one day. By then, I was already a master at the Smile, and there really was no going back.

You knew the Smile when you saw it, and Chris's was ancient—well-practiced and overused, with that real distinct look to it, like it'd been broken before, but he sure as hell wasn't going to tell you about it.

When Todney frowned, Chris rubbed his shoulder. "I didn't mean it like that, man. It's okay. You know I don't care anymore."

"It's not okay." Todney glared and flicked a couple grains of sand off his shoelaces. "My dad is an idiot."

"Yeah, but you're not your dad. I used to be close with the fam, see, but then they found out about my 'lifestyle'." He made air quotes with his hands. "And they got in a big fight. Todney here stood up for me, and his old man didn't like that. That was the last I heard from him. After high school, we got an apartment together and have been living our sitcom life ever since." He squeezed Todney's shoulder while shooting him a look of utter admiration. When he spoke again, his voice was subdued, all joking temporarily set aside. "You couldn't ask for a better friend."

Frankie smiled. "All right. That gets you some brownie points. But let's put that to the test." She threw her hair over her shoulder and looked Todney dead in the eye. "Mind if I ask you some questions?"

Chris used his fingers as drumsticks and his thighs as the drum and then hummed the *Jeopardy* theme song. I stretched out on the sand.

"This is the speed round," Frankie said. "Favorite color?"

"Green," Todney replied.

"Favorite song?"

"'For Sentimental Reasons,' Nat King Cole."

Frankie grinned. "A classics man. I like it. Lucas, add that to the point book."

Chris pushed an invisible book and an equally invisible pen into my hands. I pretended to make a note.

Frankie continued, "Favorite movie?"

"Anything with Jessica Alba in it." Todney flushed, but Chris high-fived him and Frankie just shrugged.

"Fair enough," she said. "Favorite—" Frankie froze suddenly and closed her mouth, focusing instead on something over my shoulder.

I turned just in time to see Rylie and Clay arrive beside the group, both with their arms crossed over their chests and tense, pinched expressions on their faces. "Are you interrogating him?" Rylie asked. She kicked off her shoes and took a seat next to her fiancé. "Guys, you're supposed to be bonding, not going full bad cop."

"It's fine, baby." Todney moved close and rubbed a wide circle over Rylie's shoulder blades. She moaned and leaned into the touch. "We're just having a bit of fun. I'm enjoying getting to know your friends."

"They're not giving you too hard of a time?" she asked.

Todney shook his head. "Not at all."

Clay sat down next to me, his frown deepening as he watched Rylie and Todney catch up. After a long moment of discreetly glaring, he cleared his throat, put on his picture-perfect smile, and turned to face the group. As I watched Clay's expression do a complete one-eighty, I was suddenly reminded of everything that was wrong with the suburbs, all the identical perfect front lawns brought on by chemical fertilizer and—if you had enough money—turf. For one brief moment, I could see it: Clay relaxing on a perfect plastic lounge chair on a perfect turf lawn, on the perfect day, a glass of chemical lemonade in his hand. The American Dream.

"Let's go in." He nodded toward the ocean where the waves broke over the sand in quick succession—a crashing, pounding force that would never be ready for spring break and girls in bikinis even if we'd given it all year to prepare. Summer was here, and the beach simply hadn't gotten the memo.

"Are you crazy?" Rylie stared up at the sky and shook her head. It was barely midafternoon, and already, the sun was low in the sky. Clouds surrounded it in every direction; the storm was nearing quickly.

"It'd be fun," Clay insisted. "People do it all the time. Look at the Polar Bear Club. Come on, you're getting married here. Don't you want to explore all that this place has to offer? We could just—"

"Clay, just stop." Rylie glared. There was a light burning behind her eyes now that I'd never seen before—a hard, blazing look that made Clay's jaw go slack in what I could only assume was complete dumbstruck surprise. "Don't you ever know when to give up? Just stop." She breathed out and rubbed a small circle over her temple. As though on cue, Todney surged forward and renewed his vigorous massaging of her back.

"Whatever you say," Clay snapped and went quiet.

"So your favorite TV show?" Frankie said. She tapped Todney's shoulder, her eyes practically screaming for help; my sister, who always seemed so content in silence back home, was suddenly a social being, unraveling before my eyes.

Chris leaned close to my ear. "You know, you never answered my question."

"Yes," I said.

Chris grinned and gestured at my phone. "Can I?"

I nodded, so he pulled my cell out of my pocket and entered his number into my contacts. As he handed the phone back, Chris smiled that full-faced, goofy smile of a man who knew what he wanted. It occurred to me, suddenly, that I just might be it.

I texted him "hello" just to hear the conformation of a beep in his pocket. "Ta-da," I said. "We're connected."

Crushes are very strange things; they're a warning sign in the word itself—crush: to deform, pulverize, or force inward by compressing forcefully. Whoever decided it was a good idea to equate deformity and compression to blooming affection was either very high or a genius—or maybe lost somewhere in between. But for good or bad, I could feel it: my heart pressing inward until the sound of it beating filled my ears again. I had a deformed, pulverized, compressed force on Chris, and there was nothing I could do about it.

By that point, Todney had covered the first two seasons of his favorite show in great detail and had moved on to his favorite sitcoms. Frankie was nodding, her eyes glazed over; I'd have been impressed if she'd heard a single word he said. Clay and Rylie sat nearby, arms crossed over their chests again, glaring silently out at the horizon. One great, happy family.

"I'm going in." This time, Clay stood up. He tugged off his shirt, his pants, and then without further hesitation jogged away. When he reached the water, he tried the waves one toe at a time, wincing with each move. Then all at once, he threw his whole body in face-first—one long, sweeping dive that took him past the first set of waves and into shoulder-deep water. His head bobbed up a second later, brown hair turned black and stuck to his forehead in thick, uncoordinated strips— like weeds on turf.

Rylie's mouth twitched, but otherwise, her expression remained annoyed. "You're nuts, Clay!"

Frankie laughed and rose to her feet. "Clay, sweetie, you're going to get frostbite. I know we signed up for a nice fun day at the warm beach—" She turned and glared at Rylie. "—but that's not this. So get out of the water, will you? You know, you're going to have shrinkage!"

Todney snorted, peeking out beneath his eyelashes; ten seconds later, he was watching as fully as I was while Frankie ran forward and tried to tug Clay out of the water by his flailing hand.

"I'm fine!" Clay said, splashing her and then ducking back under the waves.

Frankie gasped. "Clayton Ortiz, you did not just get my two-hundred dollar pants wet!" she screeched, and my eyes went wide as I thought of my parents' penny jars on the counter, the hand-me-downs, the college loans.

Clay surfaced again, his eyes wide. "You paid two-hundred dollars for those?"

"Well, no," said my sister. "I got them at a thrift shop for twenty, but they were originally two hundred!"

I let out a sigh of relief, and Clay laughed. "I'll buy you real two-hundred dollar pants if you get in the water."

Frankie shook her head. "No way."

I stood up, completely unaware of how damn cold it would be up in the open air—bitter ocean wind biting at my revealed legs and all. But as I'd already made the big dramatic gesture and could hardly take it back, I resignedly crept forward. By the time I reached the wet sand and the first tiny rolling waves, my teeth were chattering. How the hell did the Polar Bear Club do it—strip down in January when even the May-time weather had my bones shaking?

"Come on, not you too, Lucas," Frankie said. "We still have to drive back, you know. Do you want to be wet in the car? Mom is going to kill us if we drip water in the house!"

I ignored her and looked back at Rylie, expecting a reprimand that never came. I never thought in a million years I'd actually *want* to be yelled at, and I didn't—not really—but the silence was just, well...strange. No "if you track one drop into my van" or "you'll catch a cold" or even the new "don't you care about anything anymore?" No frowns. No disappointed shakes of her head. She simply shrugged, her eyes saying what I knew her mouth never would: you chose him; you chose Clay over me.

I jumped into the water and let the waves take me. From somewhere up above, I heard Frankie's voice—though what she was saying, I couldn't tell—then there was nothing but silence.

Truth be told, I'm not sure that the noise actually stopped—that my friends stopped shouting, or the waves stopped turning—just that I stopped listening, perhaps because my ears had filled with water or because my mind had frozen over. All I knew was that the world was fuzzy and everything that mattered was blue. The blue of the waves and the blue of my cold skin. The blue of the sky up above.

Beneath the waves, the sky seemed to be worlds away, a cloudy oasis and a burning sun a million, trillion miles in the distance—a place I would never reach.

The noise returned the second my head breached the surface; Rylie speaking to Frankie in a whisper so loud it became nothing more than buzzing, Todney arguing with Chris.

I shook the water from my ears and listened.

"You can go in, you know. The doctor said—" The voice came from the tallest blur on land. My eyes foggy from the water, wind, and cold, Todney appeared as nothing more than a well-dressed shadow.

"I'm fine, all right?" The other blur—Chris—snapped back at him. "I'm fine, and I'm good here. On land."

"Chris, you love the water."

"Loved. With a big fat ED. Just drop it, okay? I'm fine. Go in if you want. I don't care. Your fun is not limited by mine. Just go."

I blinked—again and again—until slowly the world came back into focus. Chris caught my eye over Todney's shoulder and waved. "How's the water?" he asked.

"Like icicles are licking my testicles," I said.

Chris laughed. "That rhymed. I like it. From frostbite, with love."

As he spoke, my heart did that funny pounding thing again, which was strange seeing as descriptions of my testicles—sexual in nature as they might be—weren't exactly my biggest turn on, especially when the parts in question were threatening to permanently freeze to my thighs.

"You should come in," I said, but Chris just shook his head.

"You enjoy it for me." He rubbed his knee, his fingers tracing circles over the places where the metal must have pushed beneath his skin. His smile flickered and then fell off entirely. "You'll have to remind me later what the water feels like."

Something inside me ached for him—a feeling a bit like leaving San Francisco behind or like getting punched in the face by my first schoolyard crush because boys weren't supposed to kiss boys. It wasn't the sort of ache that had a name, but the type that sat on top of your heart—dull and throbbing and easy to ignore if you piled enough on top of it, the kind you could swim away from with one easy move.

Nodding at Chris, I ducked back under the ocean's surface. The waves passed by overhead, obscuring my view of the horizon and the steadily setting sun. Visions of orange and pink escaped through the ripples. The next wave—bigger this time than the last—pressed against my nose and mouth. If it hadn't been for my legs kicking beneath me and my lungs preserving my next breath, I might have known what it was like to drown.

Four

WE ARRIVED BACK home a quarter after midnight. By then, everyone was either asleep or pretending to be. It was hard to tell with Frankie, who lay silent and eyes closed with only her fingers twitching occasionally, or Clay who turned back and forth in his seat endlessly as though trying to outrun some invisible monster. Chris's snores, at least, left no doubts, and Todney was quiet if nothing else. Rylie sat in the front seat, yawning behind the wheel while she hummed a Backstreet Boys' song under her breath. She'd tied her long brown hair up into a bun and seemed quite oblivious to her passengers, at least until she pulled up in front of Clay's house and nearly kicked him out of the car. He left, grumbling and yawning all the way to his front door.

Frankie, Todney, Chris, and myself remained in the backseat. Chris's head lolled across my shoulder, his arm haphazardly thrown across my lap.

"Chris is staying with us," Rylie said. She glanced at me through the rearview mirror and then at Todney beside her. "At least until we're married."

I blinked. The way she said it, so casual, so...normal, made the wedding far realer to me than the venue ever could have. I knew rationally that they were dating, that they were *engaged*, but dating had been so very arbitrary in high school that I still couldn't quite imagine Rylie, a nineteen-year-old ex-cheerleader who'd made out with a cheeseburger on a dare just nine months ago, picking out shared drapes and arguing with her husband over whose turn it was to do the dishes.

"Where does he normally live?" I asked.

Rylie shrugged. "I think he's always just lived where Todney did. His parents kicked him out when he was fifteen. He lived with Todney's parents until they found out why. Todney told you the rest, didn't he?"

I nodded. I wouldn't be forgetting Todney's father anytime soon. I'd never met the man, didn't even know what he looked like,, but I felt that

I knew him better than I knew anyone in that car. I'd known Todney's father my whole life—as a mailman, a sixth-grade teacher, a pastor, and a baseball coach, as the bigots on TV, and boys in the locker room.

"Yeah," I said. "He told me."

"Well, they're both from North Carolina," Rylie said. "Some small little hick town I can never remember the name of." She looked around, her gaze landing on Todney's sleeping form. She smiled. "He tell you how we met?"

I shook my head.

"It was in the hospital. He and Chris had just moved here when he was diagnosed, and Todney was checking on him. I was in visiting my grandma before she...well, we bumped into each other at the vending machine. We were so, so exhausted that we just didn't see each other, and we both tried to put our dollar in at the same time." She chuckled, but her eyes were dark. At some point during her explanation, a strand of hair fell out of her bun, but she did nothing to fix it. "Don't tell anyone that, Lucas, okay? At the wedding we're saying we met at college and that our first date was at a romantic little restaurant with roses and candles." She sighed—a long drawn-out breath that sounded more tired than anything, though that small lingering dose of hope was unmistakable. "Sounds romantic, doesn't it? Like a fairy tale."

Rylie stopped outside my house and put the car into neutral. "You're the only one who knows that."

I unbuckled my seat belt and carefully lowered Chris's head off my lap and onto the seat instead. His hand flopped down beside him, long fingers curling into a fist. "Why'd you tell me?"

Rylie shrugged. "Who are you going to tell?"

She had a point. I scrambled out of the car, overtly aware of the way my pants were sticking to my crotch and thighs. Several hours after my ocean exploration and they'd dried all wrong—wrinkled and stiff. I shook Frankie's shoulder, and she stirred—wide-eyed under the moonlight, her hair sticking up in every direction.

"We're here," I said.

Silent, she nodded and exited the vehicle. She hugged Rylie through the open driver-side window and headed into the house.

I watched her go and then said into the darkness, "Good night." But before I could leave, Rylie reached out and squeezed my hand.

"Thank you for coming," she said. "I'm really glad you could make it. I'm glad you're here." She looked back at Todney, then Chris, and then out the window, obviously seeing something I couldn't. "I'm going to need you, Lucas."

I didn't know what that meant, but I nodded anyway.

Rylie squeezed my hand a little tighter. "I love Clay. As a friend. I love him. You know that, right? That I love all of you, that this wedding...it doesn't change that? Don't go picking sides just yet, all right? We're still friends. We're all still friends, aren't we?" Her voice grew steadily higher and higher with each word. Her smile appeared, but it was lopsided. "Right, Lucas?"

It was like listening to an old tape when the film inside got tangled—the voices cracking and merging and then disappearing entirely. Where seconds ago, Rylie had been dancing around, seemingly without a care in the world, she now seemed to be chipping away in front of me. I didn't have any choice but to nod, to say "right," and try to mean it, if only to keep her smile from melting away entirely. When I looked up again, her eyes were wet.

"Good," she said, and there was the smile again—big and bright and plastic all around. I wondered if she'd learned it from Clay. "Good. I...Okay. Have a good night, Lucas. Thank you for coming. I'll see you soon, okay?" She squeezed my hand tight enough to hurt and then leaned back into her car and drove away.

I stood on the sidewalk, rubbing the feeling back into my fingertips as her rear lights disappeared into the darkness. In the city, it wouldn't have mattered; in the city, there'd be a car following, and then another dozen, and a few hundred after that. The skyscrapers above would be shining down, too many lights all around to notice a couple insignificant headlights. But in the suburbs at 12:30 a.m., Rylie's car was the only one out for miles.

My house should have been as dark. My parents should have been curled up in bed after tucking in my siblings, fallen asleep to the latest documentary on ghost sightings. But a single light remained—a small orange glow coming from the kitchen—and my mother's shadowed form, mumbling and cursing under her breath. The slam of a knife came down on the chopping block, the oven squeaked open, a bag was shook and a mixer turned on, and all the while, my mother repeated under her breath, alone in the sleeping house, "Not right, still not right, still not right."

UPSTAIRS, I COLLAPSED into my bed, my awkwardly wrinkled jeans still clinging to my legs. I shifted, and the stiff fabric shifted with me, chafing and stinging. I couldn't find the energy to do anything about it.

Just as my eyes grew heavy, just when I felt sleep creeping in around the corner, my phone rang from inside my crinkled pocket. I pulled it out and stuffed it between my ear and the pillow.

"Hello?"

"I was going to ask if I had the right number, but no one says 'hello' in quite the same grumpy way that you do," said Chris.

I tried to roll my eyes but somehow ended up smiling instead. "I'm tired. It's late."

"It's barely after midnight! The night is young!"

"Said the guy who fell asleep in my lap at ten."

There was a short stab of silence, then, "I did that? Well, that's embarrassing. I'm not going to lie, that was not part of the plan."

"I didn't think so." I tried to sound indifferent like the will-they-won't-they couples always did on TV, but it was easier thought than done. Really, all I could think about was how soft Chris's hair had been against my arm. He probably used shampoo. Most boys at school didn't bother, not when they were always rushing to class or to work or another party.

"I guess I have to step up my game then, huh?" said Chris.

"I guess so."

"Should I start reciting Shakespearean sonnets to you now, or should I jump right to the writing my own poetry with a rose between my teeth part?" he asked.

"I think it'd be hard to recite your poetry with a rose in your mouth."

Chris laughed. The sound was warm—deep but soft at the same time, not all that different from that day's ocean waves. But I imagined Chris's beach would be filled with sunshine rather than vortexes of death and cloudy eclipses.

"Okay, forget the roses. And forget the poetry too. I'll write you a song."

"I like rock," I offered.

"Rock-rock or indie rock?"

I glanced at my desk where my iPod lay, blue and scratched, the headphones still plugged in. "Indie."

"You're such a San Franciscan. Would you protest to a well-written rap?"

"Profusely."

Chris sighed—a drawn-out, wavering sort of sound that had me biting my lip to keep from laughing. "I'm not sure this relationship is going to work out," he said.

"Shame."

I thought I could feel Chris smile into the phone. "Hey, Lucas?"

"Yeah?"

"What was it like? The water?"

"It—" I broke off and scrubbed a hand over my pant legs. "Well," I said as I finally slid them off. I rose from the bed and hung the stiff jeans over my desk chair. "It was like letting go."

Chris didn't say anything for a long time. When he did, his voice was hushed, subdued. "That's it? Lucas, when did you give up on words?"

"What? You don't like my explanation?"

"It was vague! But that's okay. I was just wondering. You know, my dad always said it was the curse of the teenaged mind: we think everything we say is important, and that we always have to talk or our voices might die away. It's like the *Little Mermaid* syndrome or something. I talk too much. Maybe you just beat it already."

I lay back on the bed and rested a hand against my bare thigh. "It was like coming out of your body. Like you weren't heavy anymore. And you could move up and down and sideways and diagonal if you wanted. And you can't do that on land."

"Sounds nice," Chris said.

"Don't you remember?"

"Sure, I remember. But you can't feel a memory."

"You can't feel a story," I said.

Chris hummed. "Sure you can." He didn't explain, and I didn't ask.

For a moment, we stayed in a silence that should have been awkward but simply couldn't be when just the sound of Chris breathing had my eyes closing again.

"Good night, Lucas," he said later—maybe minutes, maybe an hour; I couldn't tell.

I smiled into my pillow. "Good night, Chris."

The line went dead, and for a moment, I simply enjoyed the peaceful silence before I forced my eyes open one last time. I dialed a new number—or old number, I suppose. Depends how you look at it.

Seconds later, a rough, faded voice answered. "Lucas! I thought you'd never call!" The boy on the other end hiccupped, clearly no more sober than he had been that morning. "What are you wearing?" Always the same question.

"A parka," I said. I rubbed a circle over my thigh. "I can't do this anymore, okay?"

The boy whistled. "Oh, we're skipping right to the good stuff, huh?"

"No," I said. "I can't do any of this. No more calls. No more late night...conversations."

"Come back, and we won't have to talk."

I seriously contemplated ripping out my hair. "No. Listen to me. I'm done. Completely. Okay? We had fun and...thanks. But I'm not going to be calling you anymore, and I don't want you to call me either."

"What's got your panties in a wad?" said the boy.

"Nothing. I just...nothing. Have a good night or...morning, I guess."

I hung up.

94 Days Before

The next morning found my house in complete chaos. My siblings ran wild around the halls, the girls in flowing white dresses and the boys in slacks. I staggered down in my boxers and yesterday's T-shirt, unaware of when my body reached the table or the food reached my mouth—just that both happened, miraculously, and that I thanked God for my muscle memory with every tired neuron flare of my half-working consciousness.

"Everyone, table, now!" said my mother. One by one, my siblings shuffled back to the kitchen, fighting over seats and placemats and the different colored cups. The only one left unquestioned was Sharon, the "baby" of us all. She was immediately gifted the "name the countries" placemat and the Dora the Explorer cup.

The twins sat closest together, both in slacks I used to own. "This itches," Daniel said, scratching at the collar of his purple dress shirt—also mine.

"Yeah," said Anthony, following his brother's lead and tugging at his blue hand-me-down shirt. "Can I take it off yet?"

My mother rolled her eyes. "They look great. Now eat your pancakes."

"Mom, why can't we go to the old church?" Sharon asked.

"Yeah, the old church!" echoed Daniel and Anthony in unison.

The old church had let us wear jeans. The pastor—Pastor Joe or Pastor Bob, or Philip, or some other classic, old-man type name—had a goatee and a tattoo sleeve and said things like "the lord commands it, yo," while he translated classic church hymns into rock songs. If religion and cool could ever go hand in hand, then Pastor Joe Bob Phillips was its personification—proof that God wasn't as uptight and rigid as all our old churches had made him out to be.

My mother cringed. "The old church did not work out," she said, glancing briefly at me and then back down at her plate. After a moment where she did nothing but nudge her eggs around and cut her pancakes into very, very small pieces, she said, "Are you going to come with us today, Lucas? Pastor Rogers would love to see you again. A lot of the kids are returning home from school now, and it's always nice to see the familiar faces. I'm sure he'd be very pleased."

At that moment, my father entered the room and sat in front of his plate of egg whites and sliced fruit. He glared at each piece in turn and then stabbed the closest melon. "Yeah, come with us, Lucas," he said. "You haven't been in ages. I'm sure you've missed it. Lucas, you'll really enjoy it." He looked up at me expectantly, meeting my eyes as though to make absolutely positively sure I knew who he was talking to—as if all the name dropping hadn't been hint enough.

My parents had this strange must-use-first-names-at-all-times thing. I still wasn't sure if it was because they had so many kids that they'd lost track or if they just thought they were being "personal," but it was always the same story. *Lucas, come here, and Lucas, do this, Lucas, don't leave, and Lucas, that's an interesting sweater you're wearing today, are you aware that it is all black and churches are "white suit" occasions?*

I looked down at my pancake. That morning, it was shaped like Mickey Mouse. Classic. Easy. I thought of my mom's frantic whispers the night before, that hysterical edge in her voice that in no way matched up with her present, cheery smile. It stretched fully across her face, her aged and yellowed teeth showing, and the longer I took to answer, the bigger it got.

I cut off Mickey's ear. "I have to go someplace today."

The corner of my mother's smile twitched but, for the most part, stayed upright. "It's Sunday, Lucas. Don't you want to spend some time with your family? With God?"

I cut off Mickey's other ear and then chopped his head clean in half. "I do spend time with God. And I'll spend time with you guys soon. I was going to go see Nathan today."

Silence fell through the kitchen. My mother stopped slicing her fruit, my father stopped mumbling curses at his egg whites, and Frankie—who, at sixteen, was old enough to remember Nathan with his eyes still open—swallowed her food and stared at me across the table.

"It's just been a while," I said. "Nine months, actually. And a couple other people were going. I'll go to church next week."

"Who's Nathan?" Sharon batted her eyes over the top of Dora's head and then gulped down the remainder of her orange juice. She slammed the cup back on the table just like the twins always did and announced, with a proud smile that was ignorant to the conversation, "Done!"

"Nathan is a friend of Lucas's," my mother explained. "Finish your fruit, and you can leave the table." Just seconds into the conversation and Nathan was already placed alongside the likes of fruit.

"I'm going to go." I rolled up my pancakes and stuffed it all into my mouth at once like a sweet burrito. I didn't look back to see my mother's expression—I couldn't—but grabbed my phone and walked to the hospital where at least it was quiet.

NATHAN LOOKED LIKE he always did in those days: still and pale, with more tubes coming out of him than I could name. Tubes came from his wrists and from his throat, tubes that connected to liquids and machines that never stopped beeping, making him both the quietest and the loudest of my high school friends. His curly black hair, once filled with product and perfectly combed, now lay plastered against his forehead. His eyes were closed, and so he couldn't see the flowers in the corner, and the "get well soon" cards on the countertop, the signed note from his baby sister on the wall. If you waited long enough, his hand would twitch and, for a moment, he was almost human again.

Our whole original crew was already gathered around Nathan's bed. As I looked at the two of them—Clay and Rylie sitting in absolute silence—high school suddenly seemed very small. In a class of a hundred and fifty, we were the only leftovers—no prom queen in sight, no baseball team at my side, Nathan as quiet as a statue.

I took a seat next to Clay, who clapped me on the shoulder and squeezed just a bit too tight. "Glad you came." As usual, he was dressed to the nines—a baby blue dress shirt over black slacks, brown eyes decorated with deep bags. In the stillness of the room, his smile was absent.

"Lucas is here. Can you believe it?" Rylie said. She held Nathan's hand and smiled when his fingers tightened against hers. Once upon a time, we'd thought that had been a sign of him waking up. In the early days, when the doctors still said "soon," we'd send the nurses in with every little muscle movement. These days it was nothing new. Nathan was still asleep. Nathan still wasn't Nathan.

"Hey." I pulled my chair closer to the bed and reached for his arm. "The prodigal son has returned."

Everyone laughed but Clay. He leaned back in his chair and took a couple deep breaths, his attention fixed on a machine over Nathan's head.

When no one said anything else, Rylie cleared her throat. "The wedding is coming up in a couple months." She stroked Nathan's dark hair from his face. "In August. I haven't gotten my dress yet, but when I do, I'll show you, okay? I had some flower choices I wanted to ask you about." She reached into her pocket and pulled out a crumpled notebook page. "Phalaenopsis Orchids or Juliet Roses?"

"No way in hell he knows what either of those are." Clay's hands shook, but he tucked them into his pockets and tried for a weak half grin.

"Okay," Rylie agreed, smiling first at Clay and then at Nathan. "Pretty white and yellow flowers, or pretty pinkish reddish flowers?" She traced a manicured finger down her list. "Oh. And centerpieces. More flowers, or something more creative? I was thinking fishbowls with little colorful rocks and maybe some reeds. And real fish. That'd be awesome, right?" She nudged Nathan's shoulder. "Can you imagine sitting down to eat, one fish on your plate and the other one staring you down while you eat its cousin?"

Silence fell again, and while Rylie braided the frayed edges of Nathan's hospital blanket, I leaned forward and studied the lines of his IV. If I closed my eyes, I could still see Rylie in pigtails, grossing out with the rest of us when someone kissed on TV. Not so long ago, we'd spent our Peter Pan days in back alleys and school yards, promises to never grow old yelled across swing sets and stolen booze. The day Clay brought a briefcase to the fifth grade rather than a backpack, I was sure I'd looked adulthood straight in the face; and yet here it was, staring me down in baby names and wedding flowers. This was real life—like some Nicholas Sparks movie playing out in front of me—while drop by drop, the bag of who-knows-what liquid that kept Nathan alive eased quietly into his veins.

"My dad's coming home tomorrow." Clay stood up and moved to the foot of Nathan's bed. As he spoke, he massaged Nathan's ankles the way the nurses had instructed us all—one small little action to keep up his circulation, one small little action that could decide whether or not Nathan ever walked again. That is, if he was ever awake enough to walk.

"He just finished a deal with Japan. Some big company merger. So if you were going to wake up, now would be a pretty great time. If you thought I was rich in high school, you can't imagine how I'm about to be rolling in it now. My dad's been working this deal my whole damn life." He paused to bite his lip but continued rolling and kneading his thumbs over Nathan's unworked muscles. "I'll buy you a Cadillac if you wake up. Any color you want. Dad won't notice if I take a few grand, I promise. It's for a good cause. Just—" He pushed a thumb hard into Nathan's leg and froze—everything from his hands to his billboard smile stuck in limbo—then, finally, breathed and pulled away. "Just come back."

Clay returned to his seat, and Rylie, her head bowed and lips tight, reached for his hand. Their fingers intertwined with all the ease and comfort of two people who had been doing it their whole lives. I glanced over my shoulder, though I'm not sure what I was expecting. To meet Nathan's eyes and gossip about our friends? To see my sister—the infiltrated spy in our midst—staring back at me with surprise? Whatever it was, I didn't find it. There was nothing behind me but buzzing machines and blank walls.

"You really don't want to miss the big day." Rylie scooted her chair closer to the bed, her eyes trailing over the IV, the machines, the veins in Nathan's unworked hands—anywhere but Nathan's frozen, blank face. "You know me; it's time to go all out. It's going to be a huge party. And Todney is a pretty good guy. You'd like him. He's a good dresser. Always in a blazer. Your kind of guy."

Clay tensed in his seat but otherwise gave no sign to indicate he was still listening; his eyes were on the ceiling, his hands fiddling in his lap. Rylie watched him from the corner of her eye.

"Let's go get some lunch, yeah?" Rylie said. She rose to her feet and straightened out her black-and-white checkered miniskirt. Clay nodded and stood to join her.

"I just ate," I said. "Big mom breakfast."

"Ohhh," said my friends in unison.

"A Momma Burke Extravaganza," said Clay. He ruffled the top of my hair. "We'll be back in a bit then." The two shuffled out all at once—unnervingly in sync.

When the last footstep disappeared down the hall, I took over Clay's seat, then Rylie's, then Clay's again, until finally I found a comfortable position—somewhere I could see both the twitches in Nathan's ring finger and the shallow rise and fall of his chest. There were always the little signs: the red flags that said his lungs still worked and his brain still functioned. The Nathan Marshall show wasn't over, but the hiatus just kept stretching on.

I don't know what it is about a guy in a coma that makes everyone feel like talking. It didn't mean anything; he couldn't hear us. We could talk until our voices bled dry, and he wouldn't notice. When he woke up—if he ever did—he wouldn't remember a word. But the thought always remained, like maybe if you say something shocking enough, something interesting enough, he'll open his eyes.

I didn't have anything shocking to say, nothing mind-blowing or new to reveal. I was home, I'd had really good pancakes that morning, I'd maybe grown half an inch over the last year, and for the first time since the eighth grade, I might have been ready to start dating. Big whoop.

Rylie was getting married, Clay was poised to take over his father's company or blow it out of the water with a newer, better one if he could stay sober long enough. Chris was a cancer survivor, an almost Olympic swimmer. And here we all were, stuck in a dead town while Nathan's heart monitor beeped, beeped, beeped.

"In San Francisco, they do social experiments in the park." Why did I say it? I had no idea. Nathan didn't flinch. He didn't open his eyes. He didn't care. "The week before I came back, they made two lines, and you got partnered up with a stranger. The stranger tells you about a problem they're having, and you give them advice. Then you tell the stranger a problem you're having, and they give you advice. My partner cheated on her boyfriend. I told her not to tell him. I told her it would hurt more if she told him. You think that's the right call?" Nathan didn't answer. "I think it's the right call. What's the point? Hurting someone just to have a clear conscience? That's bullshit." Nathan's leg twitched. Maybe he agreed; I doubted it.

"What did I tell her? I said I didn't want to go home. Ever." I dug my fingernails into my jeans until I could feel each nail like an individual knife. "Sorry. You get it, though, right? You were always going to go to L.A. You should have gone to L.A." The heart monitor beeped some more, but as far as answers went, all I got was silence. I reached for Nathan's hand and held it tight in my own. It was warmer than I expected—warm, but not warm enough, still corpse-like, still wrong. With one finger, I traced the veins on the back of his hand, followed them from his wrist up his ring finger. I'd heard once that the vein in your ring finger ran all the way back to your heart, but it seemed impractical. Chop off a finger and you killed the man. Drastic, wasn't it?

"You know what she said? She said 'it's only for the summer.'" I laughed. Nathan didn't get the joke, so I squeezed his hand a little tighter and leaned forward. He'd been shaved recently; his emotionless face was smooth but for a few missed places of stubble under his chin. "How do you do it? How do you stay so still? How can you stand not going anywhere?"

"Because he's dying."

I turned to find Clay leaning in the doorway, his arms crossed over his chest and an airport bottle of vodka hanging from two fingers. From where I was sitting, there didn't look to be a single drop left.

"He'll never wake up," he said. "Don't know why we keep pretending he will." He moved forward into the room and took a seat to my left. He groaned and hung his head between his knees. "Hey, Nathan," he whispered. "You want to trade?"

Five

90 DAYS BEFORE

Over the next couple of days, Chris and I became what I'd consider casual conversationalists. I'd like to call us texters, as I certainly texted him every time I felt like talking, but Chris didn't text; he called. Every. Single. Time. It didn't matter what I said, either. I could have been talking about the weather—and was more often than not because the summer heat was unbearable, nothing like the cool breezes of San Francisco—and Chris would still call to reply. One-sentence agreements and yups said across the telephone line, hang-ups before I'd registered picking up the phone. And you could bet your ass he'd call if it was his idea to talk. And it usually was.

Four days since we'd seen the wedding venue and we'd yet to meet up again in person, though I had been dragged to Rylie's place twice to pick between different napkin holders and followed Clay on two liquor gathering expeditions. The phone call came just after dinner and in the middle of my dishwashing adventure. I'd never had to do the dishes at school, where everything was compostable and if you did use real dishes, someone cleaned them for you. But between the soapy smell of lavender and my sisters singing an awful rendition of "I Will Survive" in the background, it was not completely unbearable.

"I need your help."

"With what?" I wiped my hands on a dishtowel that Sharon immediately transformed into a cape and took the phone upstairs.

"I've just spent six hours—*six hours!*—helping Todney pick out a tux. If I never see another suit again, I'm still going to have nightmares of dancing suits strangling me with their creepy classy sleeves." Chris huffed, and for a moment, I imagined a grumpy little toddler on the other end of the line, bottom lip protruding, rather than the attractive twenty-something whose face had yet to leave my mind those four days.

"Well, that was vivid."

"It was traumatizing," Chris corrected me. "He tried on a purple one. For his wedding. He tried on a purple tux."

"Do you need a paper bag? Maybe you should put your head between your legs. I hear that helps. Give yourself a moment to calm down. Maybe some crackers," I said.

"You know, I liked you better when you didn't talk."

"Liar."

Chris laughed. "Yeah, I am. Can we do something? Todney is pulling ties out of the closet. I need to get out of here. Please."

"Will you owe me a life debt and forever be my indentured servant?"

"Sure."

"Cool," I said. "Where we going?"

"How about that French theater downtown?"

I blinked. "We have one of those?"

"Yup."

"Who knew?"

THE OLD FRENCH theater was a little run-down building on Fifth Street. The last time I'd been home, it had been closed. I recognized it not by the shining lights out front, the ticket window, or even the movie posters on the walls outside, but by the broken glass permanently littered across the sidewalk and the window patched up with duct tape. I'd never got around to watching a movie inside it, but I knew the theater was a hot spot for vandalism, and that one time in the eighth grade, we'd snuck in to drink whiskey in the dusty back seats.

That night, the theater was up and running, and a little man sat behind the newly reinforced ticket window. With a thick German accent, he charged us for two overpriced tickets. He waved us along, past the door that had once been boarded up and through hallways that still smelled like fresh paint.

"French theater, huh?" Chris said, mimicking the man's not-so-very-French accent.

"Oui, oui," I said, and Chris laughed.

"You know you're just saying 'yes' twice, right?" he said.

I shrugged. "I don't speak French. That's literally all I got."

We picked a row midway through the theater and sat directly in the center seats. It wasn't hard; there was no one else in the theater but two old ladies several rows down where I assumed they could actually see the film in their inch-thick glasses. They were gossiping, as I'd come to believe all old ladies did—not a lot of new happened when you were that old, so anything even *slightly* exciting was worth discussing.

They didn't look back when we entered. When I was alone somewhere and someone new came in, I always looked back, always memorized his face and his clothes and every little detail I could just in case I had to tell the police about it later.

"I've always wanted to learn French." Chris leaned back and threw his legs over the seat in front of him. The theater repairs had been minimal, and there were still scratches and dents and places where huge chunks of the fabric were missing in every seat. "Before I die, I mean. When I was in high school, I always thought I'd grow up and go to some fancy college and study abroad in Paris or something."

"You end up going anywhere?" I asked. I didn't want to say "after the cancer" or "when you stopped dying" or anything, but once you lived your life in a hospital, where'd you go from there?

Chris shrugged. "Community college. I'm still there."

"What are you majoring in?" Immediately, I hated myself for the question. I couldn't have counted the number of times I'd asked that same thing on my fingers and toes and the books in my closet combined. When you were a freshman in college, "what's your major" replaced "hello," replaced "how are you" and anything even closely resembling general human politeness. *What's your major, and what dorm hall do you live in, and where did you live before you lived here? What do you want to do when you graduate? Have you decided the rest of your life yet?*

"Undeclared," Chris said. "Can't pick what I want to know everything about until I know a little bit of everything, right? I'm behind. Way too behind. I got a lot to learn." He looked up at the screen and then back at me. "But I always thought if I learned French, I'd feel really cultured or something."

"I took Spanish in high school," I said. "Haven't taken any languages in college yet."

"I see I chose my date wisely. So neither of us is going to understand a single word of this movie, are we?"

I shook my head. "Nope." I waited for the moment when Chris would suggest "alternative" activities for us to do, waited for his arm to snake around my shoulders, or at the very least for him to ask to leave, but the words never came. If anything, he sunk back into his seat even farther, stretched out as though he'd never been more comfortable in his life, and watched the screen with obvious interest as the pre-preview commercials played. I couldn't understand a thing they said, and neither, I guessed, did Chris, but he laughed all the same.

For a long time—two commercials, to be exact, and these French commercials were pretty damn long—I just sat there, overtly aware of every breath I took, of how the oxygen left my lungs, how heavy the muscles in my legs were, and how, if I touched my knee, it was solid, but not metal solid. And then I started wondering if my breath smelled okay, and I thanked God that dinner's mashed potatoes hadn't been garlic—which was all pretty damn stupid because Chris wasn't even looking at me, let alone thinking about kissing me. There were two women on the screen, pretty and very, very French in that sexy way I could still appreciate, even if I wasn't thinking at all about kissing *them*. If his attention would be focused anywhere, it would be there.

My hands stupidly sweaty, I pulled out my phone and googled "basic French phrases."

"*Excusez-moi,*" I said to Chris. He blinked and then smiled.

"I know that one," he said.

I looked back down at my phone, read over a couple of lines to avoid more "easy ones," and then tried again. "*Comment allez-vous?*"

Chris smiled. "No idea," he said. He turned away from the screen now and gave me his complete attention, his mouth twisting up around the corners. "That sounded dirty. Was that dirty?"

"I said 'how are you?'"

Chris shrugged, and his smile grew even wider. "Could be dirty if you wanted it to be."

"Do you want it to be?" I asked.

"We'll see." Chris shifted in his chair. With his "good leg," he moved seamlessly and tucked it under his body; with his bad leg, he fumbled around for a good thirty seconds before finally thrusting it straight out in order to leave his fake knee unbent. "So *comment allez-vous?*" he said finally.

How was I? "That's your opening question? Pretty big for a first date."

Chris shrugged. He placed his hand against the armrest; his fingers traced little circles over the fabric. "You think so? I think it's pretty simple. You know, you're happy or you're sad or you're angry. How many emotions do you think there are? Ten?"

"Thousands," I said. Perhaps they weren't all named, but words couldn't cover everything.

"All right," Chris conceded. "From the thousands then. Coma alu vas. Did I say that right?"

I shook my head and laughed—not out loud or anything, but internal laughing counts for something too, I think. "Not at all," I said as though I remembered the real saying myself. How was I? Cooment all—something. "Well, how I am depends on a lot more than just me, you know."

Clay came to mind first—bloodshot eyes and a bottle permanently fused to his hand; then Rylie—fading makeup and watery smiles; Nathan—still as death. Then a glimmering image of my dorm room and my quiet roommate who never tried to drink himself to death or get married to someone he hardly knew, and the only things he ever asked me to do for him was to wear headphones when I listened to music. Then I saw a big city where there was more than just one McDonald's and a shady diner, and you could eat at a different restaurant three times a day for a year and still not exhaust your options. In English, French, Spanish, and every accent and language in between, the image came with possibilities and a life not held back by the endless expanse of nothing that existed outside the walls of this French theater.

"I'm tired," I said.

Chris's eyes narrowed. "You're on summer vacation. What are you doing besides sleeping all day? That's what I'm doing."

I shrugged. I'd slept until noon that day. I was still tired. This town was tiring. Life was tiring. I was starting to wish I could hibernate. "We have this friend," I told Chris instead, "who got in a car accident last year. Night of graduation he drove into a tree. He's in a coma. All he does is sleep, and I think he's the most exhausting person I've ever met."

Chris didn't say anything for quite some time. At least one commercial passed—a long, "insider's view" into an upcoming film—before he finally looked at me again. "I'm sorry about your friend."

I shrugged. So was I. So was everyone. Sorry just didn't do much about it.

"I'm serious," Chris said. He turned until his entire body was poised in my direction, all trace of a smile gone from his face. "I know what that's like. At least a little bit. Lying around in a hospital bed day after day. There's nothing more exhausting than doing absolutely nothing. Do you know why he crashed?"

I shrugged again. "He was drunk. We all were. We all took a cab, but he didn't want to leave his car, and he kept telling us he was fine. We didn't stop him. Surprised you didn't see it on the town welcome sign; the story singlehandedly fed the newspaper staff for months." I crossed my arms over my chest. My fingernails left marks along my skin, but I couldn't imagine caring. The last time Nathan's eyes were open, they were as bloodshot as Clay's were every day. The last time Nathan spoke, he'd been slurring. I didn't notice any of it then; I sure as hell noticed it now.

Chris moved closer and knocked his shoulder against mine. "Not your fault. If you were all drunk, you wouldn't have known what was okay and what wasn't. It was an accident."

I shrugged but took the Nathan approach and said nothing.

The previews started, ads for more movies we couldn't understand with plots we couldn't follow, but the two old ladies ahead of us kept laughing, so I guess the ads couldn't have been that bad. While we waited through the opening credits, I pulled up more basic phrases and read them aloud to Chris.

"You have to guess," I said. "Guess what you think it is."

Chris nodded. In the darkness, his expression appeared uncertain, but he pushed it away with a blinding smile. I was starting to doubt he was capable of dim. "All right, I'm in. Throw 'em at me."

"Comment vows apple vose?" I said, which was supposed to be *comment vous appellez-vous*, but I wasn't French, and I was never going to be.

"Will you marry this apple?" Chris said, completely straight-faced.

I rolled my eyes but still laughed out loud this time. "I said 'what's your name?' Now you say *je m'appelle Chris*."

"I call my apple Chris," Chris translated.

"Wow, you are a natural at this."

Chris laughed—hard—and at the same time, both old ladies turned around and shushed him at the top of their old lungs. Each woman held a single wrinkled finger over her mouth and glared us down until Chris and I went completely silent. Only then did I realize that the movie was playing.

From what I could gather, it was a love story between a poor, young farmer boy and a rich, well-to-do French girl. The girl flipped her hair over her shoulder a lot and wore dark lipstick, and when she said things dramatically, her boobs sort of stuck out more than they had in the scene before. Maybe it was her character—I didn't have a clue what was going on—or maybe just the actress herself, but her eyes seemed depressingly sad the whole time: smiling but sad, yelling but sad, making love but sad.

Chris's first "move" came after the French girl and the farm boy broke up for the second time (I think). The classic slide around was slower paced than any date I'd ever been on, but I also kept my pants on the whole time too, so it sort of made sense. It wasn't until halfway through the film that his arm completely draped around my shoulders. It was such a worn-out move, but for some reason, I didn't even care. Chris's arm was warm and firm; he wasn't the bulky type, and he certainly wouldn't have won any weight-lifting competitions, but I could feel the muscle against my shoulder blades, and that was enough.

The couple on the screen started making out then, their noses squished together all funny like—as smashed as the silly putty I used to play with as a kid.

"Do you think they can breathe?" Chris asked me.

I shrugged. "I don't know. Maybe they practice a lot. Could come in useful. For when all the plants die and oxygen is limited."

Chris nodded. His profile was sharper in the dark, more defined and mysterious. For a moment, he almost looked edgy rather than the handsomely goofy I was used to. I couldn't decide which one I preferred.

"Should we practice?" he asked.

"Probably," I said. "It could save our lives."

"I do like to save lives. And I like to live," Chris agreed.

He moved closer. His shoulder brushed mine. His hand lingered over my forearm. His fingers brushed my fingers. The pre-kiss prelude was always such a strange moment: should I bend to the left or to the right? Did I shave this morning? Did I need gum? What if it was bad? Sometimes really cute guys were *really* bad kissers, and it sort of ruined everything, like why put all this effort into one human being, crafting every little detail of their existence so perfectly just to ruin it all with an inability to properly use your lips? The pre-kiss prelude was all about eye contact and close breathing and *proximity*, and I was counting Chris's eyelashes up until the very moment my own eyes closed. That was when our lips touched.

I'm not going to say it was fireworks or anything, and no sparks came shooting out of our lips, but it was good. I mean, really good. His lips were soft, but not too soft, and the little bit of stubble on his jaw stung at just the right level of pleasurable. Chris's arms were heavy on my arms in that way that said "I got you" but not "I'm going to kidnap and kill you," and when he smiled, I could feel it. I could feel the light.

"A first kiss in a dark movie theater. So cliché," Chris said when he pulled away. He smiled again, or maybe he'd just never stopped. "Good thing I don't have the time to be original."

TODNEY PICKED US up from the theater. It was like being fifteen again and having your parents drive you around on your first date—embarrassing because there's no possible way of feeling like an adult when your mommy and daddy are still asking how it went, but oddly comforting too, like if it did go wrong, you had someone to complain to. Someone to understand. We didn't do any complaining, at least not about the date, but Chris did grumble nonstop during the drive, saying things like "I'm twenty-one years old, I do not need a babysitter" and "My legs work, Todney! That was the whole point of the surgery." Eventually, he resorted to just sticking his tongue out at the back of Todney's head and called that good enough. I never stopped laughing.

When Todney pulled up to my house, he put the car in park and faced the backseat with such a serious dad look on his face I half expected to get the safe sex talk right then and there. Instead, he smiled—a little forced, a little tired—and told me to have a great rest of my night. I kissed Chris's cheek and got out.

The car clock had read eleven something, and though I was nineteen years old—officially part of the "and older" demographic of "eighteen and older" and didn't have a curfew anymore—I still crept in like I used to. Slow and quiet, careful of every step, every little noise that might tip off my parents that I was coming in late.

It didn't matter. They were waiting for me in the living room.

"Where were you?" My mother was dressed in a pink and yellow flowered nightgown, which might have been funny—used to be funny—

except that she'd worn it every night of my life. When it got dirty, she had a second, identical backup. I'd always daydreamed of burning it.

My father sat in the worn armchair beside her, plucking bits of fluff from its many holes. He didn't say anything.

"I was out," I said.

"Out?" My mother stared at me, her eyebrows raised, and then looked to my father.

"Out where?" he asked.

"Out with a friend."

"You know you're supposed to tell us when you're going out and how long you'll be *before* you leave," my mother said.

"I'm nineteen, Mom."

She didn't hear me, or if she did, she didn't care. Waving her hands around with every word, she continued, "Sharon is coming down with a cold. We could have used your help today. You're already gone most of the year; the least you could do is be home when you're here."

"She's not my daughter," I said.

"But she is your sister."

"I know that." I knew every freckle on her tiny little face, knew the way her hair curled in the back, and the way she'd cried for days when she was five and fell out of a tree. I'd been gone, not dead. Of course I knew.

"Well, you'd think you'd want to spend more time is all." My mother stepped forward. The way she was looking at me—her eyebrows lowered, her arms crossed over her chest—you would have thought I'd left home to travel the country as a bank robber, not to go to school. She reached out and placed one hand on my shoulder. With the other, she tilted up my chin. Forget "eighteen and older;" I might as well have been five, about to get a time out. "Family is the most important thing in the world, Lucas. Don't go forgetting that. You know, if you stayed home next year and went to the nice little community college down the street, you'd have a lot more time. And I worry about you all by yourself in that big city."

I stepped back, away from my mother's hand, away from her hopeful gaze. "I'm not staying here."

My father chuckled. He leaned back in his chair and stroked a hand across his stubbled chin. "Don't be so dramatic, Lucas. You say that like you're being tortured. What's so bad about here? This is a good town. There's a lot happening."

"Right." If you liked backyard gardening or selling drugs to minors then, yes, there was quite a lot to do. But my father worked two towns over, so he almost never passed by the dented tree where Nathan had last seen the world, and he didn't know that Mrs. Cartor, the widow next door, wailed out her window each morning, or that the whites of Clay's eyes hadn't been white since we were in the sixth grade. But my mother, who would say everything was fine until her lips turned blue, knew. My mother—who stood in a classroom all day begging her students, "please don't grow up the way the last generation did"—knew and still she came home preaching about the big, glorious world we all lived in.

My parents didn't say anything more, so I slipped past and went upstairs. Sharon's room—well, Sharon and Frankie's shared room—was two doors down from mine and still open. I stepped inside. Frankie was passed out, face flat into her pillow, snoring and clutching the small blue blanket she'd clung to for the last sixteen years of her life. Sharon was awake but pretending not to be, one eye open to size up her bedroom intruder.

"Lucas?" she whispered.

I nodded and went to sit on the edge of her bed. She sat up. "How'd your date go?" She giggled. "Did you kiss him? Was it gooood?"

"How'd you know I was on a date?" I placed a hand on her forehead. Sure enough, it was warm and clammy—a flu in the making. I grabbed a bottle of water from her bedside table and handed it over.

She took a small sip and then set the bottle down and giggled again. "Frankie told me." Sharon pointed across the room at her sister's sleeping form. "She said she heard you talking on the phone about a boy. Is he cute?"

I nodded. "He's very cute."

"Did you kiss him?"

"Yup."

Sharon clapped both her little hands over her mouth and laughed between her fingers. "Was it good?" she asked again.

"Yeah." I smiled. "It was really good. But I heard you didn't have such a good day. Sick, huh?"

Sharon nodded and then sniffled, undoubtedly for added effect. "Very sick," she said. "I might die."

I frowned and ruffled back her tangled brown hair. "Can you try very, very hard not to? I'd miss you if you died."

She smiled, and then, as though remembering the seriousness of her "condition," frowned, coughed a little, and shrugged. "I'll try." She fake-coughed a couple more times—a sound like "ahem, ahem, ahem"—then drank the rest of her water.

I kissed her forehead and headed back to my room. My phone started to ring before I'd even reached the door. I couldn't remember ever having so many people to talk to—at least not in school because everyone I knew lived across the hall or camped out in the library, and if my phone did ring, I didn't answer it. But there didn't seem to be a lot of options now. I picked up on the third ring.

"Lucas?" Rylie's sobbing across the line almost stifled her voice. I could just barely decipher the words through her heavy, watery gasps. "Lucas, are you there?"

"Yeah, I'm here. What's going on? Is everything okay?"

She hiccupped. "Everything's fine."

"Then why are you crying?"

"Because I'm sad."

I tried to think of what the correct response might be, but the more platitudes that came to mind, the more it all felt wrong. "Why are you sad?" I asked.

"I had a dream. About the wedding. We were all dancing, and then Nathan's car came crashing into the ballroom. He died. Everyone died. All of the wine was blood, Lucas."

I sank back into the bed, into my warm sheets, my warm pillow, with my twenty-first century phone pressed to my ear and no blood on my hands. Eighteen and older. Adulthood and family life, marriage, booze, and dead ends—everything slipping through everyone's hands like ash, and all I really wanted was to sleep and make the world sleep with me.

"That's probably normal," I said. "Prewedding fears and all that."

Rylie laughed—a sound so hysterical, so high-pitched and unreal it could belong only in a horror movie. A knife-wielding, sobbing, crazy-eyed villain. Or a woman desperately looking to the future when the past kept twitching—asleep—in a hospital room: a constant reminder.

"Prewedding fears are about the groom leaving you. About divorce. Not death. You're never going to understand."

"Then why'd you call?" I asked.

"Because you don't know anything."

"What's that supposed to mean?"

"It means you weren't here watching Nathan's parents cry every day; you weren't the one hugging them when they were sobbing into your shoulder about burying their child; you weren't here when Todney proposed and couldn't tell his family, when Clay got his stomach pumped over Christmas! You call yourself his best friend, but you weren't there for him. I was. *I* was, Lucas! You weren't here when your sister landed a role in her school play. She's really good, did you know that? You weren't here for anything, so you don't know anything." Rylie's voice wasn't watery anymore. It wasn't muffled. Each word came through clear as day, each one angrier than the last.

"Then why'd you call?" I said again.

"I don't know," Rylie said. "Because I miss you. Or maybe because talking to you is like talking anonymously on the internet; I can get it all out and no one will pat me on the back and say a bunch of positive shit that doesn't matter. I don't need sympathy."

"You don't think I'm sympathetic?"

"I don't think you care."

"You're wrong."

"Maybe." Rylie paused. After several beats of silence, she sighed. "Yeah, maybe. I'm sorry. Maybe I just want you to tell me things get better. You got out. I could get out too, right?"

"If you want to."

"I think I do. I do now. Todney and I. We can start somewhere fresh. We could be happy. Maybe. I don't know. You ever think about getting in your car and just driving until the gas runs out?"

I pictured it; disappearing in some beat-up, old pickup truck, coffee cup in the holder, music blasting, and a copy of Kerouac's *On the Road* sitting in the passenger seat. Just the pavement and me. *There was nowhere to go but everywhere.*

"I take a bus," I said. "I don't have a car. In the city, I take a bus everywhere."

Rylie laughed. The watery note was back, that lingering desperation, that frenetic, panging, broken nothing. "Then you don't really get to choose where you're going, do you?"

I shrugged, though she couldn't see it, though it didn't matter. "You choose which bus to take and where you get off."

She sighed. "Maybe that's good enough."

Six

79 DAYS BEFORE

Since the French First Kiss, I had talked to Chris every day—whether it was on the phone or on a date or at the diner for burgers—and yet I had never really planned to be talking to him over assorted wedding cakes. But Frankie had been unavailable and Todney uninterested in cake flavors, and so here we were, sitting at a table big enough to feed an army—Rylie, Chris, and I, ten cakes between us.

"You know gay guys aren't inherently better at this stuff, right?" I said.

"And I'm not gay. Bisexualllll," said Chris through a mouthful of pumpkin-stuffed something. The names—things like Blissful Romance in Classic Vanilla—had been lost on me after the first twenty-minute long cake description.

Rylie rolled her eyes and tried a bite of the brown cake to her left. Like with every bite before it, she took her time, rolling it over her tongue, looking up to the heavens for cake-tasting advice, and then swallowed dramatically.

"This one tastes too tangy, don't you think?"

Chris reached across the table and took a bite the size of a child's fist. "Tastes like orange cake. Very..." He paused to savor. "Orangey."

Rylie rolled her eyes.

SOMEWHERE AROUND THE twentieth cake, I was beginning to feel more than comfortably full and more than a little ready to unbutton my pants in public. Rylie left the table to find the baker, and for a long time, they spoke in the corner, discussing sizes and designs while Chris and I stared at frosting samples.

All was still and quiet until Chris jumped up from the table. "Come with me." He placed a finger to his lips. "But don't let Rylie see us."

All soft steps and hushed moves, we slid past the table, past the rows of uneaten cakes, past the other couples feeding each other off ornate forks, and snuck into the store closet near the back. Chris pulled a joint from his pocket and used a lighter to illuminate our too-close faces.

"In here?" I asked.

Chris grinned. "In here."

He lit the joint and we shared it, one hit there, one hit here, and several long minutes after the butt end died out, I felt like I could eat twenty more cakes. Whole. My munchies had always come fast—faster even than the high, and I was craving everything. Chris gestured for me to stay where I was, so I took the joint, lit it one last time, and sucked up the last nonexistent bits while he darted out the closet. A minute later, he came back, laughing through his teeth and holding a sample plate. We dug in.

I'm no business man, but if you ask me, this was the way to sell cakes: stoned out of my mind in a too-cramped closet with a good-looking boy, and I was ready to buy every cake in the shop. The pumpkin was suddenly more pumpkiny, and the strawberry more *real*, the sugar more sweet, and the frosting to fucking die for. Cake heaven was the best of them all. I slumped back against the closet, using my phone flashlight to illuminate our surroundings.

It was kind of a dump—just a bunch of brooms and a vacuum and more cobwebs than I liked to see in a food establishment—but I was so focused on Chris I barely noticed. He had his legs kicked out in front of him, his head back against the wall. Everything about him was loose, from his lazy smile to the slump in his shoulders. I didn't get it. I didn't get him. But honestly, I wasn't even sure I wanted to because for the very first time, I understood the mystery boy cliché, and I sort of liked it; give a man a puzzle, right?

Chris scooted closer in the dark and reached for the last cake sample. He ate a bite and then slid his finger through the frosting and placed it on the tip of my nose. "Ah, Rudolph, there you are." He laughed.

I scrunched up my nose, and maybe because I was too high to be my properly socially inept self or because the dark of the closet made me brave, I kissed him and reached for the zipper on his jeans.

"Whoa, Casanova." Chris's hand fell over mine, stalling any future movements, but his mouth stayed, a mouth that tasted like weed and cake and something minty I thought was probably toothpaste but could have also just been more cake. "Give me a second to count our dates," he said into my mouth. "I don't do the nasty until the third."

"This is our fifth."

"You count making out in a broom closet a date?"

"It's not?" I asked.

Chris laughed. "I'll take it."

We made out for a while then, his tongue in my mouth, and my hands on his back, his leg wrapped around mine until I couldn't tell quite where he ended and I began, but it didn't matter. All that mattered was that he was warm, and when he laughed, nervous or amused or somewhere in between, I could feel it vibrate over my lips and through my bones. I'd made out with a lot of boys, and I was no stranger to taking off a man's pants, but when Chris's hand finally found mine and brought it to his belt loops, I could actually taste my own anxiety—thick and overwhelming, like overeating at Thanksgiving.

I undid the button on his jeans, pulled down his zipper, and had his pants to his ankles—a hard job in our cramped closet, mind you—by the time he got my shirt over my head. It was all very fast after that, hands wandering, mouths everywhere, teeth grazing skin, and my pants were suffocating me. I had them halfway off when the closet door opened, blinding us both in vivid white light.

Rylie stood, arms crossed over her chest next to the very distraught-looking baker.

IT'LL SUFFICE TO say that we were kicked out, that Rylie claimed we were both mentally unstable, and if the baker would please, please consider still making her cake, she would promptly throw us into a volcano or under a bus or whatever would be most pleasing to the baking gods.

"We didn't *actually* do anything," Chris said on our way back to the car, jogging to keep up with Rylie's "I'm pissed off and not talking to either of you" pace.

It was kind of hard to back him up what with us both getting stoned and exchanging spit in a bakery closet, which I thought was at least *something*, but I shrugged and added, "All underwear stayed on," for good measure.

Rylie rolled her eyes.

"Hey, remember that time I almost died and you were going to miss me?" Chris said.

Rylie blinked and nodded, looking like she'd seen a ghost.

"Yeah, can you drive me to the diner? Todney wants to grab a beer." Chris held up his phone to show the supporting texts.

"Why couldn't you have just said that?" asked Rylie. "What was that intro about?"

"I wanted you to feel motivated to help me." Chris shrugged. "Got to use the cards I have."

Though she bitched about it the whole way—admittedly, with good reason—Rylie drove Chris to the town diner. He kissed me goodbye, and she and I left for my house then parked idle in the driveway.

"You can't play him," she said. Rylie never had beat around the bush. "It's not like he's fragile or anything. Because he's not. It's that he loves hard. And he's a good person. He'd take a bullet for Todney or me, and I've never known anyone like that before. He's very loyal and you..."

"Are a slut," I finished.

"I wasn't going to say that."

"But you were thinking it." I leaned back in my seat and shrugged. I could still taste Chris on my lips, this tingling excitement on my taste buds, and perhaps that was the strangest part. I was out of the moment, but the moment had stayed. It had been a long time since I'd felt infected by just a kiss.

"I like him," I said after a while. "Don't look at me like that, I *do*. They've all been good dates. We're having fun. You know, some people do that. They have fun." I might not have been ready for marriage at nineteen—which I liked to think was true for most people, minus my current company—but I was more than capable of dating. Chris was interesting. Funny. Nice. Good-looking—*fuck*, he was good-looking. Playing someone made it sound so serious; a witch with a voodoo doll, sticking in the pins. I'd just wanted a good fuck.

"And that's great," Rylie said. "But I don't want you to *hurt* him. You understand?"

I nodded. Saluting her as I slid out of the car, I said, "He's in safe hands," and then marched up the steps to my front porch, yanked open the door, and let it slam behind me.

74 DAYS BEFORE

On Saturday, the twins had their first soccer match of the season, which Chris and Clay joined me in watching—that is, if you count sitting idly on the sidelines with no clue what the score was to be watching. Chris said he'd never understood soccer, that it moved faster than baseball and slower than swimming, and so naturally he'd always been lost. Clay didn't watch sports at all. I just didn't care.

The twins were good in the "occasionally kicked the ball and never let the team down so badly that it made you wince" sort of way, and the weather was nice—sunny but not too hot—so all in all, the day wasn't a complete waste. But I longed to do something important, even if it meant another peace rally in the city, or a recent college grad's pretentious art show. In little league soccer, they didn't even keep score. Nothing lost, nothing gained; a wash of a day.

While we watched, Chris braided two strands of grass together idly and made a ring. "Did your brothers choose to play soccer?"

I shrugged. "I don't know. Why?"

"Well, I've always wondered if I had kids if I'd make them do sports or not. I mean, part of me thinks when kids are little, they don't know what they want, so you sort of have to give them a nudge? And so it's good if you get them into a ton of things while their brains are all spongy. I mean, I wish someone thought to teach me a second language while it was still possible for me to learn it. But at the same time..." Chris sighed and looked out over the field, at all the five-foot twelve-year-olds chasing after a mud-splattered ball that wouldn't even earn them points. "I don't want to push my kids into anything they don't want to do. Or give them some weird expectations they can't live up to, you know?"

I shook my head. I didn't know. I'd never even thought of kids before, let alone what I'd teach them and what I wouldn't. "You already have all that planned?"

It was Chris's turn to shrug. "Yeah. I mean, it's always been part of my picture."

"Your picture?" Clay asked.

"Yeah," Chris said. "The way I see my life. Once I get all my pieces together—you know, school, health, yada yada—I'll have the picture. And I think there will be kids. Probably. Maybe adopt, though. Don't want to pass on the cancer gene." He turned back to the game, stared at the field for a while, and then shook his head and looked back at Clay and me. "Nope. Still don't get it."

THEY WON. FRANKIE kept score on her phone and showed us the whopping 10-2 that had occurred without any of us boys noticing. Feeling vaguely incompetent and more than a little sluggish, I rose to my feet, said goodbye to my family, and nodded for my friends to follow me behind the park. We pulled out a few cigarettes, smoked until the sunlight ran out, then headed to a bar with the help of Clay's fake and a couple of uninterested and unobservant bouncers.

Chris was the only one of us legally old enough to order, but Clay was friends with the bartender. So while he got the drinks, Chris and I found a booth and picked at the peanut-filled bowl in the center of the table. An old Buddy Holly song played on the radio.

"Looks like I'm going to spend this whole week intoxicated with you," Chris said. "Man, when I was on chemo, I couldn't drink anything. I mean, not even beer. And no, I wasn't twenty-one yet, but seriously? I'm getting too old for this *now*; I missed my prime." He shook his shoulders in time with the music and then reached for a peanut. One crack of a bite, and he gasped and spit it right back out. "Wow, that is nasty. Do not try that."

"They've probably been here for years," I said. A lot of things were old in this town: the peanuts, the music, the people. Thinking of Nathan's old car and my friends' old relationships, I looked away and tapped my fingers against the counter until Clay returned with three shot glasses. We clanked them together and then drank as one. It went down like heaven.

I guess I was just ready to be drunk, or maybe tired of being sober, but four shots did me in, and soon I was so damn focused on the dots on the ceiling—fifty-four and counting—that I barely noticed Chris's arm come sliding around my shoulders.

"You, my friend, are drunk," he said.

"Am not," I said.

"Are too." Chris handed me a peanut. I took it, but before it even touched my lips, he confiscated the nut and threw it to the ground. "That was a test, Lucas, and you failed! You almost ate the poisonous peanut."

I blinked. With his arm still around my shoulder and his lips close to my ear, his words didn't really register. The nuts looked perfectly fine in the haze, but his lips looked better. I wondered, briefly, if his lips were different than any other lips, and I tried to remember the last time we'd kissed and if I'd liked it. I thought I did. But I thought it needed more experimentation. Slumping down into the booth, I hiccupped, laid my head in his lap, and stared back up at the ceiling. Fifty-five dots.

Chris's fingers slid through my hair. I thought: *not bad*, and closed my eyes. I wasn't in a bar anymore, just lying with a cute boy, listening to old music, eating bad peanuts.

"This is cute and all," said Clay. "But certain single people are still present." He pointed at his own chest and then sucked up his drink loudly—something with a straw and umbrella, though I couldn't remember when he'd gotten anything that wasn't in the form of a shot. Lifting my head above the table, I took in the collection of drinks—a couple of which looked like they might have been mine—and a basket of onion rings. I took one and lay back down.

"Good," I said.

Chris laughed and resumed petting my hair.

73 Days Before

I woke up the next morning to a raging headache and the sight of Chris sitting in my desk chair. He looked over as I sat up, smiled, and offered me a bowl of cereal. "Your mom let me in, hope that's okay. She said, and this is a quote, 'I like you. None of Lucas's other boyfriends ever brought him food when he was sick.' Am I your boyfriend, Lucas?" He smirked. The bastard.

I groaned and reached for the cereal. At least I'd have something to do with my hands while my mouth flailed. Clearing my throat, I twirled the spoon through the milk. "You're...the boy I've gone on five dates with," I said after a minute.

"Six."

"What?"

"Six," Chris said. "We've been on six. Last night counts."

"Okay," I said. "Six. But I don't like the term boyfriend. It's...childish." I shrugged and started up on the cereal. Never in the history of humanity had Honey Nut Cheerios ever tasted so good. God himself must have poured the milk because it was actually perfect. I spooned the rest into my mouth while trying not to focus on the way Chris's bottom lip twitched or how bright the room still was. Light bulbs really should have been illegal in the presence of the hungover.

"Fair enough," he said.

They say all is fair in love and war, but this was neither. Head pounding, body aching, and lost in that troublesome, nameless relationship bubble of "where are we now," I sunk down into my bed and resisted the urge to groan aloud. I was the ass, of course, for keeping him in limbo, the commitment-phobe, and he'd see through it eventually, say Rylie was right. But you couldn't blame a boy for enjoying the good times while they lasted. Pinocchio, terrifying as he might be, was right about some things: life was better without strings.

Two minutes of silence and then, "Want to go get some coffee?"

I nodded. "Desperately."

WE MADE IT as far as the park and then stopped and made out under the oak tree.

Seven

Every dinner was a full-family affair in my house. I often imagined that what my family ate on an ordinary Thursday evening was equal to that of a normal family's Christmas, or, at the very least, a Super Bowl feast. Seven mouths took a lot to be satisfied. Seven mouths that included two growing boys, a man trying to cheat his diet, and a starved college kid who had lived on ramen and cafeteria food for nine months were *impossible* to satisfy.

We all squeezed around the dinner table, my mother shushing us because she said the noise in the kitchen made it difficult to concentrate. She sprinkled in the seasoning and counted the measurements under her breath.

"Why'd you call us in if dinner wasn't ready?" asked my father.

My mother glared over the top of her mixing spoon. "Because it's dinnertime. Sit down."

It was ten more minutes before she actually put the food out, and I swear we hit that pot like lions on the savanna—pounce and devour. My mother never took the easy way out—the way I would if I had an army of kids—never bought us pizza or takeout or mass amounts of TV dinners. She never cut corners, never bought premades to heat up, never skipped steps, and if my father ever offered to help, she pushed him away with whispers of "you don't understand a thing about food." Dinner was all homemade—homemade stew with homemade bread, fresh vegetables and just-cooked noodles. I was on my second helping before my mother cleared her throat and reminded us what real food actually cost.

"How was everyone's day?" Her face lit up as she waited for answers.

My mother tried so damn hard to be traditional, to uphold the family values her mother had taught her and her grandmother before her.

Lessons of civility and grace, of place settings and forks and knives all in neat little rows, of happy family conversation and napkins in our laps. Her face lit up, her frown lines evened out, she clapped her hands together, and for that one moment, while stew dripped from all our lips and hunger had us still eager to be there, I think she forgot who she was sitting with. She sure as hell couldn't be seeing the truth.

She couldn't be seeing her overweight, balding husband who dripped mushed carrots over his chin with every bite while his cholesterol levels continued to skyrocket. She couldn't be seeing the daughter she never meant to have, the one who kept the family from retiring, the one with uncontrollable hair who didn't look like the rest of us. She couldn't be seeing the twins, who, the night before, had had normal dirty-blond hair that was now suddenly streaked with lime-green strips that none of us wanted to ask about. She couldn't be seeing her gay son, the one she left her favorite church for, the one who ran away, the one the papers talked about because he and his batshit crazy friends didn't save the boy in the coma.

Frankie, for what it was worth, had normal hair, and last I'd heard, she'd brought home A's and B's from school every term, so she couldn't be turning out that bad. Anyway, she answered first.

"I hung out with Jackie today. We went to the movies. It wasn't very good. Well, I didn't like it, but I think Jackie did."

My mother smiled. "That's lovely, dear," she said. Which didn't really have much to do with what Frankie said, but then, I wasn't entirely sure that the content of *what* we said was as important to my mother as the mere fact that we said it.

It felt sort of like an AA meeting or a confession or something else far too serious. *Hi, my name is Lucas, and today I drank a quarter bottle of scotch with Clay in the park. Forgive me, Father, for I have sinned.* I half expected my mother to say "thank you for sharing" and point at the next guest, but she just smiled and looked to Anthony.

"Uh, I, uh," he said. "I played video games with Daniel, and I totally won." He shoved his twin, and the two boys dissolved into laughter, whispering about cheat codes and who actually beat who and how the game was probably rigged. It wasn't, but last summer, Clay *had* put all their games on expert level while they were sleeping. Also, they just weren't very good.

Daniel was next, bouncing around in his seat until a single look from my mother stilled him entirely.

He folded his hands in his lap, cleared his throat, and said with all the dignity a twelve-year-old could muster, "After I epically defeated Anthony, I read the newspaper because *I* am a grown-up."

"What did you read about, sweetie?" asked my mother.

"Rylie's wedding. Do we have to get dressed up for that?"

She nodded. "Of course we do. It's a special occasion, and we want to celebrate her happy day, don't we?"

Sharon leaned forward in her seat. "We dress up for grown-up days. Is Rylie a grown-up now?" The curliest parts of her hair fell across her face and dipped into the night's soup. She didn't seem to notice.

"Yes," my mother said. "She's a grown-up now."

Sharon's brow furrowed in confusion. "Does that mean Lucas is a grown-up?" She looked at me, her already large eyes even bigger now. I thought of playing dolls with her before high school graduation, of tea parties and funny accents, of her laughter. But mostly I thought of mine—of *my* laughing and *my* smiling and my countdown until my eighteenth birthday, of the days when Clay was sober and Nathan was still talking. The days when we were kids.

I nodded. "I'm a grown-up."

My phone went off before we'd finished our second helpings. I checked it under the table.

Clay: *I'm outside.*

I waited for another text, an explanation of some sort or a request. Come get me, or take me home, let me in, get me food. A minute passed and still there was nothing. I wiped my chin with my napkin, excused myself from the table, and went around to the back door.

Clay stood behind the glass, his arms crossed over his chest and a ratty backpack hanging off one arm. His left eye was a mess of black and blue. He shrugged when he saw me, that abused smile giving a last ditch attempt at a cheery appearance before it fell off. He looked down at his sneakers. They were the oldest, dirtiest things Clay owned—laces ripped, sides scuffed, every inch covered in Sharpie drawings because in high school we never had anything better to do than pretend we were artists.

I opened the door, and his smile widened. "My dad's home," he said and then peered over my shoulder to see who was around, I suppose. My family was still at the table enduring a long-winded work story of my dad's.

"Smells good," Clay said. "Burke Stew?"

"Not everything my mom makes is patented. It's just stew," I said.

"Amazing stew."

Up close, Clay's eye was worse than your old classic black and blue; it was splotchy and raw, a long red cut running up through the middle like it had been done by a ring—a Harvard graduate's preppy, unnecessarily large, obnoxious ring. And if the framed diplomas all over Clay's house weren't enough evidence of who it belonged to, Clay's picture-perfect smile summed it all up real nice. I'd been there for the after-school lessons, the Ortiz family motto of look good before all else, and I knew who taught Clay to smile even when his world was falling off by the hinges. I might not have been a very good friend, might not have been much of a friend at all, but I sure as hell was aware. After nineteen years, you sort of put the pieces together.

"Stop looking at me like that," Clay said. He leaned against the doorway but winced when his arm rubbed against the metal. I had a pretty good guess where the rest of the bruises were hiding, but I didn't say anything, pretended not to notice, tried not to look *like that*. I thought I had a decent poker face—should have after all these years, and hell, I practiced—but Clay just frowned even more. "That's not better," he said. "Now you just look constipated."

I rolled my eyes. "What happened?" We were both adults here—sort of—and I knew the start of a subject change when I heard it.

Clay shrugged. "He was drinking. It's not a big deal."

"*Not a big deal?* Clay, it's dinnertime. My *mom*'s dinnertime. The last time you showed up during dinner, I ended up waiting in the emergency room. I'm not buying it."

Clay crossed his arms over his chest and studied his shoes again. While he rubbed the toes together—one covered in an American flag and the other a skull and crossbones—he mumbled, almost inaudibly, "It blew up, okay? My big project that was supposed to change the world is now just a bunch of ash and broken parts scattered across the garage. And I'm not in school, and I'm not doing anything, and he kicked me out, so if you have a corner of the garage or something where your parents won't see, I just need one night." He spoke too fast, each word blurring into the other, no breaths in between, and by the end, his knuckles were white where they gripped the sleeves of his ratty sweatshirt.

Before I could say anything, my mom came rushing up behind me, her arms spread wide like freaking Mother Mary. She ushered Clay into the house with cries of, "you'll catch a cold out there!" though it was summertime, and "Lucas, is this how we treat guests?" though Clay had been around so much in the last two decades that he hardly qualified as a guest anymore. She didn't ask what had happened, had seen it too many times, but I noticed the pinched look in her face that would have adopted Clay in a heartbeat should he have ever allowed it.

The crappy part was that Clay didn't even look surprised, just endlessly *grateful*, like my mom's too-loud voice and overbearing ways were the best damn thing to ever happen to him.

My mom looked at Clay and saw a project she could fix, someone to pamper, someone to mother because five kids just weren't enough; I looked at Clay and saw dead ends.

MY MOTHER HAD Clay seated at the dinner table in under a minute. There was an eighth chair ready at all times just in case we ever had guests, and though sometimes it had been Rylie sitting in it or maybe Nathan, we'd all come to calling it Clay's chair because he used it the most. Clay sank into it. He grinned and thanked my mother for everything. Though he was rich and could probably afford three-course meals worth a hell of a lot more than Momma Burke's homemade dinners, he devoured his stew like he'd never had anything so good before in all his life.

"Mrs. Burke, you really are the best cook in the world," he said.

My mom beamed and patted his head affectionately. It was the same sort of pat she'd reserved for the one and only dog we'd had when I was in first grade, the pat she gave my father when he got home early from work, or the one she used on us kids when we brought home good grades.

I finished my second bowl of stew and was filling my third when she struck up a conversation with Clay about the cooking process and how she had a secret ingredient she was taking with her to her grave.

"Well, whatever it is, Mrs. B, it works wonders," Clay said. He rubbed his stomach, all smiles until he caught my eye. His brows furrowed and he shrugged in some sort of unspoken apology—for what, I had no idea.

AFTER DINNER, MY parents disappeared upstairs—only after pulling out every extra pillow and blanket we owned for Clay to sleep on, that is. My siblings, Clay, and I gathered in the living room to humor Sharon in a game of tea party. We sat in a circle, everyone with their own empty cup of tea while Sharon taught us the etiquette of proper tea drinking and tea party behavior.

"You have to put your pinky out." She thrust out hers and took a sip of nothing just to demonstrate.

We all followed her lead, Clay more enthusiastically than anyone. He downed his nonexistent tea in one nonexistent gulp and then pushed his cup forward and batted his eyelashes at Sharon. "Can I have some more?" he asked. She blushed and filled his cup with more air.

Frankie sat on Clay's other side, occasionally showing him her phone screen. Whatever was on it—more science jokes or theories or whatever it was the two talked about—made Clay laugh and spit out his nonexistent tea all over the carpet.

"Clay, why do you always have dinner here?" Sharon asked.

Clay laughed. "What, you don't like me here?" He clapped a hand over his heart in a gesture of great offense. "And here I thought we were friends."

Sharon giggled. She moved her cups out of the way and scrambled to his side. Kissing his cheek, she said, "Of course we are. But Momma says dinner is for families. And you're not family...are you? Don't you have a family to eat dinner with?"

Clay's face darkened, but it was a move so fast, so seamless, that if you hadn't had nearly two decades worth of practice looking for it, you wouldn't have noticed; after a second, it straightened out again, all careless smiles and empty eyes.

"My family isn't home very much, but that's okay because I have you guys. And you can have more than one family."

"You can?" Sharon asked.

Clay ruffled her hair but looked at me. I shrugged. He smiled. "Yeah," he said. "You can."

This game went on for an hour or so, everyone drinking their tea and then passing around these invisible little cookies Sharon swore were to die for. Then one of the twins knocked over the pot, and Sharon, yawning, her little eyes barely opened, announced that they'd spilled it all and it was time for bed.

Another of my friends might have been surprised by the declaration—for what it was worth, Clay used to be, *I* even used to be—but Clay reacted now only with the tired smile of a man resigned to his own inevitable seduction. Sharon was the only under-ten-year-old I'd ever met who announced her own bedtime, and for years, my mother had praised her as her "responsible child," but we all knew the truth now. Her bedtime tuck-in—full of "read this to me," and "read that to me," and "sing me a song"—could keep my father busy for an hour; an outsider as susceptible as Clay could be up there for a lifetime.

Already, Sharon was batting her eyelashes and pushing out her bottom lip with the talent of a much older woman as she asked, "Clay, will you tuck me in?"

As he scrambled to his feet, nodding and promising her an epic story of a princess and a dragon and a ninja raccoon, he knocked into his backpack, and a flask and two bottles of pills came tumbling out of the open zipper. He stuffed them back in before my siblings could really get a look. Though—with the exception of Frankie who was busy on her phone—they were too young to really understand and having too much fun to really care, I wondered for the first time if I was the only person at all who ever saw Clay.

AS PREDICTED, IT was over an hour before Clay sauntered into my bedroom, carrying his backpack over one arm, a pillow over his shoulder, and a pile of blankets in his hands.

"She made me read her the entire book," he said. "Lucas, there were thirty stories in there. Thirty *long* stories. I had to act them out. With voices. And songs." He threw the blankets onto the ground and kicked them around until they resembled a nest. He dropped the pillow in the middle and lay down, curling his body to fit.

Up on my bed, a good two or so feet above the floor, I could barely make out Clay's silhouette in the darkness. It was like his whole body had turned to shadow, nothing light about him anymore, and if I squinted, he disappeared entirely.

"What happened?" I asked again.

"I told you," he said.

"You told me about tonight. What *happened*?"

His shadow twitched—an arm moved or a leg kicked out, just shadowy limbs in a shadowy oblivion. After what felt like forever, with my breathing too loud in my ears and my wall clock ticking obnoxiously in the corner like some bomb about to go off, he said, "We grew up, Lucas. Mistakes don't get erased anymore. Being a grown-up means writing in pen."

"What the hell does that *mean*?" I scrambled out of bed. My feet weren't soft on the floor; they came down with none of the grace or skillful stealth of the heroes I'd always watched on TV—always bigger and bulkier than I was and yet far more poised. My feet crashed. They boomed. I was so very present in the darkness, and Clay, lost somewhere in the tangle of blankets, seemed a forever away.

I crouched down, fumbling until I felt an ankle. I sat next to it. "Can you just talk like a normal person?"

The ankle twitched, and Clay sat up; his silhouette appeared through the dim strip of moonlight that shone through the crack in my blinds. "Do you remember when we learned to play soccer?" he asked.

I shrugged, not sure if he could see me but not really caring either. The question was just so damn random. "Yeah, you sucked."

Clay laughed. "You weren't so good yourself."

"I was better than you." I folded my legs, and my calf knocked against Clay's. He didn't move, so neither did I. Instead, I crossed my arms over my chest and tried to hold everything tight inside me, like if I squeezed hard enough, I could compact my ribs and heart and everything inside into one small, insignificant pile.

"Yeah," Clay said. "You were always good for such a small kid."

"I'm not a small kid," I said.

"Well, you're not now." Clay's silhouette twitched before disappearing, and I supposed he was lying down. I lay beside him and contemplated the splotchy darkness that was my ceiling. The moonlight cast shadows from wall to wall, and though I hoped I was creative enough to find patterns in the gloom, all I could see were stripes from the tree outside and the waves made from the blinds.

"You were such a small kid," Clay said. "If I was going to pick a kid to have a rough childhood, it would have been you. You were so fucking small, and then you go and come out, and I thought 'fuck, he's a goner. I'm really going to have to watch his back now.' But you were fine. You were always fine. How'd you do that?"

"I didn't do anything."

"Yeah, you did." Clay's arm bumped mine. His fingers twitched against my elbow and then dug in until it hurt. But the pain was nothing—nothing but nights spent under crap-job pillow forts and soccer tournaments in the backyard. Nothing but dragging Clay and his smoked-out lungs across the track in P.E. Nothing but watching him cry for the very last time as his mother packed up her things and drove away.

"You never gave anybody a chance to pick on you," he said. "You always knew who you were. You didn't care what anyone else thought. How'd you do that? I thought I was going to be the one taking care of you. How the hell'd you end up being the one taking care of me?"

I thought of all the nights I'd cleaned Clay's vomit off the carpet in my bedroom, and of me, crouching over the toilet in the stall of a dorm room bathroom, of all the boys pulling up their pants and slamming the door, of all the "Major Change" forms that littered my desk and the textbooks piling up and the voicemails from my mother that I'd deleted.

"I don't know," I said. "I guess I've just got everything figured out. Knew who I wanted to be and what I wanted to do." I patted Clay's arm in the dark. "I'm sure you'll figure it out too." I paused. "You drunk?"

He laughed. It wasn't a yes, but I was pretty damn sure it wasn't a no either.

After a long while where neither of us said anything and the shadows started to look a lot like demons, Clay said, "Rylie still loves me." I wished I could say he whispered it, that it was just that sort of mumbled bedtime talk that came out when dreams interrupted your waking brain and pulled you down, the sort of talk you could ignore. But Clay didn't whisper. He didn't stutter, and I knew it wasn't the alcohol talking but some poor attempt at hope. No matter how bad he was, he always thought he'd win our soccer games.

"I know she does," he said. "She told me. She still loves me, Lucas." He yawned. His body twisted, his arm coming to rest over my chest. I thought of rolling him onto his side. Years of experience and months of college drinking education classes had taught me it was the safest position—kept you from choking on your own vomit—but it had been hours since Clay had drank, and his breathing was fluid, calm almost. I let him be and listened as he repeated it over and over. "She loves me. She's got to. Someone's got to."

Maybe ten minutes later, just when sleep was finally growing heavy on my eyes, Clay asked into the darkness, "You ever loved anybody?"

For a second, I wasn't sure he was talking to me—didn't know why he would when he damn well knew the answer—but then there was no one else in the room, and his body sort of shifted closer to mine, like he was leaning in for the answers. Suddenly, irrationally, I wanted to rattle his brain up until all the pieces fit right, until he just *understood*. Or maybe I just wanted to sleep.

All I could think of were the little pink and red hearts you see in store windows on Valentine's day, or the girls in my eighth-grade class that yelled "love ya!" before every period, like if they didn't say it, if they didn't hug and declare their deep, temporary feelings of friendship, they'd lose it all.

While I was busy philosophizing, giving myself an existential crisis and all, Clay started to snore. He was sleeping, and here I was, going through the chorus of Nat King Cole's "L-O-V-E" trying to find meaning in "the way you look at me" and "very, very extraordinary."

My mom was pretty damn extraordinary, and I guess I loved her—those were the rules, after all, what with that womb pushing out business and the nineteen years of meals. Clay was alive and hoping, and that was something. Chris, too, was pretty extraordinary; not everybody beat cancer and lived to tell the tale, not everyone almost went to the Olympics. And I wasn't complaining about the way he looked at me either, that look of genuine interest when I was speaking. But those were letters. Just a little L and a little V. I didn't know what strung them together, how you got all four to line up, but maybe Nat King Cole knew something I didn't.

Not feeling all that tired anymore, I lay in bed and stared up at the ceiling, at the shadows that only really looked creepy if you squinted, and listened to Clay's slow breathing.

L is for a liver that hasn't given up yet.

O is for oxygen intake.

V is for very, very still alive.

E is even more than I can take.

Eight

59 DAYS BEFORE

Clay was gone in the morning. My mom showed up outside my door at 9:00 a.m.—late by her standards, but early for Clay, so I supposed she'd thought it a worthy compromise for our "guest." She entered the room, smiling and holding a tray of breakfast, looking happier than I'd seen her in months, only to find a pile of folded blankets on the floor where Clay should have been. There wasn't a note—Clay wasn't big into writing, and if he did, he was more likely to draw you a blueprint than actual legible words—but everything was clean, everything in its place.

I sat up in bed as my mother tilted her chin to one side and blinked, her eyes watering. I jumped up just in time to save the tray.

"Mom, it's fine," I said. "He's fine. We worked everything out last night." We didn't.

She nodded and handed me the tray. I set it on the edge of the bed, picked up a biscuit, and took a bite just to see her smile. She did, but only partially—a loose gesture with downcast eyes. For a moment, I remembered her in the kitchen, remembered how distressed she'd sounded while baking, and I hugged her just in case.

"It's great, Mom."

"Thank you, sweetie." She ruffled my hair, glanced at the pile of blankets, and then picked up the tray and turned to go. "You should invite one of your friends for dinner."

IN THE MONTHS leading up to graduation, I had someone different over every night. Usually Clay was there too—always Clay and a "guest"—and for months, my sisters played dress up with the baseball team and braided Rylie's hair.

Nathan only came once, ten days before the accident.

I don't remember much of the night, only that he shook everyone's hands and raved about the chicken. We had mashed potatoes with some sort of raspberry dressing, and when he kissed me in the doorway at the end of the night, his lips still tasted like it—sweet with a sour tang as sharp as a bite. I don't remember if he used tongue, can't quite picture his face in my mind, the way our eyes locked, or if he closed them when he leaned close. Just the raspberry.

It's funny, the things you remember.

56 DAYS UNTIL THE WEDDING

A few days later, I met up with Chris at our town's local park. I hadn't been to the place in months, not since I was in high school, but it hadn't changed much—the same scattered square of oddly placed trees, oaks and pines and this one lone willow that always seemed depressed. No one sat under that tree, but then again, most people didn't care about the trees at all. They were here for the playground: little kids sliding down slides and swinging on swings, and parents ignoring them for a good book or the morning paper. You started to feel like a creep if you stayed around the trees long enough—just you resting, staring, and a bunch of kids all around—but the trees had shade, and in those summer days when the temperature was skyrocketing, you took all the shade you could get.

Chris, who said he had no interest in shorts of any kind—Bermuda and "manly" or not—showed up in a loose pair of black jeans and sat under the shadiest oak. I, in cargo shorts and a tank top, plopped down beside him and felt a shiver creep up my spine as some loose bits of tree bark poked through the thin fabric over my back.

"I don't care," I said, thinking of Clay's pinched expression in the dark. "I don't. And I wouldn't even be getting involved if he didn't keep making me. I mean, if my sister is such a good replacement friend, she can take the job. I don't want it."

Chris nodded but didn't say anything. He'd called an hour earlier and said almost nothing then either when I told him about Clay and how he used my house like a hotel and how he perpetually stunk like a liquor store, and I, for one, was growing tired of the stench. He didn't say a word when we met up at the edge of the park and I told him how I was the only one Clay had, how I was his last defense, and really, it was a lot of responsibility for someone my age. Chris didn't say anything but just nodded some more while we found a good spot. For a man who claimed to love words so much, he sure knew how to keep the silence stretching.

"He's my best friend. So I understand that gives me some sort of responsibility to take care of him, but you'd think he would have figured out his life by now, right? He's the one always saying how we're adults now." I folded my arms across my chest. With the sun beating down all around us, it only took a minute for the sweat to build up between my limbs. All too aware of Chris sitting so close beside me—looking good and calm and cool in a band T-shirt and sunglasses, like he was immune to the heat somehow—I quickly unfolded my arms and straightened.

"He's had it hard. I know that. Most of it's not his fault. But..." I paused. "You don't even know what I'm talking about."

Chris smiled. "Nope. You've told me nothing about his life, situation, background, or circumstances. All fine. Please continue." He waved his hand as though to usher out the remainder of a rant I was only now realizing was insensible and probably unintelligible. I contemplated the freckles on my upper arm as it would have been easier to string them into a line than to string my thoughts into any sort of rational notion.

Beyond the grove of trees—if you could call the five scattered trees a grove—a few kids around Sharon's age raced off the playground to meet an approaching ice cream truck. That overplayed, slightly eerie music rang through the whole park.

"It was just bad, you know," I said. Having no rights to Clay's story and not quite evil enough to go sharing his secrets to his supposed enemy's best man, I figured bad was enough to sum up the tale. "His home life was bad, but he was smart. He *is* smart. In first grade, he must have been at a...fourth-grade level or something. He skipped to the third at least, and then a couple months later, he came back. He didn't like the kids, I guess. Wanted to be on the same level as the rest of us. That's how it's always been. Clay dumbing himself down to fit in. What am I supposed to do about that? I can't do anything about that."

Again, Chris said nothing.

I wrinkled up my nose, and then, not wanting to look like I was offended or angry or anything, pretended to be sniffing at the ice cream across the street—some strawberry sherbet that shouldn't have smelled as sweet as it did. But then, maybe I was imagining it the way I'd imagined the interest in Chris's eyes.

It wasn't like he owed me anything, wasn't like he had to sit here and listen to me if he didn't want to. Sure, we were up to kissing every day, and it was good, and he called a lot, but we weren't having sex, and even that, I knew, guaranteed me nothing. People are only around when they want to be.

"It's not like I'm a prude," I said. I couldn't help it; the less Chris spoke, the more the words kept pouring out of my mouth, like I had to fill the deficit he was leaving in the wake of all his silence. "I don't care that he drinks. I mean, I drink too. It's fine. It's just..." I ran a hand over my face, felt the beads of sweat pooling in the creases on my forehead and the spaces under my ears. Chris might have it all together, but I was melting. I was oozing out and dripping away, and I smelled nothing like the sweet strawberries in the air. I wasn't pretty. I wasn't cool. My head spun like I'd just stepped off a plane—heavy and floating and unaware of the day or time. Jet lag and disease and tingling skin from every touch that didn't last. I'd often dreamt of ripping that skin apart, thought of tearing, scratching, clawing my skin away until I found me. Strawberry sweet and untouched. "We already lost one of us. We can't lose anyone else."

I looked up to find Chris smiling. His face was loose and easy, his sunglasses pushed up into his hair. His teeth showed, and his jaw looked sharp as a knife. I wanted to cut myself on it, thought it would be worth bleeding to be part of it. Damn, he was beautiful.

But like all unfortunate things in this world, the truth hit me—that here I was, throwing my soul into the void of the universe, hoping he'd catch at least a word; and Chris, the man I was trusting, the man I had *hoped* would understand, was smiling. Like it was a joke. Like me finally doing what he wanted—talking, using words—was nothing to care about, nothing to pay attention to.

"What? What are you doing? What is that? Why are you smiling?"

His grin didn't falter for a second. "You're talking a lot."

I glared. "What? I thought that's what you wanted. That's what you've been saying—"

He quite effectively cut me off by grabbing my hand and giving it an intimate little squeeze. "It is. It's good. It's *really* good, Lucas. See—" He leaned forward, his smile widening, his spare hand coming to rest on his fake knee. "—I never thought words were an endangered commodity, but it looks like the more I shut up, the more you shut...down?" He wrinkled his nose, which was really unfortunate, honestly, because it only made him more attractive when all I wanted was to see him melting, oozing, dripping all over this depressing little park like I was.

"Okay, that doesn't make sense. You know what I mean." He waved his hand. "Talking. Sharing. It feels good, right?"

I nodded. It sure hadn't felt bad.

"Want to try something?" he asked.

I nodded again.

"Okay." Chris lay down under the tree, his body falling into the overgrown grass at the base of the oak. Little blades of it obscured his face and made it look as though he had a green beard and green mustache and strange wavy green eyebrows. It should have been stupid—too silly to be attractive—but my heart raced.

It's a strange thing, but when you like someone—and I mean really like, not that high school tolerance "well, they have the same lunch as me, and I don't want to be alone" bullshit—that like tends to turn stupid into cute. It's like all these expectations, these words you build up in your head that are supposed to make up perfection—beautiful and sexy and sophisticated—only draw you in. They don't hold you. It's grass beards and grass stains, snorted laughter and stupid faces that start to spell out "want."

I lay next to him and tried to stare at the sky though my eyes kept wandering back to his face—to the shadow of stubble creeping up on his normally well-shaven jaw, to his hair, tangled and wavy from where the sunglasses had slipped off into the grass, to his lips. I could appreciate the sentiment as much as the next guy—Chris taking that step back to give me room to speak—but I liked his lips better when they were moving.

"Are we cloud gazing?" I asked.

Chris's eyes narrowed. "What, are we in the second grade? No. We're philosophizing." He put his arms straight up into the air and spread his fingers, his eyes focused on the places in between. "Everyone who has cancer thinks they're dying. Even if you have 'good cancer' and they say you've got a few years, or maybe you'll beat it, you still feel like you're dying. Usually you are. And usually everybody gets pretty depressed about it, and even if you aren't depressed, your doctors think you are," he said. "So they start teaching you these 'be happy' strategies. Like different ways of thinking about the world and little things you can do to stay positive. You ever seen those cat posters? Those 'keep hanging on' ones? It's like that, but... I don't know, better?"

I nodded. I put my hands up in the air and spread my fingers the way he did, looked through the places in between. With my hand pressed over the sun, my skin appeared a translucent red while bursts of blue sky and white clouds came shining through like missing puzzle pieces.

"Now what?" I said.

"The doctors said that when life starts to get you down, to do this and remember that this is how we see our world. We're limited by our scope. When all you see are the spaces in between, the sky doesn't look that impressive but..." He paused and dropped his hands to the ground. His fingers brushed my thigh. I felt it all the way up to my scalp, a tingling sensation that spread through my nervous system like a virus. "It's a big sky," he said. "It's big, and it's beautiful, and you can't see it all, but it's still out there. All those possibilities."

Chris turned until we were face-to-face. Drops of sweat rolled down his forehead. His face was flushed, but I couldn't figure out why. "Maybe you're only seeing the pieces," he said. "Clay's got this problem, right? And you're seeing the side effects. The consequences. Maybe you need to try to look at the whole picture. What's his whole story? What's going on with him? I don't know, and I don't expect you to tell me, but I'm guessing you've probably got a pretty good idea if you really think about it, right? I mean, how long have you known him?"

"All my life." You tended to remember your joint diaper days when your mom was always bringing the pictures back up from the grave; moms sure were good at making certain you never forgot your most embarrassing moments.

"All right," Chris said. "Well, there you go. Dive into the problem. Look at all the angles." He paused. "This isn't very helpful, is it?"

I shook my head and smiled. "Not really. Did it help you?"

"Nah." He folded one arm behind his head and used it as a pillow. "I always thought it was a bunch of bullshit. If I'm going to die, I'm going to die. No point trying to make it sound cheery."

"But you didn't die."

Chris tapped his nose. "No, I did not." He stared long enough to make me wonder if I had something on my face or if my hair was beginning to resemble the aftermath of a tornado—both were likely. Grass sitting wasn't exactly great for the stylish self, and though I hadn't eaten in hours, there was bound to be something stuck in my teeth. It just wouldn't be a date without an embarrassing piece of broccoli to mark the occasion. And then, of course, I started wondering if this was a date at all, and if it was, I'd probably already screwed it up by talking about Clay.

And then Chris's fingers were touching my chin, and he asked, almost breathless and definitely smiling, "Can I kiss you?"

I nodded.

A KISS WILL be a kiss will be a kiss, and believe it or not, lips aren't all that different from one person to the next. Every mouth tasted a little different—some good, some bad, some you'll never forget, and some you wish you could—but at the end of the day, it was still just a mouth, and a mouth is a very weird thing to get turned on by—just a saliva-filled, food-chewing machine.

I'd always thought I was strange for not getting it, that there was something endlessly alluring that I just wasn't seeing. And then Chris was leaning in, his hand caressing my cheek and his eyes burning holes all over me, like he could see *into* me. And in that moment, I got it. It wasn't the mouth or the tongue or even the lips that were the secret: it was all of it. It was eyes locked together, it was skin on skin, the twitch of a tongue, but mostly it was just knowing—knowing that the person on the other side of the kiss was not engaging with you out of some won or lost lottery, some pick of the litter, but because they were focused solely on you. They picked you. Chris, who had faced death head-on and had no time for mistakes, for sideshows, had picked me.

I'M NOT PROUD to admit it, and it certainly wasn't planned, but after the first swipe of Chris's tongue against the roof of my mouth, I tackled the poor man until I was straddling his waist and kissing him with all the vigor I possessed. He laughed into my mouth, and I swore I could feel it vibrating all the way down to my fucking bones.

"So I take it you're more of the 'action therapy' sort of guy," he said in one of those small moments when we separated to breathe. "I don't know about this, but physical therapy actually exists. I mean, obviously." Kiss. "It exists if you've got a physical problem. Like when my dad got a herniated disk in his spine, he had to go to physical therapy all the time to like learn"—kiss—"these stretches, and I think they even made him do yoga." Kiss. "But I mean, for the depression, they'd be like 'take a walk' and 'play with your dog,' as if we all had a dog because I guess all sad people have dogs, and I swear one of the nurses told us to have sex." Kiss. "You taste like pineapple."

I splayed my hands over Chris's chest; his heart beat wildly under my fingertips like a drum solo set on repeat. "Do you know you have the least sexy make-out talk I have ever heard in my life?"

He laughed. His hands, which had been holding my jaw and my neck and sliding everywhere in between, moved down to his own chest, and his fingers curled around mine. "I know, bad habit." He kissed my fingertips.

All the breath went rushing out of my lungs, more exhausting, more stunning than any make-out session could dream to be.

It was a long minute before I caught myself and smirked instead. "You were talking about your dad."

Chris winced. "I was?"

"You were."

"Any chance I can make you forget that happened?"

I shook my head. "I don't want to forget. I've never made anybody ramble before."

"That going to be your superpower?" Chris asked.

"Yeah," I said. "I'm making T-shirts and everything. You going to wear one?"

"Only if you call yourself Doctor Death Ramble."

"Deal."

Somewhere behind us, a woman cleared her throat and whispered for her child to look away. I rolled off Chris to face a stout, sixty-something grandma holding the hand of a little girl with pigtails.

"This is a family park," said the woman. "Show some decency!"

DECENCY, AT LEAST by Chris's definition, turned out to be sitting hip to hip with a French book slung over his lap and the page turned to the "basic items" lesson. It was all kindergarten shit—pencil, pen, book, paper—and I would have thought that was a good thing if I didn't sound like the dumbest kindergartener in all the world.

By my fifth try at "computer"—*l'ordinateur*, but more like lablatur on my tongue, Chris was on the ground laughing. "You're terrible," he said, red-faced and hiccupping back to normality. "At this rate, we're never going to make it in Paris."

"I didn't know we were going," I said.

Chris grinned—that blinding smile I'd known from day one, the one that said I know something you don't, and it's great on the other side. "Oh, we're going to Paris." He brushed his hair back, and his smile only grew wider, all teeth and gums. "We'll hide out in some crappy little apartment because we'll be starving artists—I'll be the wannabe athlete, and you'll be the superhero in disguise—and it'll be all we can afford. But it'll be okay because we'll have this great rooftop that looks over the city. Not the *city*-city, like the expensive tourist part because we're still poor, but the grungy artist part of the city, and we'll see the real world; you know, everyone living their lives. Buying groceries and talking to strangers in the street and smelling fresh-baked bread every morning." He paused to look wistfully out across the park. I wondered if he was seeing it—a cityscape and a life in the clouds, little artisan streets and painters on every corner—instead of the three-year-old picking her nose on the swing set and the two boys burying each other alive in the sandbox.

"Then I get kidnapped," Chris said. "Because you're a superhero, and I'm the love interest, and I'm pretty." He batted his eyelashes. "So they're going to string me up somewhere, probably without my shirt because every good story needs a gratuitous shirtless scene, and you'll come barging in to save me, but because this isn't some cliché afternoon special and it'd be too easy for you to just defeat the villain *like every other superhero in existence*, we die in a fiery explosion."

I blinked. "You sure you don't want to be the storyteller?"

Chris wrinkled his nose and shook his head. "Nah. Athlete. I'm the athlete. Did you miss the bit about the gratuitous shirtless scene?"

"No," I said. "No, I did not. But I thought it was usually a gratuitous sex scene."

"We can have one of those too." Chris winked.

I held his gaze and tried to look sexy, but honestly, it's a talent only women have really perfected—a pursed bottom lip or a flash of exposed skin; hell, just a low-cut shirt will do it. But men only really have the one asset, and pulling it out—especially at a kid's playground—was more of a call for arrest than good flirting. All I had left were five semiworthy abs—four if I'd missed the gym for a week—and that was on a good day.

Chris laughed first—his sexy smolder dissolving into amusement. He soon gave in and completely doubled over. I followed, and for a long time, we didn't say anything but laughed and mumbled out a few more butchered French phrases, like at least we were sophisticated even if we couldn't be flirty. For the record: words like pen, computer, and paper sound a hell of a lot sexier in French than they ever do in English. Don't translate French; it's just disappointing. *La papier, un livre.*

After a few minutes, Chris stopped laughing and winced instead. With both hands, he rubbed circles around his knee and then pulled up his pant leg.

I stopped laughing myself to stare at the scar, four inches long at least, that stretched along the left side of the joint. "Does it still hurt?"

Chris shrugged. "Sometimes. Sometimes I think I imagine it." While he continued to rub his knee with one hand, he placed the other across the center of his chest and rubbed circles there too. "Pain doesn't mean anything. It's just a sensor in your brain."

"Definition doesn't really stop it from hurting, though, does it?"

"I'm trying to enlighten you with scientific facts," Chris said. "Are you questioning my genius?"

I nodded. "Yeah. That going to be a problem?"

He leaned back against the tree. His left hand still tapped against his collarbone, which was growing redder with every passing minute. "You know, I like this sassy you. He planning to stick around?"

I shrugged.

With one hand still placed firmly over his knee, Chris looked out over the park and sighed. "I don't know how you could hate this town so much. It's beautiful. Beautiful trees. Kids playing in the park. Look, look at that dad playing catch with his son. It's like a movie. The sun is even out!"

"You don't know it like I do." I wanted to add that the sun was *always* out over summer, and that sometimes even beautiful trees got dented when a car barreled into their trunks, but before I could barely do more than think it, my phone rang. It was some awful metal song I hadn't listened to fully since middle school, which meant Clay was calling, and nine times out of ten, Clay's calls were an emergency—or at least he liked to think they were, or maybe I'd just deemed them so over the years. I couldn't remember anymore, but I picked up after the first screeching note anyway.

"Hello?"

"Lucas, Lucas! You picked up. Good." Clay's voice was high-pitched and nearly hysterical. The alcohol was present in every wavering syllable. "You're there. You're there."

"I'm here," I said. "What's going on?"

"I had a brilliant idea," he said. "It was going to change the world, Lucas. This was it. This was the one. You would have liked it."

"Yeah, what was it? What happened to it, Clay?"

Something shattered on the other line—something delicate, fragile, and I could picture the millions of broken pieces as easily as I could hear each broken note in Clay's tone. "Doesn't matter. None of it matters. Just wanted to stay goodbye. I love you, man. I love you."

"Clay." I rose to my feet. Chris looked at me, concerned and confused all at once, and then stood up too. "Clay, what's going on? Why are you saying goodbye?"

Clay hiccupped. "You—" He paused. Something broke again. "You are a great friend. Have I ever told you that? Great. You're great. Always been great." Another crash. More broken pieces falling over the line— falling and clattering to the floor. "Ouch. I gotta go. I'm sorry. I love you, man. I love you. You're a good friend. Such a good friend. I hope you hook up with that cancer kid. Shit, was that bad? That was probably bad. Don't tell him I called him that. I didn't mean that. I take that back. He's good for you. You should—you should be happy. One of us should. Fuck him and have a really big fucking wedding because you should get married. But don't fuck up with choosing your best man, okay? Just...don't give it to Todney. Give it to Frankie. Frankie's the best. She'll get the best strippers. Or—or Rylie. Rylie would be a great best man. Tell her...tell her I love her. Okay, fuck, got to go."

The line went dead.

I'd always sworn by my ability to keep a cool head—a strong man in a storm, my dad used to say—but by the time the beeping started on the other line, I was already soaking in sweat, and this time it wasn't from the heat. While my heart made a WWE lunge at my rib cage, I stuffed my phone back into my pocket and turned to Chris.

He was slouched against the tree, holding his leg with one hand. The other dug fingernail marks into the heart of his T-shirt. He looked winded, red in the cheeks with sweat dripping from his forehead.

I moved to help him, to offer a hand, a call—anything—but he waved me away with a breathless, "Go get him. I'm fine. I'll call Todney to pick me up. Just go."

I nodded, but compelled by some sideways gravity or sorcery or whatever unexplainable force it is that draws one person to another, I still leaned in, grabbed his chin, and kissed him for maybe half a second. Though I could still hear Clay's voice in my head, and my palms were sweating, and my heart was racing, and everything about the moment was the opposite of romantic, I realized something in those few split seconds between the moment I pulled away and the moment I set off running to Clay's: if you got to pick your last moments in this world, I would have picked kissing Chris.

I didn't have time to look back, would never know if he smiled after, or if it was as good for him as it was for me, or if he was as terrified as I was. I'd never even know if he got home safe.

What I did know with earth-shattering certainty was that in nineteen years of friendship, Clay had never once said goodbye to me until now.

Nine

I HEARD THE sounds of breaking glass long before I reached Clay's front door. He hadn't bothered to lock it, so I walked in and followed the crashes until I was front and center at the Smack Down Show of Clayton Ortiz. That afternoon, the show featured a Clay with shaking hands who stood in the middle of his father's expensive kitchen, throwing expensive plates and expensive mugs at the expensively painted wall. There was a gun sticking out of the waistband of his jeans that I'd seen before—just once when we were still too young to know that life really sucked, and Clay thought it was a good idea to show me where his dad kept the "adult items." Just in case.

Clay breaking down was problem number one—smile gone, clothes disheveled, hair sticking up in every direction, like for once in his life, he wasn't ready for a press conference. Problem two was his bleeding hands. I could see the little chips of china and imported dishware from who-knows-where poking out from the bloody places on his palms—bright blues and greens against scarlet red. How deep, I wondered, did the glass run, how much was breaking from inside Clay when so very much was breaking around him?

Three glasses left in his hand—I'd price them at a hundred bucks each, easy—Clay arched one arm back and threw, threw, threw, until there was nothing left but pieces—tiny and unsalvageable. With no ammo remaining to unleash, he let his shoulders hunch, and he took several wavering breaths as though steeling himself for the comedown. But the muscles in his back were still tense, and his hands still shook, and I knew this storm was far from over.

When he finally turned around, his eyes widened, and he staggered back several steps. "You weren't supposed to be here." He sounded like he'd just seen Zorro or God or a ghost or whatever it is that makes eyes go inhumanely wide. I rather thought it was the other way around—that I should be the one surprised—but, well, semantics.

I surveyed the room and found a stack of shiny, silver-colored plates in the cupboard above Clay's head. I pulled them out ten at a time and handed them over. "Don't let me interrupt."

He looked at me, at the plates, and then back at the mess on the floor—shattered pieces of every color, like some warped, sadistic rainbow broken at his feet. Without warning, he snatched two plates from my hands and threw them both at the fridge. They shattered and fell to join the glass graveyard on the floor. Over and over he did this—grabbing the plates from me and destroying them—and over and over, I found new things for him to throw. There were only so many dishes in the cupboards, but there were coffee mugs that were never used and wineglasses for entertaining clients, shot glasses that were supposed to be hidden but weren't, and a blue mixer that looked just like the ocean waves when Clay snapped it against the granite countertop. It was beautiful in an eerie sort of way, like seeing the bright surface of the ocean when you were already drowning.

And then he wrapped his hands around the coffeepot, strangling what could not die, and I figured it was time to step in. I wrestled it out his hands. He growled, but after a moment—ten seconds, by my count, where we stood eye to eye, no one breaking focus, no one wavering—Clay's whole body seemed to collapse, and he turned away. He grabbed onto the countertop as he slid to the floor. I cleared a butt-sized path in the shards of broken kitchen and sat beside him.

"We going to talk about it?" I asked. I eyed the gun that still created an L-sized lump in the back of his jeans. Beneath it, little shards of glass stuck to Clay's legs—weapons just waiting to pounce. I brushed them away and ridded the spot around him of any more potential mini knives.

Clay shrugged. He picked up one of the larger glass pieces—almost a palm's widths of unbroken plate—and tossed it back down so hard it broke into another dozen shards. "There's nothing to talk about."

I raised an eyebrow at the sea of broken kitchenware.

Clay sighed. "Almost nothing?" When I shook my head, he frowned a little more, folded his hands into his lap, and cried.

In movies, you always see these actors crying the "hero's tear"—that one lingering single tear that trails down his or her face and just makes the actor look brave and stoic and nothing like real people do when they cry. It's like by crying they confirm their status as protagonist—bigger and stronger and braver than the rest of us even in their moments of weakness. But real crying is ugly—puffy faces and pink cheeks, eyes running red, and sniffling noses.

When Clay cried, he didn't look heroic; he just looked sad; he looked broken. He looked like the storm had finally died and maybe it'd taken him down with it. His cheeks flushed, his hands quivered, and when he buried his face in my shoulder and sobbed into my cheap white T-shirt, I could feel him shaking all the way through.

I patted his shoulder while I waited for some light bulb to hit me and tell me what might actually be helpful. It was always easy to say the words—I'll be there for you, and you can always lean on me—but friendship was different up close. Being there was the simple part; what did you do once you were there? How helpful was it really to sit and pat and say "it's okay" until your voice ran dry?

Clay hiccupped and pulled away. His eyes were puffy and his cheeks wet, but his jaw was solid—his mouth a set, unwavering line. "Do you want to see it? My project?"

I nodded.

CLAY'S GARAGE WAS a kaleidoscopic world and one almost impossible to navigate. His father had very little use for cars—he always took an airplane or a limo or some expensive cab on his trips—and this had left Clay with an unlimited and unimpeded access to the entire area for almost twenty years.

He took advantage of every inch. Corner to corner, the room was stacked with boxes, with tools, with wrenches tucked under tires, and something green and oozing in a beaker. There were blueprints and white papers and green chalk drawings on the ground, scribbled equations in orange Sharpie. There were buzzing black machines and squeaking purple machines and something that looked very much like a robot rolling around the floor and bumping into the walls.

When we were kids, I'd thought of Clay's garage as a wonderland—as Disney's playground and our escape. Now, I thought of it as an unguided tour into Clay's mind, all the wires twisted around the desks, twisted around your ankles, twisted around you. One wrong step, and they'd pull you under.

I stepped carefully over the robot and then over several boxes before I reached a place of empty, solid ground.

Clay led us to the far corner of the room where his personal desk was located, and it should be noted that this was different than his work desk, though I don't know why. The desk was just as messy as the rest of the room, though less sticky. It was covered more in papers and crumpled notes than actual experiments, which was good, seeing as the green goo on his work desk looked slightly lethal. One deadly experiment, I figured, was more than enough.

Clay reached for a stack of papers and placed them in my hands one by one. "It's an advanced computer system," he said. "Like the one in your phone, but...well, smarter. I wanted it to work in hospitals so doctors had instant access to information and assistance in high-stress situations."

I looked over the notes and scattered designs, but they didn't really mean anything to me—like trying to read a language when you previously didn't even know the words existed. The sketches, at least, vaguely resembled a time machine.

"It looks great," I said; it wasn't a lie so much as a bit of hopefully well-placed optimism.

Clay's face lit up. The swollen pink patches on his cheek were brighter for it.

"So what's the problem?" I asked. "You said on the phone that it *was* going to change the world; why can't it?"

Clay shook his head and took the papers back. "I can't actually do it."

"Why not?"

"I can't."

I snatched the papers away from Clay and held the designs up to the light. The notes around the sketches were in English—I was sure of it— but it was some advanced dialect meant for scientists and engineers, for geniuses, but not for washed-up college kids. Clay reached out for his work, but I tugged it away, squinting to read every scribbled word.

"You're smart enough," I said.

"I'm not," he said.

"You are."

"Doesn't matter. I don't have funding. Dad won't pay for it."

"You can get a grant."

"Can't." Clay crossed his arms. He shifted from leg to leg. "They only give them to students or people doing important things with the school. It's all about making the school look good."

"Well, you're in school. Shouldn't that be enough?" I gave up trying to read his work and looked him in the eye instead; I raised an eyebrow, questioning. Clay went to the community college just out of town—the brick building squeezed in between the auto shop and the closed swimming pool.

"Actually," he said, "I'm not. I dropped out first semester."

My fingers dug nail marks into the papers. "How? Why?"

"Never went to class."

I froze. A strange tingling radiated in my hands and up my arms and into my chest. I just kept seeing this picture: Clay sitting on the side of the road with a cardboard sign, and his brain—always too big for his head—oozing out his ears, and all of a sudden, I was sick to my stomach. I set the papers on the desk and sat in Clay's chair. He grabbed my arm, his face drooping more than I would have thought possible a moment ago.

"You all right?"

I nodded. "I just...why you got to be so stupid?"

He chuckled. Easing up a bit, he took a seat on the edge of his desk and shrugged one shoulder at a time. "Got to stay on your level."

I rolled my eyes. I splayed the papers on the desk in front of me—all those scattered black and blue lines, faded pictures, bright red marks to note the important parts. Clay was nineteen years old and a disaster, yes, but nineteen-year-olds were supposed to be getting jobs at diners, not designing advanced computer programs. I was the one who had it all figured out, but Clay saw the world.

"Why?" I asked. The edge of the blueprint folded upward, but I pushed it down and held it tight to the desk. "Why are you wasting everything?"

Clay's eyebrows shot into his hairline. "I'm not wasting, I'm—"

"You are!" I sure didn't plan it, but then again, I sure wasn't thinking either as I jumped from the desk and scattered the papers. The blueprints flew across the room and fell to meet the rest of the chaotic floor—one tucked under a box, one on top. "You're wasting everything! You think everyone gets this? A plan? A—a talent? You have something, and you do *nothing*!"

The kaleidoscope closed in—too many colors, too many projects, too much of everything, and all I could see was Clay kicking a soccer ball around my backyard with a clean face and hands that didn't shake. And he never made a goal.

"And you don't need this." I snatched the gun from his waistband. It was heavy, a solid weight to keep my own hands steady. If I'd known more—if this were a movie—I would have emptied it then and there and ended this whole mess. But instead, I held it out dumbly and imagined blowing holes in the floor.

Clay held both hands up. It took me several long, stretching seconds to realize he was laughing; his red eyes were filled with unshed tears, his whole body shaking with it. "Oh, it's a fun idea, isn't it, Lucas?" He stepped forward and moved my hand until the gun was pressed to his temple. His smile widened. His eyes closed. He stilled, and the more peaceful he became, the more my heart raged, pounded all the way up into my lungs. All I wanted was to drop the gun, but my hand wouldn't let me.

"It's empty, you know," he said.

I stepped back. The gun fell from my grip, and the sound—a sharp clatter like the footsteps of a thousand metal beasts—echoed around the garage. "You weren't trying to kill yourself?"

Clay laughed. "I'm not that brave." He bent to pick up the gun. "It's for protection. A bluff. I don't know. I thought I'd pick up some bullets at the store or something after I left. The open road can be a dangerous place, Lucas Burke."

"Don't call me that. Where are you going?" I felt something wet on my cheek and realized for the first time that I'd been crying; I wiped it away with my arm and hoped Clay hadn't seen. "If you weren't trying to kill yourself, what the hell were you saying goodbye for?"

Clay plucked a bottle of pills out of his front pocket and swallowed a few down before answering. "I'm getting out of here. I can't stay in this place anymore." He looked around, and I wondered if the garage was as chaotic for him as it was for me. Maybe he was used to the mess, but then maybe he was drowning in it. "I thought I'd go look for my mom maybe. I mean, she's got to be out there somewhere, and even if she doesn't want to see me, it'd be nice to know where she is. I mean...she went there—wherever there is—for a reason, right? Maybe it's nice."

That, or accidental babies in loveless marriages just gave people the running away sort of vibe. Clay tossed the bottle into the air and caught it again. "Here," he said. He handed it over. I left my palm open, not ready to touch it. I didn't want it. Honestly, I didn't even want to look at it.

"I won't need it where I'm going."

"That's it?" I turned the bottle over so the prescription was facing down. "You think you're going to run away and everything gets fixed? That what? The only solution to fixing your life is to just leave?"

Clay shrugged. "Isn't that what you did?"

His words were calm, quiet, but they might as well have come on a freight train the way they hit me at full force. It wasn't like I'd ever been so delusional as not to realize what I'd done, like I hadn't heard Clay's and Rylie's and my mother's voices all cluttered in my head these last nine months saying "don't you think we should all be together right now?" But I'd never thought of it as running away. I'd thought of it as not having to see Nathan in limbo or Clay rotting. I'd thought about San Francisco, about all the new that was waiting for me, and that was *good* even if the rest wasn't. This town was a trap; to leave was not running but escaping.

"It's okay," Clay said. "I get it. I'm not judging you, man. That's what I'm saying. There's nothing in this hellhole but bad memories. Screw this shit, right?"

"Right," I said. I opened the bottle of pills and dumped the remainder into my hand—there were only a few left, not enough to make it through the day at Clay's pace, and suddenly I understood why he'd given them to me: an empty gesture.

There was a little sink in the corner of the garage that probably saw chemical spills and oil messes more than it ever saw soap. I added the pills to its metallic stomach. Clay didn't say a word as I washed them down, nothing when I threw the empty bottle into the trash, but when I turned to face him, I could see his face paling.

"What?" I said. "I thought you didn't need them."

"I don't."

"Clay, where's your dad?"

"Does it matter?" Clay's shoulders tightened again. His lip curled.

"Sort of." I crossed the room and stopped when we were face to face. "Thursday he was messing with you again, and today you've got a gun and you're trying to skip town. So yeah, I think it kind of matters where he is."

Clay raised both eyebrows. "What? Do you think I killed him or something? Yeah, Lucas, I shot him with the last bullet in the gun—no, hell, I shot a whole round into the bastard's cold heart, and then I chopped him up in little pieces and let you waltz right into my crime scene. He's in fucking Florida, okay? The investors called two days ago, so he got on a plane, and he left. That's all I know."

"Two days ago? Then what happened today? Why'd you...call?" The word sounded awkward on my tongue, like calling a war a misunderstanding, but what else did I have?

Clay froze, hesitation written in every tired line of his face, and then he crossed the room and pulled a picture out from under the stacks of paper on his desk. There was a hole in the top through which a ribbon had been strung. "I found this tied to a bottle of scotch." He handed me the picture.

On the glossy side—the picture side—were two smiling people. In fact, they were beaming, happiness radiating off them like heat, so strong I could almost feel it through the photograph. I barely recognized the man as Clay's father: he was like Clay with piercing green eyes and a wicked smile, but older, and the lines on this man's face were still from smiling rather than screaming. Time hadn't changed him yet. The woman could have been anyone, very pretty and very thin, but I had a feeling I'd seen her jaw before, seen it shaking and yelling and rattling on about a scientific world I'd never understand.

"Okay, it's your parents, and?" I pushed the picture back at Clay.

"And they're happy. And this is before she left, and before me, and they're fucking *happy*. Look at that." He snatched the picture out of my hand and tapped both his parents' shiny photographic faces. "I fucked everything up, but it doesn't have to stay that way. If I find her—"

"If you find her what? She falls back in love with your dad? She apologizes for leaving you? What," I said. "You're going to play matchmaker?"

"Maybe!" Clay looked at the picture and then back at me. "Maybe that's what I'm supposed to do. Maybe that's the thing I'm good at. I don't know. But I do know that everything I've tried to make has literally blown up in my face, Lucas, and the only person I've ever loved is getting married in two months! So what am I doing here? Nothing good ever happens in this place, and even if you find happiness"—he waved the picture in front of my face—"it falls apart. It doesn't last. Ever."

I stared. There were avalanches of words I *could* have said then, but none that seemed appropriate and none that could have helped. There was nothing but standing, slack-jawed and dumb-looking, replaying one of my last classes before summer break. My professor had taught us about existential crises and how in a split second, the infrastructure that made your life feel secure could vanish. You'd be left in the void, understanding nothing no matter what you knew. It was not difficult to feel unintelligent in Clay's presence; it was irritating at best and intellectually damaging at worst, but I'd always been able to rely on the unflinching fact that Clay, a man of science, would always be there to reassure me of the world's purpose when my crises began. For the first time since I'd come home, it occurred to me that I might not know the man in front of me as well as I thought.

"Look," I said. "I'm sorry about Rylie. Losing the person you love sucks, but it's not a reason to run away—"

Clay laughed in a way that held no amusement but a touch of hysterics. "You hypocrite."

"What are you talking about?"

"Nathan."

"What about him?"

"You loved him!" Clay threw his hands into the air. "You loved him, and you lost him, and you ran away. So blame it all on this town and on me and on your friends all you want, you asshole, but you weren't the only one who cared about him, Lucas, and this year was really fucking hard, so you don't get to stand here and tell me I'm being selfish when you, you bastard, ran out on all of us when we needed you. We didn't make him crash, okay?"

"I didn't love Nathan."

"What?"

"I didn't love him." I crossed my arms over my chest. There seemed to be less and less breathable air available in the room each second, and I wondered how Clay could just stand there, his chest heaving, breathing, wasting it all, when we were clearly experiencing a crisis.

Clay frowned. "He said—"

"That we went out? Once? That it was nice? Yeah, it was," I said. "It was great. He was great. You know that. We all know that. I didn't love him. Maybe I would have learned to, maybe something would have happened, I don't know, but I do know that I kissed him once, and then he was pretty much dead, and I wasn't going to stick around here and watch him die when I'd already been doing that with you!"

Silence fell between us, the kind that made running away or breaking something—something loud—start to feel like the only solutions. Then Clay picked a bottle of scotch off his desk. The words Happy Anniversary were scrolled in glittery writing over most of the label, and the neck was tied in a ribbon that matched the one on Clay's picture. It was half-empty.

"Then I guess you don't want to help me finish this," he said.

I grabbed the bottle and took a swig. "But we're going to talk about sports and boobs," I said once the burn began in my throat. "No more of this emotions and love bullshit. What is wrong with you?"

Clay laughed. "A lot. You don't even like boobs."

"Everyone likes boobs."

WE DIDN'T TALK about boobs. Clay said the only boobs he could think about were Rylie's, and it was all very mushy and vaguely inappropriate when talk of her boobs inevitably led to talk of her wedding.

"What's she working on now?" Clay asked.

"Drapes for the reception."

"Tell her that setting the drapes on fire makes a lovely addition to any wedding. Free heating, decoration, and a free show," Clay said.

"You've got to pay for lighters." I located the cleanest, un-experimented-on cushion and settled down. "And probably the drapes."

Clay shrugged. "She could cancel the wedding. That'd be a hell of a lot cheaper."

I rolled my eyes and positioned the cushion beneath my head. I yawned. "You know she loves him, right? That this wedding is a thing that's actually happening?"

"Yeah, I know." Clay sat down on the couch across from me. "But she loves me too. She said so. She loves me. I'm just..." He brought the bottle of scotch to his lips and took a sip. After a moment, he frowned and turned the bottle upside down, shaking it until the last drops fell out. "I'm a bad choice. Obviously. She said she doesn't trust me. Which, okay, is not great, but it's different than not loving me. I have a chance."

I doubted it, but the alcohol was just pleasantly warm enough in my stomach to remind me to shut my mouth. Anyway, Clay just looked so damn hopeful, his sunken eyes wide like he was still dreaming of all those possibilities that might never be. I was mean, but I wasn't mean enough to ruin that. Not yet.

"Whatever you say."

"She says I'm not good for her."

"Hmm." I thought of Chris and his big goofy smile—the one that took up half his face. Though the scotch burned hot and heavy in my gut, it couldn't quite extinguish that instant burst of happiness, a feeling like I was lighter than what was inside me, lighter than the booze sloshing around in my stomach or the memory of Nathan's blank eyes and the boys with their pants down—lighter than air.

There were two slits in the garage door, and through it, light from the moon and the streetlamp shone inside; for one small moment, I didn't miss the city lights. For one small moment, the streetlamps seemed like enough.

"I don't think anyone's good for anyone," I said. Chris smiled too big. I'd get lost in it. Maybe I already was.

"You sure? You know, I meant it before," Clay said. "That Chris guy? He's good for you. He likes you. And I know you like him."

"Oh yeah? When'd you become such a love expert?"

Clay shook his head. "Love? Fuck, I don't know anything about love. I don't know about love, but I know you, Lucas. And I know when you're faking it and when you're really happy." He smiled. "You're happy. Even if you don't know it yet."

I tucked my arm under my head and closed my eyes. It seemed improbable that someone could be happy and not know it, but, well, my time at the park that afternoon hadn't exactly been terrible.

Clay brought me a blanket and slung it over my shoulders. He moved back to his side of the couch and curled into a ball. "Night, Lucas."

"Night, Clay."

Minutes, or maybe hours later, my phone rang from inside my pocket, but it might as well have been miles away. Too tired to care and too worn out to move, I rolled onto my side and fell asleep.

Ten

55 Days Before

I woke up in the passenger seat of Clay's most expensive red convertible. I couldn't remember moving over the course of the night, but when I opened my eyes, my face was plastered against the dashboard in a pool of drool. Light streamed in through the crack between the garage door and the cement floor. The panic took two full groggy, sleep-blinking minutes to settle in.

"Your dad is going to find us." I sat up and scrambled out of the car, careful even in my haste not to dent it or break a window or anything. I didn't know what the car cost, but whatever it was, I couldn't afford it. "Your dad is going to come home, and he's going to kill us. Fuck, fuck, fuck."

No one answered.

As far as I knew, Mr. Ortiz was not *actually* evil. He never came home with a pitchfork and red tail, and I wasn't even scared of him—not exactly. But I *was* scared of what he'd say to Clay if he knew he had a guest over, scared of what his face might look like when he realized someone *not* of the noble Ortiz bloodline had infiltrated his kingdom and breathed on his most expensive things. I was scared of being interrogated about what I'd touched and what I hadn't and asked if my mom was still in that "awful teaching business."

Mostly, I didn't want to *deal* with Mr. Ortiz, especially not when my mouth smelled like death and my clothes were sticking to me and my stench was actually making me sick. Like this—hungover and reeking of morning breath—I didn't stand a chance of making a good impression.

But Clay was nowhere to be seen. The door to the workshop was slung open, and I could hear voices from inside. For one heart-stopping moment, I was sure it really *was* Mr. Ortiz, and I froze just outside the convertible. The way I saw it, I had two options: stay there and potentially overhear a very uncomfortable conversation, or barge in and get caught up in a private family affair that could easily make everything a thousand times worse.

I thought about sneaking out through the back or finding that gun just to pull a good bluff in self-protection, but then the door opened completely and Clay stepped out looking as scared as I felt. He stopped several feet away, his phone held in one shaking hand.

"Your dad—" I started, but he shook his head.

"My dad won't be back for days. But we've got bigger problems."

I raised an eyebrow. It seemed unlikely. Seriously, I smelled *bad*. High school locker room after P.E. bad, and even if Mr. Ortiz wasn't around to ridicule me, I was desperate to get home.

"Chris is in the hospital," Clay said. "The cancer is back."

WE TOOK CLAY'S convertible and ran two red lights to get to the hospital. "Don't worry about it," Clay had said. "I can afford the tickets."

Rylie was already there and pacing outside Chris's room when we arrived. "Todney is in there with him now," she said. Half her face was covered in makeup, half of it was clean, and she had false eyelashes glued to only one eye. "I was testing makeup artists. I was in the middle of an appointment when Todney called." Her voice was watery. Her knees shook. "He's a mess. I've never seen him like this."

"What's the diagnosis?" I asked.

Rylie shook her head. "They've been doing tests all morning. We don't know. Todney just said Chris has been running a fever for a couple days, and his chest was swelling up, and they thought he had a flu or something. But, you know, they're careful now. Got to check all the options. So they did some lab work a couple days ago just to be sure, and..." She ran both hands over her face. Every nail was a different color, some glittery, some with flowers on the edges, some striped or polka-dotted. "And the results came back yesterday, and it doesn't look good."

"Yesterday?" I said.

"They wanted to be sure before they told anyone."

"So we don't actually know yet?"

"They're doing an X-ray right now."

"But he already beat it. He's cancer free."

"These things come back, Lucas." Rylie wiped a tear from her cheek. It had fallen from the makeuped side of her face and smudged quite a lot of her mascara. The black lines covered her cheek like a dark watercolor painting. She must have seen me looking, because she smiled through her oncoming tears and said, "Cheap stuff. I'll have to get the waterproof version for the wedding. I'm sure I won't stop crying all day. Chris is going to look so handsome standing up there with Todney in his suit."

She said it confidently, like the future was inevitable, but then another tear slid down her face, and I clenched my fists and looked away.

"This is crazy." Clay crossed the room until he was face-to-face with Rylie. He wiped the tears from her cheek. "He's going to be fine. Lucas said it; he *beat* cancer. It's probably just a flu, just like they thought."

Rylie sniffed. "Todney won't know what to do without Chris. He's got to be okay. He's just got to. They need each other. They're like brothers. It just came out of nowhere. I mean, I know he'd been sort of sick for a few days, but he was fine. He was fine. And then Todney calls me screaming because he found him passed out and he wouldn't wake up, and he didn't know what to do, and I don't know what to do." She coughed and scrubbed at the wet spots under eyes. She squinted at Clay's hand as though noticing it for the first time and then quickly swatted it away. "I know I don't need *that*."

Clay backed up. Before anyone could say more, Todney stepped out of Chris's room with tears streaked down his face.

TODNEY EXPLAINED THAT Chris had developed what the doctors liked to call metastatic Ewing tumors—metastatic because unlike last time, where the tumor had been localized in just his leg, these tumors were spreading like wildfire. Though they'd started just on his chest bone, they'd jumped ship now and were running uncontrolled through his lungs, and it didn't look like they were stopping there. We looked it up online: localized tumors had a 70 percent five-year survival rating; metastatic tumors had 20 percent. They'd be starting chemotherapy that week.

"Can we see him?" I asked.

Todney ran a shaking hand through his hair and shrugged. He didn't look like Todney anymore; no more nice clothes or straight posture, and even when he reached for Rylie's hand, it was a loose, flimsy gesture.

"Yeah, I mean, the doctors said it's fine. You just have to be careful, okay? I mean—"

"Oh my gosh, just let everyone in!" Chris called from somewhere inside the room.

Despite everything, I grinned.

The three of us piled into the room one by one, though the doorway was hardly small enough to deem it necessary. There was an awful lot of tiptoeing and hushed voices, and we all stopped a good five feet from the bed. Everyone but Todney, that is, who rushed over and refluffed Chris's pillows.

Chris glared. "I'm *fine*." He sat upright in bed, wearing the blue and white clothes the hospital provided—the clothes Nathan lived in every day.

Chris didn't look any different, but then I guess that's why they say you can't trust appearances and not to judge a book by its cover, because the outside never shows what's within. But still, it was strange—to say someone was sick, for someone to have something as fear-inspiring as cancer—and then to see him looking perfectly normal. Like it was all a joke. Some elaborate prank. *You're supposed to look dead*, I thought. I imagined cancer as a source of decay from the inside out; I saw bald heads and pale skin, and, well, zombies—though I certainly wouldn't admit that one out loud. And though I knew somewhere in the darker, more rational parts of my mind that these things take time and a diagnosis was just the beginning of a long, painful journey, I couldn't understand. Not fully. Maybe not at all.

Chris had been fine a day before; in fact, he seemed more annoyed now than anything, his arms crossed over his chest, two fingers flicking his IV line until Todney tugged it out of his grip. He'd been fine—laughing and kissing me in the park, fine and living and not sick. He *was* fine. He was healthy just a day before, and things couldn't really change that fast.

But had he really been okay? Hunched over, sweating, grabbing at his leg and chest all day long, and what had I done? Sat by and complained; *you only see what you want to see, Lucas.*

Chris flicked the IV again.

Todney grabbed his wrist. "Do you want to make things worse?"

Chris looked from Todney to me to the rest of the group. He gritted his teeth. "Could they be worse?"

No one answered; we all knew the truth, but no one was cruel enough to say it.

A window filled most of the wall behind Chris's head. The sun streamed in and lit up every corner of the hospital room with warm yellow light. It outlined the more prominent angles of Chris's jaw and painted golden highlights in his dark brown hair.

I'd say he looked like an angel just to make the picture prettier, but it wasn't true. He wasn't serene, wasn't peaceful; he was glaring and flushed, and his already messy hair now appeared to have seen both sides of a tornado. He looked exhausted, not holy. They say people search for miracles when things get dark—that they think they see Jesus in their toast, and that we're stronger when we're suffering—but what doesn't kill you doesn't *really* make you stronger; it just makes you weak, and Chris was drowned in the light, not amplified in it.

Todney leaned on the edge of the bed, and slowly, my friends pulled up the visitors' chairs. We all sat. Chris stared at us, his eyes red and dark, and we stared back, and then after what seemed like eons, Rylie coughed. She reached for Chris's hand and gave it the same sort of squeeze my mother always used to after we'd received bad news.

"I know it seems scary right now," Rylie said. "But you're going to fight this."

Chris certainly looked like he wanted to fight, though I'm not sure what he was fighting was cancer. He bit hard on his bottom lip, his jaw tightened, and then he nodded. "Thank you. I will."

"Do you need anything?" asked Clay.

"We can get more water," said Rylie.

"I uh..." I scratched the back of my neck. "Ice chips?"

Chris laughed. "Thank you, Lucas, but despite popular belief, I'm not actually giving birth. See, I know the flab can be deceiving—" He patted his very firm, very not-flabby stomach. "—but this is not actually a baby. Actually the baby is up here." He touched his chest. "I'm growing in the incubator of my lungs a village of baby cancer cells, and I, as you can see by my numerous charts, am an excellent mother. Todney, where are my charts? I'd like to see my children again. We should name them. Little Fucker One, Little Fucker Two..." He trailed off as Todney's glare turned livid. "What? I'm *lightening up the situation.* That's what you told me to do."

"You don't sound light; you sound homicidal," said Todney.

"I thought that was the goal. Cancer is the big *fight*, isn't it? I'm getting in the fighting spirit." Chris flicked his IV again. "Can I take this out?"

"No, seriously, what is wrong with you? This is serious. Can you act like an adult for a second here?"

Chris's eyes grew so wide it might have been comical had they not looked so very close to tears. "*What*?" he asked in obvious, biting sarcasm. "I had no idea it was serious. What would I do without you?"

"Chris." Todney placed a hand over Chris's shoulder and gave it a squeeze. "I know this is hard right now, but we're all here for you."

Rylie nodded in agreement. I thought it was obvious we were there for him, that gathering around his bed and offering our condolences was a clear sign of that, because, you know, we were literally *there*, but since it didn't seem to be enough, I nodded too.

Clay didn't. Clay leaned back in his chair and crossed his arms over his chest and looked at Chris like some science experiment he hadn't figured out yet. He'd looked the same way at our sixth-grade class pet and the outdated computers in the high school lab. I thought about kicking him under my chair to get him to play along, but then Chris's eyes locked with Clay's, and they exchanged this sort of nonverbal, secretive nod, and Clay stood up.

"We should all get lunch," he announced.

Todney's eyebrows rose dangerously high. "Excuse me? Why would we—"

"Yeah," Chris said. "You guys should get lunch. I bet you're starving. Bring me something back, will you?"

Todney rolled his knuckles together and then sighed so deeply that it rattled down his spine; I wouldn't have been surprised if even his socks were crumpled from it. "Okay. I guess we're getting lunch. Are you going to be okay while we're gone?"

"I'll be fine," Chris said. He didn't look at Todney. He didn't look at any of us.

I wanted to reach out to him, wanted to take his hand, to kiss him, to do something other than just sitting here like a lame duck, but my feet wouldn't move, and my brain wasn't any more help. Chris had beat this.

He was the 70 percent that got out alive, and he'd boasted of his cancer-free body since the moment I met him. Chris was the straight bet, the one I didn't have to worry about. When everyone else in this forsaken town was ripping apart at the seams, Chris was the survivor—the proof that things got better if you made it to the other side. What was the other side now if life was just a cycle?

Without another word, we all trudged out of the room. Todney closed the door behind us but not without shooting one last questioning look back at Chris. Chris shot him two thumbs up, but he didn't smile, and the motion tugged at his IV, so he dropped his hands again and closed his eyes. Todney sighed.

Once the door clicked behind him, the noise of the hospital finally seemed to kick in. Nurses bustled in every direction, crying families exited rooms across the halls, and laughing kids ran up and down, singing that grandpa was going to be okay.

"Well, that went well," Rylie said.

"What'd you give him that idea for?" Todney pointed a finger at Clay.

Clay shrugged. "He wanted us out. He was practically begging for it. I'm sorry, but the guy just got the worst news in the world. He deserves some alone time to think it over."

"That wasn't your call to make—"

Rylie placed a hand against Todney's chest. "It's not your call either," she said. Todney opened his mouth to reply, but when no words came out—even after several long *Jeopardy*-esque seconds—he closed it again and nodded.

"Um, should we get food?" he asked.

SO WE GOT food. We walked to this fast-food joint across the street, and several greasy burgers later, we returned to the waiting room to eat and wait and wait and eat. Though the hospital itself was loud, not a single sound penetrated our little group but for the crinkling of wrappers and the smack of a last bite.

I felt this strange obligation to break the silence if only just because that's what Chris would have done, but the second I opened my mouth, the thought hit me that taking his role would be like declaring him dead. So I shut my mouth and tried to trust fate, tried to imagine Chris running back out into the hall, declaring himself healed and talking up a storm.

My imagination had never been my strong suit.

Todney was the only one who didn't eat; he held his burger up in front of his mouth, stared at it, stared at Chris's room, and then sighed and stared at his burger again. This went on for quite some time. Then Rylie grabbed the burger from his hands and took a bite.

"Delicious," she said with her full mouth. Flecks of bun and mustard scattered over the floor. "And not poisonous. So eat it." She pushed the burger back in to Todney's hands and didn't so much as blink at the wide-eyed look he gave her.

Slowly, he took a bite.

"Not bad, huh?" Rylie patted his knee and grinned, but it didn't quite meet her eyes. After a while, she threw away her half-eaten burger and walked toward me. She took a seat and placed a hand over mine. "How are you feeling?"

I shrugged. I knew what they expected me to feel—that they expected me to cry or freak out or something else extreme. And I knew that *I* expected nothing—that I'd get this sort of awful news and I'd just carry on—acknowledge it was sad, and that was it. But as is the way of life, nothing went according to plan. My heart wasn't broken on the floor or anything, but I wasn't as numb as I would have liked either. All at once, I was very aware and unaware: aware in that I could feel the blood running through my veins, and I could still taste Chris on my lips; and unaware in that I could barely hear the sounds of my friends' voices, and I tasted nothing even though the wrapper on my burger said it was one of the best in town.

Chris had cancer, and that sucked, not because I loved him—because loving him or anyone at this point would have been crazy—but because cancer sucked, and no one deserved to die at twenty-one. Chris had cancer, and we were all piled up in a white, death-filled sterile prison, waiting for him to come to terms with his own demise, and that was awful, and 20 percent was shitty odds. So, no, I wasn't happy; I was shitty, and I was supposed to be shitty, and that didn't mean anything, just that I was another person hearing bad news.

I would have said this, of course, but before I could put it into speakable words, Rylie squeezed my hand, leaned in close, and whispered, "You're not going to run, are you?"

In all fairness, I should have seen it coming. History is bound to repeat itself, and after my first day at the hospital with Nathan, I'd disappeared for months. I was the flake, the runner, or, as Rylie had so beautifully put it, *the one who got away.*

"I'm not going anywhere." I didn't bother keeping my voice low, not like Rylie did, did not use the secretive whisper she'd always been such a master of; I had no reason to keep it covered up. Not here. Not now. "I'm right here. I'm staying right here."

Todney looked up, and our eyes met. I'd always thought I'd have to impress him to stay on Rylie's good side, at least until the wedding; it had never occurred to me that one day I'd have my own selfish reasons for making him like me. I wasn't sure Chris was capable of existing without his own personal Todney.

"I'm here," I said again. "I am. And I'll be here as long as he wants me to be."

The second the words came out of my mouth, I wanted to rip them back, to pull them from the air and stuff them where they belonged: unheard and unspoken. Who did I think I was, making a declaration like *that*? It was a lie, or at least it should have been—I thought it was, was *sure* it was—and this wasn't the time for lies. Certainly, it was inappropriate to say the least. Except, well, I couldn't stop looking back at Chris's door or hearing him laugh in the back of my mind, and every time I clenched my fist, I imagined Chris's fingertips trailing along my palm. It was the little things—the way he butchered French and the shadow of his arms in the sunlight—that haunted me now.

Todney reached for my hand, and like Rylie, he squeezed it tight, leaving me in the middle of this strange grieving couple sandwich. I looked between the two of them and tried to smile.

"Thank you," Todney said. "Chris needs you now."

"I need a drink." Clay stood up and, without further explanation, walked away.

I watched him go, his wrinkled T-shirt—such a strange sight to see on the always impeccable Clay—becoming just a dot in the distance, and I tried not to notice when my throat went dry. I stood up and paced the hall just to give my feet something to do. I'd been at it for five minutes or so when the door to Chris's room opened up and a nurse stepped out.

"He's asking for you."

I looked around the hallway, meeting eyes with Rylie and Todney before the nurse pointed directly at me. "You. Are you Lucas? Chris is asking for you. Would you like to come in?"

I nodded.

Chris was lying back in bed, his arms over his head and his fingers spread. His eyes focused on the spaces in between. *We're limited by our scope.* I choked on the sudden onset of tears in my throat.

I coughed and stepped forward. "I learned some new French words today."

Chris lowered his hands and smiled over at me; it was a weak gesture, not quite up to snuff with his normal beaming flashlight of a grin, but it was a start.

"Oh yeah?" he said, ushering me over. I crossed the room and sat down on the edge of his bed. When he raised his eyebrows and looked at the empty space next to him, I moved closer. I positioned myself against the headboard so we were hip to hip and I could stroke his hair while I tried to remember my words.

"*Boire comme un trou,*" I said. "It means 'drink like a hole' literally, but it *really* means we should get really, really drunk."

Chris laughed. "We really should."

"Um." I scratched my head. "*Avoir une araignée au plafond.*"

"What's that mean?"

"You have a spider on the ceiling."

Chris looked up, but the ceiling was as clean and sterile as the rest of the room. He looked back at me, questioning, and I barely held back a smile. His eyes were wider when he was confused, big and brown like an oversized puppy.

I shrugged. "Apparently it means you're crazy."

Chris smiled. "I like French."

I told him all the words and phrases I knew: *casser les oreilles* (breaking someone's ears, AKA to get on someone's nerves by making the wrong kind of sound; I had to google that one to remember it), *possibilité* (possibilities), *navet* (turnip, though apparently it could also be used derogatorily, like "what a turnip of a situation we have found ourselves in!"), *pain* (bread). Soon, Chris was laughing and shouting about all the turnips in his life, constructing a horrible French accent as he threw his hands up in the air and said, in English, "turnip this!" and "turnip that!" and neither of us could breathe from laughing.

When we calmed down a bit, I pulled out my phone and found an online translator. I knew they were notoriously unreliable, but since I wasn't about to be fluent in French any time soon, it was all I had. "*Il est grand, et il est beau, et vous ne pouvez pas tout voir, mais il est toujours là. Toutes ces possibilities."*

"What's that mean?" Chris said.

"It's big, and it's beautiful, and you can't see it all, but it's still out there. All those possibilities."

Chris's eyes crinkled around the corners and then grew watery, and I looked away. It was quiet for a long time, and then he said, "Most people have a list."

I looked back, met his eyes, and raised my eyebrows. "What?"

"Things to do before you die," he said.

"Do you have a list?" I asked.

"Yeah."

"What's number one?"

"Don't die."

Eleven

AN OLD NINETIES romcom was playing on the TV in Chris's room when the nurse finally came back. I'd always hated romcoms on principle mostly because, well, I was a dude, and also because the time between meet and love was so notoriously short. But Chris watched with at least mild interest, his hands propping his head up so he could see properly. It wasn't until the nurse cleared her throat that he looked away from the television and blinked his way out of an apparent daze.

"You're free to go, Mr. Wood," she said, and he beamed.

To give him the privacy of dressing alone, she left the room, and I offered to do the same, but Chris just waved his hand and told me that "we all have the same parts."

I didn't see what good that did or why it was supposed to be comforting when he knew full well I wasn't very interested in *opposite* body parts, but I stayed anyway and tried to focus on the ceiling when he climbed out of bed in nothing but a flimsy hospital gown. Problem was, peripheral vision was still very much a thing, and as good as I wanted to be, I couldn't help but notice the firm, tanned expanse of Chris's back that ended in the band of his boxers and the curve of his ass underneath. Chris had a swimmer's body, and I'd been excited enough in *hearing* about it, but *seeing* it—the lean muscles of his arms, the abs, the long legs, the tanned skin—was a bit of wet dream in more ways than one.

Someone coughed, and I nearly jumped out of my skin before turning to face Todney. He closed the door behind him and raised an eyebrow just as Chris finished buttoning his jeans.

"What's going on in here?" He sounded way too much like a dad—arms crossed over his chest, eyes narrowed, posture ready to attack.

"Strip show," Chris said without pause, not even looking up. "I'm practicing for my new job. I didn't tell you? Right, Todney, I'm a stripper. I'm practicing lap dances next. I mean, I can give you one if you want, but Lucas sort of asked first."

All the heat in my body rushed directly to my face. Chris pulled his shirt over that last lingering strip of stomach and flattened out the wrinkles.

Todney rolled his eyes. "If you two have sex in a hospital room, I will leave you."

"I want you to leave me," Chris said. "I mean—" He paused and scratched the bridge of his nose. "You've been here too long. You need a break. Take Rylie home, and Lucas can take me home." He looked to me, his eyes wide and hopeful, and I nodded without thinking. I didn't need to think. A whole life spent overthinking, and here I was, reacting to anything and everything that had to do with Chris as though it was basic instinct.

"Yeah, I can take him," I said. "Clay left me his car." He'd walked home an hour ago after wishing Chris his best. Chris, waving and smiling, had seemed happy enough with the attention, but I'd rather thought he could've done more. Given the circumstances, goodbye felt like a curse.

Todney nodded, an action that seemed to take all his strength and willpower to accomplish. Jaw tight, eyes dark, he clapped Chris on the shoulder, gave me a weak sort of smile that was probably a warning, and then left the room.

When he was gone, Chris turned to me, his expression suddenly very serious, and said, "I'd like to meet Nathan, if that's okay."

NATHAN HADN'T CHANGED since the last time I saw him, not that I expected him to or anything. He was still pale, still, well, *still*, and it was difficult to make out his face behind his overgrown bangs and the darkness of the room. The shades were pulled down over the window, blocking out all afternoon sunshine, and it was there that Chris went first.

"Light heals," he said, shrugging as he pulled the blinds up and opened the window to let in a weak summer draft.

Only after the light came streaming in did Chris stop and fully look around. He sucked in a deep breath and then sat in the chair beside Nathan's bed without a word. For a long time, he stared at Nathan, and I stared at him, and only the sounds of the beeping machines and monitors filled the room.

I kept waiting to get used to the sound of the machines, to walk into Nathan's room one day and not feel that sinking rush in my stomach. The noise wasn't new anymore—it was echoed in the streets of this city every time I stepped foot within the town limits—and yet I could still remember what it was like to hear it for the first time, to see Nathan still as death and not know why, to not believe it. Chris was hearing the machines for the first time, but it wasn't the same. Chris didn't know Nathan; he didn't know that Nathan ate sushi every Thursday, that he'd failed out of art and he was the fastest guy on the baseball team. He didn't know the sound of Nathan's laugh, or the way he tapped his fingers over his thighs in tune to every word he said. He'd never seen Nathan moving, so how could he know how wrong it was to see Nathan still?

But Chris did look devastated, and I couldn't figure out why. He held his head in his hands and stared at Nathan's bed, at Nathan's hands, at Nathan's face. Chris's gaze roamed anywhere and everywhere, and with each passing second, his frown became more pronounced, like it actually hurt him—a stranger—to see Nathan this way.

After a long moment, he dropped his hands, folded them in his lap, cleared his throat, and said, "Will you tell me about him?"

"We went to school together," I said.

"More than that. Tell me *about* him. Please."

Nathan's finger twitched, a reminder that he was actually there—a human and not a mannequin, still a present member of the room. I pulled up a chair and cleared my throat, trying to think up all the little pieces that made a person a person and not just another story you told at a funeral.

"I met him when I was five," I said. "Same time I met Rylie and Clay. We all lived on the same street. Everyone's moved around since then but stayed in town. Clay lived right next to me, and Rylie was on the other side, and Nathan was across the street. And we played basketball on Nathan's hoop or baseball in the park. Nathan always had the baseballs, and Rylie brought the chalk when we needed to make a field or a court. And that's it. We were kids, and we were all together. We were always together. And we grew up, and we went to the same middle school and the same high school, and Rylie and Clay started dating, and Nathan and I—"

"Started dating," Chris filled in the blank.

"Yeah. It wasn't for long," I said quickly, as though I owed it to Chris not to linger on the topic, like because we were dating, I couldn't have dated anyone else, at least not for a while. It's funny how that works: like the shorter you were together, the less it meant, and yet Chris had only been in my life for a couple of months and already my feelings for him were reaching a capital L sort of area.

"I don't care," Chris said. "I've dated other people too. Was he good to you? How'd you two get together?"

I raised an eyebrow. "Why are you asking me this stuff?" Call me traditional, call me old-fashioned, but talking about an ex in front of your current almost-boyfriend was weird, and that was just if we were alone; talking *in front* of the ex was downright awkward, coma or not. Actually, particularly with the coma.

Chris said nothing at first, just brushed a hand through his hair and stared at Nathan again. Finally he turned to me and shrugged. "I just want to know."

"Why?"

"Because."

"Because why?"

"Because he's dying!" Chris's eyes widened to near impossible proportions as he gestured back at Nathan's sleeping form. "He's dying, but dying doesn't mean gone, right? It can't. *It can't.* But right now? He's got nothing. He's a bunch of muscles and bones and a sleeping brain, and if that's how his life ends, then that really, really sucks, Lucas." Chris's voice broke, and he pushed his knuckles to his mouth, his chest heaving. "He's only a person right now if you remember him. You. So please, *please* can you remember him?"

It clicked then, the "*I'm* dying" lingering under every "he." And I was damn near robotic, an unfeeling monster, a heartless runner, and *that* was what I was good at, and *that* was the way things should be, and I didn't want to hear it. I could have ended it all right then and there. Time to get out of the room, time to go home. *Pack your bags, Lucas, and get away.* I didn't want to be Chris's tether to life, didn't want to watch him disintegrate, and I had not chosen to be pulled down by his side. I fell for Chris because he was alive, because he was the one guaranteed not to fall apart. This—hospital visits and beeping machines—was not the life I picked, and if I was smart, I'd have ended it.

I couldn't remember moving, couldn't place the moment that the gears all swiveled into place and my muscles got the memo, but next thing I knew, I was out of my chair and standing behind Chris with my arms slung over his shoulders, my lips pressed to his hair. His body shook under my hands, his heart pounded under my fingertips, and when I leaned in close and whispered in his ear that everything would be okay, I could hear him choke back a sob.

"We barely dated," I said. "But he was a good friend. I always sort of had a crush on him, I guess."

"He *is* good-looking," Chris conceded. And he was: Good jaw, good hair (when it wasn't grown out), good eyes (when they were open): the facts were hard to argue with.

I laughed. "Yeah, he is. And very good at baseball. He always had my back; I always had his. I taught him to smoke, and he taught me to dance. He didn't ditch with us much, though, because he was real set on going to college, so his grades had to be okay. Clay was the smartest, but he was flunking, and Nathan kept saying he didn't want to be like that. So one day, he stopped smoking and drinking and everything, and he was on time to all his classes, and he started showing me these college pamphlets of these faraway great cities, and I fell."

"For him?" Chris asked.

"For the cities. He was going to L.A. I didn't...I didn't care. But I sort of didn't want to go to L.A. just because he was going there."

"You didn't like him?"

"I did. It's complicated." I rested my chin against the top of Chris's head. Some things you could talk about all day, and other things you could never find the words for. For me, Nathan had always been the latter. When I tried, I saw color, heard songs from kindergarten, and got this *feeling*—like when the wind rushes through your hair and you're staring through the rearview mirror on the longest road trip of your life, but I could have read the whole dictionary and not found a single word to express it. "I liked him," I tried again. "I did. I like all my friends. But they were here. They *are* here. And I wanted to be—"

"Someone else," Chris filled in the blank.

I blinked and stared down at him, feeling very Spiderman-esque as our eyes met upside down. It was oddly romantic in the awkward sitting-in-front-of-your-dying-ex talking-about-your-abandonment-issues sort of way, and I might have kissed him if I hadn't been so damn surprised.

Instead, my mouth fell open, and I stared. And Chris, his eyes still watering a bit, his hands still shaking as they moved to caress my face, smiled and shrugged.

"Am I wrong?" he asked.

I shook my head. "No." I guessed not. But it was news to me. I'd been about to say *somewhere*. "You're telling me I hate this forsaken, soul-crushing town because I don't like me?"

"It's basic psychology," Chris said. "You project all the things you weren't comfortable with or happy about yourself onto the place and the people you were with when you felt those things. You go somewhere new, and you can find new happy associations, so when you come back and the old memories come back too, you blame where you are. You blame the people."

"Where'd you learn that?"

"You have a lot of free time during chemo."

"So you read psychology books?"

"Basically."

"You are very strange."

I kissed Chris's cheek for good measure and then lifted my head again—just in time too, because all the blood started rushing to my brain, and the room spun faster than a ballerina. I blinked and steadied my weight by pressing my hands into Chris's shoulders; his muscles relaxed under my fingertips, and he leaned back.

"I never felt judged in San Francisco." Another sentence I hadn't planned, which was great, just great, when word vomit had never been one of my many problems before. *Well, too late to stop now.* "Not just for being gay. I mean, that was nice. That was really nice. But things weren't bad here. Not like for you. We had to leave a couple of churches, and some kids at school...well, you know. But we had a gay straight alliance club in high school, and that was kind of cool, I guess. And my parents supported me, and I know most kids don't even have that. But I was still the only gay kid I knew. At least until Nathan came out. And that wasn't until eleventh grade. But in San Francisco, it was more than that. It was like...okay, there were ladies on the bus in hair curlers and bathrobes, and no one would even look at them. No staring. No questions. Nothing."

"And you particularly enjoyed riding the bus in your hair curlers, Lucas?" Chris asked. Though he faced away from me, I could see the reflection of his smile in one of the many clear surfaces of Nathan's machinery.

"No, I..." What *had* I liked? The permission to be wild? License to dye my hair, wear whatever I wanted? If so, I'd barely used any of *those* liberties. In the city—same as now—I wore my basic-colored T-shirts, ratted-up jeans, and clean Converse so I didn't have to see my friends' names signed on the white strips. Hardly the clothing of a rebel.

"You didn't have to know what you wanted yet." And there it was in a nutshell: Nathan's lips hovering so close to mine and not knowing if I wanted to kiss him, a naked back leaving my room in the dead of night, and I, alone in bed, not ever sure if I wanted that stranger or the next to turn back around.

I looked to Nathan, at the little wrinkles in his hospital gown, the hint of stubble creeping up around his jaw since the last time he'd been shaved, the steady rise and fall of his chest.

"I only kissed him once," I said. "I was always going to leave, and I never told him. But he was always going to leave too. I...I don't know what we were doing." And that, meaningless and empty as it might have been, was the truth.

Chris patted my hand and then let go of me entirely and scooted his chair across the room. He stopped next to Nathan's bed and whispered something in his ear.

"What are you doing?" I asked.

"Trying to wake him up." Chris did it again—a whisper and a smile.

"What are you telling him?"

"Stories about you."

I crossed the room and sat on the edge of Nathan's bed so I was as close to him as I was to Chris. He grinned up at me, and when he tried again, his whisper wasn't so whispery anymore.

"Come on," Chris said. "I need the dirt. Does Lucas snore in his sleep? Is he the cuddling type? Will he wrap around you like an octopus, or is he one of those straight as a board 'don't touch anyone, sleeping is alone time' types? This is important stuff, and you are all I got, Nathan." He reached for Nathan's hand and rubbed little circles over the back of it with his thumb. "Wake up? Please? Come on, man, pleeeeeeease. Lucas has started learning French. Which means he's gotten really, really bad at French. Don't you want to hear it? We can gang up on him and force those weird little French phrases out of him."

I rolled my eyes. "At least I know something."

"Shh," Chris said. "I'm working on miracles here. Play along, will you?" He winked at me, and his smile tilted up to one side. It was a strange thought—one I'd deny on principle, of course—but I sort of felt like that one side was just for me, a Morse code language of mouth twitches and half smiles only we could understand.

I threw my hands up in surrender and nodded for him to continue his oh-so-important work. This time, there was not so much as an illusion of a whisper.

"I've always wanted a love triangle," Chris said. "If you wake up, we can fight over Lucas, pull each other's hair, and rip out each other's earrings. It will be a glorious battle, my friend." He waited, and when Nathan didn't jump out of bed and declare war, Chris sighed and let out a long childlike whine of disapproval. "Seriously, you are passing up such a good opportunity here. We can both try and take him out on dates. Oh! We'll recreate the Bachelor. Come on, they haven't had a gay bachelor." He looked up. "Have they?"

I shook my head.

Chris nodded. "Right, they haven't. So we'll take Lucas out on dates, and we'll compete like 'who kisses better?' and 'who buys more expensive gifts?' You'll probably win that one; I'm poor. But I will pick him the best most beautifulest flowers from one of these yards around here."

I laughed. Chris winked. In some sort of fit of desperation (probably), he lurched forward and grabbed me by both cheeks. "I'm going to kiss him," he told Nathan. "I'm going to do it. You better wake up and stop me. I'm doing it. I'm doing it." With each cry of "I'm doing it," he leaned closer and closer to my lips but never touched them. His breath ghosted over my skin, making goose bumps rise wherever it touched.

This went on for at least a minute, and self-control be damned, I couldn't take it anymore. I kissed him first. He went slack against me, and then his hands tightened against my face and drifted down to hold my neck. We kissed and kissed and kissed, and for a while, time disappeared; then one of Nathan's machines beeped, and we pulled away.

"Careful, Nathan," Chris whispered, and because we were just centimeters away, I could still feel him on my lips. His voice vibrated, tickled too, but I didn't dare to move. "You don't wake up soon, and I just might fall in love with him."

I gulped. I knew he didn't mean it, that he, like everyone else who visited Nathan, had just said the craziest thing he could think of to shock Nathan awake. We'd all tried it: the apocalypse is coming; we need your help to fight; zombies are outside; grab your sword and chop up the dead bastards like you always wanted to; we're going to have an orgy, and if you miss it, we're not recording it. Nothing worked. We never got more than a twitch, and yet no one stopped trying. Chris, like Clay, like Rylie, like me, was just trying to help.

Still, I couldn't *force* my heart to stop pounding.

"We've done everything." I pulled away fully and calculated the space between us until we were at least a foot apart. At a distance, there was no way to get bad ideas; at a distance, there was no reason to go getting my hopes up, thinking about his tongue in my mouth and love on his lips. "Clay even kissed me once to try to freak Nathan awake."

"How'd that work?"

"Not good. Really, really gross."

Chris laughed. "Not your type then?"

"Not at all."

We moved off Nathan's bed after that, but even across the room, we couldn't forget his presence; he was a constant watching force, the ticking clock, and though I'd have rather talked about anything else in the world, I knew what I had to say.

"So your cancer is back."

Chris nodded but didn't speak, so I kept going, digging my thumbnails into my arms to keep up the nerve.

"That sucks. Are you scared?"

Chris raised an eyebrow. "You don't talk about feelings very often, do you?"

I shook my head. Chris smiled. He reached for my hand and gave it a squeeze that was softer than I deserved. "I wasn't kidding when I said I love you. And I'm not saying that because I want you to say it back, so don't go getting your panties in a twist. I already know." His chin tilted up slightly, and he smiled—smiled brighter than anything I'd ever seen, brighter than every ray of light coming through that damned window. Even with his eyes red, even when his whole body shook with fear, even when his very cells had turned against him, he smiled. He was so beautiful. And I knew he was only saying it because he might be dying, and that fear made people say crazy things, but I almost wanted to believe it. He was sick, probably dying, but he loved me, and he was mine—all mine.

I never read any psychology books, hadn't begun to even think about taking any classes, and so I wasn't sure if we, as humans—as men—were taught to love, or taught not to love, but I knew one of us had missed a vital lesson, and I longed to be on the same page.

"Am I scared?" Chris said. "Of course I'm scared. But it's common. I'm a statistic. Twenty percent of people are going to beat this, and eighty percent are going to die. Everyone always says, you know, 'someone's got to be that twenty percent, why can't it be me?' They say you've got to fight. But it's not a battle. It's probability. Heads I live, tails I die, and I'm outnumbered in tails. So maybe I'll make it. But that won't be me fighting. It'll be math. I just really don't want to talk about it, Lucas."

They say you can't care about something until you don't have it anymore, and that you can't appreciate a thing without understanding its opposite. Well, I'd never asked anybody anything before. How are you doing today? And how are you feeling? What's it like to be you? had never been part of my vocabulary, and yet it had never stopped my friends from telling me their problems, from inquiring for my advice. Only now, when I was asking and getting nothing in return, did I realize the value of knowing what another person was thinking, of seeing into their brain when otherwise all you had was a blank wall. As long as Chris refused to speak, he offered me as little as Nathan did, and for the very first time, I *wanted* to know—wanted to reach in and pull out the part of him that was hurting, the part I couldn't see, the part that had just been told that at twenty-one years old, he might not live to see twenty-two. I wanted to find that part and cradle it, to hold it.

And so when the tears rolled down his cheeks, I reached for him before he could reach for me, and I held him, and I stroked his hair, and I pressed my cheek to his forehead, and I wiped the water from his eyes.

Maybe I knew nothing of love—not what it was, what it meant to be in it, or what to do when you were—but maybe, just maybe, it meant finding a boy who only smiled and then holding his hand when he frowned.

WE STOPPED AT the only ice cream shop in town before I took Chris home. He complained the whole way about how he was a grown adult and this "being carted around like a child" thing was just insulting, but also that he liked the leather of Clay's car, and asked—ten times at least— if Clay was my sugar daddy. In fact, once he got going, Chris never *stopped* talking, even when mint chip stuck to his lips, even when I tried to kiss him quiet, even when my shirt hit the floor.

When the ice cream was gone, we parked behind the high school and fucked in the backseat. When it was over, I traced the finger-sized bruises I'd left on his hips. He was gloriously sweaty, and it was a phrase I had never used before—never thought to use—because I'd always associated sweat with running and sports and the putrid smell of a high school locker room. But on Chris, it was different—the sweat dripping down the side of his face only worked to highlight his jaw, and the sweat dipping into his belly button and sliding down his still-shaking thighs had me wishing for a camera, though I knew, somehow, I'd never forget it anyway.

"You know," he said as he sat up and leaned against the foggy backseat window. "I'm sort of glad our friends are getting married."

"Sort of?" I asked.

"Well, I kind of thought it was weird." His nose crinkled up, and I wanted to kiss it, but I held back the urge. "They're pretty young. I mean, you're pretty young."

"I'm nineteen."

"I'm twenty-one," Chris said.

"That's two years."

Chris yawned. He traced his thumb over the back of my hand. "A lot can happen in two years."

"Oh yeah?" I said.

He nodded. "Two years ago, I didn't know you."

I gulped, the particular implications of those words filling up all the little corners of my brain until there was very little space to spare. "But now you're too old for me."

Chris laughed. "Yup. This just isn't going to work out." He laced his fingers with mine and kissed my knuckles. "I love you, Lucas Burke. And I'm going to tell you every day until I don't have any days left."

My heart started up that pounding thing again. This was all so very, very strange; sex meant very little when you stopped caring—just insert part A into slot B—but then, most of my sexual encounters didn't end in declarations of love either, and there really was nothing simple about that.

"And what if I don't say it back?"

"Then I'll say it again." Chris shrugged. He let go of my hand and used his own to trace the side of my face; his fingers lingered against my jaw, and then he smiled. "Love isn't an agreement, you know? *I'll love you if you love me.* You just do it. And you can't help it. I'm sorry, Lucas, but you've got yourself a selfish man. Because I would be honored to be loved by you, but don't think for one second that the way you feel about me affects the way I feel about you."

It seemed a very strange way to live, if you asked me—a life with no confirmation, no satisfaction—but you couldn't have guessed it by the look on Chris's face: gleeful and light and everything I couldn't possibly be when admitting something as unnerving, as life changing as love.

"I don't understand," I admitted.

"I love you," he said again—simple, easy, like the words just rolled off his tongue, no questions asked. "Just you. Not who you are to me, not how you treat me, not the way you feel about me, or the way you look at me. Just...*you*. And who you are is unrelated to me."

It was such a nice thought, and I tried to smile then, tried to look even a fraction as sincere as Chris sounded because I owed him that at least. He strung together such pretty words—it was a talent really—but I only wished I could believe them.

So because I couldn't say anything, and because Chris couldn't go on declaring his love forever, we fucked again, and this time he *did* top, and then we got dressed, and I drove him home.

As he disappeared into Rylie and Todney's apartment, waving at me and smiling at me and, for a moment, looking like he might not die after all, I repeated the word in my head over and over and over: love, love, love, love, love, love. After a while, it stopped sounding like a word at all.

Twelve

14 DAYS BEFORE

I always thought it was unfair to say that one event can turn your life upside down, as though we'd ever been walking with our right sides up to begin with. For all I knew, I'd spent my whole life at the wrong angle, trying to get back on my feet. But in the days that followed Chris's diagnosis, my life did, at the very least, summersault through a loop-the-loop.

To start, there was suddenly a whole lot of firsts. First appointments with the special cancer doctors, the first time I spent the night in Chris's bed, and the first time a strip of Chris's hair fell out. The doctors started chemo, and Chris started to say "I love you" like he breathed, and on most days, I spent all my time in the hospital, holding Chris's hand and reading from his stolen French book while they pumped him full of poison.

Once upon a time, right when I first started college, I'd had this dream of a summer vacation where I hung out on the beach with all my new cool college friends, and we rented a boat and lived in a perpetual bubble of fun. And that summer, I did, in fact, spend most of my time in a bubble surrounded by others, but it was the bubble of a very small clinic room that smelled of disinfectant and the heavy perfume of the woman who always sat to Chris's left. My new "friends" were always coughing and crying and telling their loved ones how much they were "fighting this for them," and a cabana boy never did show up.

In short, our days went like this: Chris and I drove to the hospital in Clay's car—which he hadn't asked me to return yet and which I hadn't offered; we then got checked into the clinic, and Chris would sit in this chair while a nurse set up a needle and this tiny plastic tube they called a catheter. The needle left and the tube stayed, and for almost an hour, it pumped into Chris all these mixed-up chemo drugs from a plastic bag.

The doctors explained it to me time and time again—how the chemo was killing all the bad cancer cells, and that this was *helping*—but after the first week, when Chris stumbled out of his chair and threw up all over the front steps of the hospital, I stopped listening.

For all the good things that the chemo was *supposed* to do, it did a hell of a lot more of the bad—nausea, fatigue, bruising. I spent most days watching Chris nod off in his chair, smile at me when he wasn't wincing, and then we'd go back to his place and lay him on the couch and hope it was the last time he'd feel this way, though it never was.

"I've done this all before," he reminded me one day while his eyelids flickered open and closed and opened and closed. He no longer had the strength to keep them open for good, at least not while the chemo was up and running. I supposed he thought his words would be comforting, that I'd just assume chemo was no different than riding a bike—once you did it the first time, there was nothing to it. But if anything, it just made it worse. You shouldn't have to fight cancer, but if you did, you really should only have to do it once.

"You know, that's not half as reassuring as you think it is," I said.

Chris leaned back in his seat and rubbed circles around the spot where the catheter met his arm. "I'm not trying to reassure you. You don't need it. Everyone else needs it."

And it was true; when Todney came, Chris's whole attitude changed. And Todney came most days, fretting and sweating and overly worked up by the smallest of things. The day a nurse dared to prick Chris while putting in the needle, Todney damn near threatened to sue the entire hospital. When Todney was there, suddenly Chris was cheerful, pretending to be unconcerned by his disease and spouting numbers like facts: "you know, twenty percent is actually a lot. That's twenty in a hundred; the lottery is one in a million, and people win that all the time. I'll be fine. I feel good about twenty."

And though he would never say it out loud, we both knew what would happen if Chris ever told Todney the truth, if he didn't say he felt great whenever he saw him. Maybe I knew even better than Chris did, because I was already on the other side. I was the one who heard Chris scream in pain, and I listened to the doctors' reports, and I pulled to the curb and held the last strands of his hair back from his face while he threw up out the car window. There were no illusions there, no *I'm fine*s no matter how much or how often I wished he'd say it. If Chris didn't lie, Todney would know just how powerless he actually was.

"You've been here all day," Chris said now. He reached for the pile of magazines next to his chair and grabbed the one with Brad Pitt on the cover. He flipped it open and looked at me over the top of the glossy pages. "Take a break. Call Clay. I've got a date." He pointed at the magazine, smirked, and then disappeared behind its pages.

I knew a dismissal when I heard one, even if leaving your cancer-ridden boyfriend at the hospital alone would always feel like a bit of a dick move. I kissed him on the cheek and headed outside, nearly blinded by the sunlight I'd almost forgotten about. It was summer, and I was seeing so very little of it.

I called Clay.

TWENTY MINUTES LATER, we found a spot on top of this picnic bench where we could see just enough of the town to feel powerful, but not enough to get depressed over. Like if you could see the ice cream parlor and the theater and the school where we'd all played hide-and-seek, but not the liquor shops or the dented tree or Nathan's house, then it almost didn't hurt to look.

Clay talked for ages about the computer he was working on while he fumbled in his pockets for the cigarettes. When he finally located the stash, he lit mine first, and as I inhaled and exhaled, I stared at the intricate lines of smoke and the way they disappeared just a spot in front of my face. Everything was so fucking temporary these days.

Clay inhaled deeply, coughed, then looked me in the eye. "How are you and Chris doing? He didn't look so good the last time I visited."

"He never looks good," I said.

"But is it working? The chemo?"

I nodded. Truth was, I had no idea if the chemo was working. All I knew for sure was that the doctors kept ordering more. But it was easier to say yes than to start worrying about what no might mean. It wasn't a possibility I—or I think anyone I knew—was ready to look at.

"So how are you guys?" Clay asked. "I mean, this has got to all be pretty hard on you too, huh? What? Don't look at me like that. I'm trying."

I resisted the urge to roll my eyes and looked away instead—away from the perfectly tailored shirt and the wide eyes. I tried to spot the theater on the horizon again. "I think I'm being emotionally blackmailed," I said.

Clay's head swiveled around—from the view to my face—so fast it had to have caused whiplash. "What are you talking about?"

"I mean, right after he got diagnosed, he told me he loved me." This elicited an impressed whistle and a clap on the back. I continued. "And he hasn't stopped saying it. It's like every time I leave, every day he tells me. And it's nice but..."

"But?" Clay repeated.

"But I think he's just scared I'm going to leave him. Like if he keeps pretending we're in love, then he won't have to be alone."

"Well, *are* you going to leave him?" Clay asked.

I shook my head. "Of course not."

"Then it's not blackmail."

"But..."

"Do you love the guy?" asked Clay.

"We've only known each other two months," I said. And maybe it was the all allusive, cliché romcoms hanging above my head, or my own bitterness at having picked a potential first love who I could barely kiss without winding, but two months was still two months. You could do a lot of things in sixty days, but I doubted you could fall head over heels in love.

"So? You both could use some love. You could at least say it. I'm sure it'd make it all easier right now. What's so bad about it? I love you." Clay slung his arm over my shoulder and beamed. "Hell, I fell in love with Rylie the moment I laid eyes on her."

"I'm not going to say it unless I mean it. And how are you supposed to know something like that?" I'd heard girls in college say "I love you" to each other the very second they became friends; they said it at night and when they left for classes; hell, they said it when they went to the bathroom. And yet in movies when it was said between a couple, it was this all-consuming moment that promised forever. I was nineteen, a full-grown adult—sort of—and still I didn't understand the difference. Why was it so very easy to love a friend, and so much harder to love a lover? The name was right there in the title.

Clay shrugged. "All I'm saying is that love isn't the worst thing in the world." Before he could say another nauseating Hallmark greeting, his phone rang, and he handed me his cigarette so he could put the phone on speaker.

It was Frankie. "I'm so bored," she whined. "We've been trying on dresses for hours. But we're finishing up, and there's this great taco place across the street. Come have lunch with us. I'll text you the address."

There was a rustling in the background, and Rylie hissed from somewhere on the other line, "Do not invite—" but she was cut off before she could finish the sentence.

"Please?" Frankie said. "I haven't seen you in ages, Clay."

SO I CLIMBED into one of Clay's many cars and ended up sitting shoulder to shoulder in the parking lot across from this little hole-in-the-wall dress shop. Everything to do with weddings in our town, it seemed, was very, very small. The taqueria was just across the street, and, go figure, there was yet another liquor store to the left, but the rest of the buildings in the lot were boarded up—run out of money, no doubt, and left to rot.

Frankie called again just as Clay started reaching for another couple of cigarettes. "Come in. We're almost done. We can walk over together."

I don't know what almost done means in girl language, but when we stepped inside, Frankie was still wearing a very pretty but very strapless blue gown, which as far as I knew was not pizza-eating attire—nor anything I had ever wanted to see in all my years on this earth. Three other girls stood next to her, two of which I recognized briefly from high school—both had been in theater, I think—and the third of which was a complete stranger.

"Hi, Lucas. Hi, Clay," said the two high school girls whose names I couldn't remember, and the third stuck out her hand for us to shake. "I'm Hannah. Todney's sister."

So Todney had a sister. I said hi to the two high school girls and then shook Hannah's hand and told her she looked beautiful.

She blushed and said, "I hear you're dating Chris," as though we were in some sort of teen movie, and my dating Chris was just as important of a topic as Chris's declining health. I nodded and sat on one of the big poofy pink benches next to Clay.

"We are in the stomach of the whale of love, and it is so *pink*," said Clay.

Just then, Rylie entered the room through some back hallway, still speaking over her shoulder—to the seamstress, I suppose—about how lovely everything was and repeating, "thank you, thank you, thank you!"

When Rylie finished speaking, she crossed her arms over her chest and beamed around the room. She wore her wedding dress—a beautiful thing that flowed down her body like a white waterfall and fluffed out around the ends. Though she should have been the image of marital bliss, her expression plummeted when she noticed us, the penis-wielding party crashers.

"Frankie told us we were eating tacos," I said.

Frankie glared. "Well, *excuse* me. I didn't realize getting out of these dresses would take longer than getting in them."

Rylie shifted from foot to foot, and for a moment, I couldn't tell if she was going to cry or scream. I figured both were well-deserved, though this still wasn't *my* fault.

In the end, though, she simply huffed and said, "Did you at least bring Chris?"

"Chris who's in the hospital Chris?"

"That's the one." Rylie clicked her tongue and surveyed the chipping nail polish on her left hand.

"No," I said. "I didn't bring stuck-in-the-hospital Chris." You'd think some things were self-explanatory, but there we were.

"Well, bring him," Rylie said as though it was all so very easy and *I* was the one being slow here. But before I could so much as open my mouth to argue, she pointed to my pocket. "Your phone, Lucas. FaceTime him. I want to see his expression. He always has the best expressions. And he'll know if Todney will like it or not."

I wondered when exactly Rylie had witnessed Chris's reactions enough to say "always"—if it was in the first month when she was neck-deep in napkinware or the second when she was fretting about cake toppings. I wanted to yell, to tell her she had no right, no reason to go about talking about him like she knew him. And I would have too, had it not hit me then—one of those fast-acting realizations that make you truly grateful you never opened your mouth—that when I dropped Chris off at the end of the day and patted myself on the back for *being there for him*, Rylie and Todney made dinner, and maybe they stayed up half the night talking, and maybe they talked about me, or maybe they just talked about life, and maybe they'd been doing it long before I ever came home for the summer, long before I'd ever met Chris.

And for a moment, I could actually see it—the hopeful, shaking gleam in Rylie's eyes, the look of a girl who just wanted a happy wedding but got an extra side dish of an ex-boyfriend who couldn't give up, a handful of crazy friends, and a very sick best man for her beloved groom.

Maybe I wasn't the only one picking up the pieces.

"Right," I said all too late, as Rylie was still staring at me, confused, and the rest of the group had begun chatting amongst themselves again. I pulled my phone out and called Chris. He answered on the first ring as I knew he would because he had nothing to do during chemo but stare at the walls. To my surprise, however, he picked up laughing, and it was a moment before he said anything that sounded at all directed toward me.

"Sorry, sorry. Hi, Lucas? Sorry, I was talking to—" He laughed again and then cleared his throat. "—this lady next to me, I swear; funniest woman I have ever met. She's letting her grandkids draw her hair on. It's the best thing. You've got to see it. Uh, sorry. What's up?"

"Can I FaceTime you? Rylie wants you to see her dress."

"Oh yeah, cool! So the hemming is done? Thank God. Last time I saw it, she was still walking on the bottom of it. 'Bout time they finished. We're getting close to crunch time here."

"I don't know about hemming, but it looks good to me." I set up the FaceTime, and once Chris appeared on the screen, I held it up so he could look around the room. Everyone waved and said their hellos, and Chris wolf whistled at all the bridesmaids.

"Are you all the something blue?" he asked. "Because blue has never looked better."

The two high school girls giggled, and Frankie rolled her eyes fondly, but Hannah, Todney's sister, stuck her tongue out at the screen.

"You're such an ass," she said. "How dare you get sick when I needed you here to zip me up? You're so selfish. I bet you planned this."

Chris laughed—a louder, happier sound than I'd heard from him in days. "You caught me. This was all just to screw with you, Hannah. Now let me see the bride being a bride."

Rylie stepped into view and did a full three-sixty, stopping at well-planned angles to best show off her "assets." Chris oohed and awed at all the right moments and made comments about the stitching and the "breast patterns" and things that I couldn't have dreamed of understanding. All the girls told her how beautiful she looked, and they took pictures for her mom who was apparently sick in bed, and they gushed about it being "the wedding of the century."

"Now get changed because I'm starving," Frankie said—and in perfect timing as Clay had begun staring at the metal fixtures on the wall like he might stab himself with one at any second.

"I'm going, I'm going." Rylie blew Chris a kiss. She disappeared behind one of the curtains at the same time that all the bridesmaids went to change out of their gowns. They were gone for several minutes, and in the meantime, Chris put the woman next to him on the phone. She entertained us by showing the camera the different stick figures and rainbows that made up her hair.

Then Rylie called from the dressing room. "Can someone come unzip me? I'm getting stuck! It is not easy taking off a wedding dress by yourself."

It was just us guys left in the room, and though we all rose to help, Clay got there first; as by the time I had stood up, he was already pushing back the curtain to the dressing room. It swung closed behind him, and then there was silence.

"This isn't good," Frankie whispered as she made her way out of the dressing room, followed by the rest of the bridesmaids in quick succession. I nudged her, worried that Hannah might overhear and leak Clay's secret to her brother, but Hannah just shook her head.

Dressed now in a ratty T-shirt and shorts, she slumped down into the nearest chair and yawned. "I'm not stupid," she said. "And neither is Todney. I know. Everyone knows. He's not going to do anything about it because he trusts Rylie, but do you really think your friend's been subtle? He's got hearts in his eyes, and it's embarrassing."

He's in love. This is what love does. I shrugged and whispered an apology for Clay's sake just to be safe. Hannah shook her head at the same time that Chris laughed over the phone. "Lucas," he said. "Do you really think you can change the way other people feel?"

FIVE MINUTES LATER, Rylie and Clay's screams started up from behind the curtains—a glorious mix of curses and insults. Ten minutes later, they were silent, and by eleven minutes, Hannah was pacing around the dressing room.

"She's probably killing him," Frankie said. Dressed again in her dark black T-shirt and jeans, she finally looked like herself again—my moody sister instead of a ballroom dancer. "Poor Clay. Rylie probably socked him in the jaw and dragged his body into a ditch." She tapped black and red nails against her thigh, and when that didn't distract her, started chewing on the tips in earnest. "Someone go check on them."

Someone, as it turned out, was me. Frankie suddenly had a burst of enlightenment that deemed her incapable of breaking up a fight; for the first time in her life, my sister, who played with spiders and wouldn't watch a movie if it wasn't rated R for violence, was now scared of blood and convinced we were going to find Clay's dead body behind the curtain. Hannah raised her hands in front of her and said it wasn't her problem, which, admittedly, was true. And the girls from high school were completely no help at all; after a second's debate, they decided they both, conveniently, had other obligations and left the store. So I handed Chris to Frankie—

"Good luck! Don't get killed in a murdery bride fit!" he yelled across the line.

—then ducked behind the changing room curtain.

What I saw was far from unexpected, and if I live to be an old man, I vow to always tell it the same way: Rylie and Clay were kissing, which might have been shocking if I were someone else—someone who knew Todney more than they knew Clay, for example, or a true believer in marriage and love. But for me, a kid who had seen Rylie and Clay kiss a thousand times and who had heard Clay declare his love for Rylie a million more, I cannot say with any honest bone in my body that the kiss was surprising. Still, it glued me to the floor.

Rylie was still in her wedding dress, the picture-perfect image of wedding love—or at least, the parts I could see of her beyond Clay appeared perfect. He leaned in front of her, his hands on her cheeks, and kissed her like he was trying to draw the very life marrow out of her body straight through her mouth. And Rylie, for all the white innocence that she wore, kissed back with vigor, though tears streamed down her cheeks.

This went on for longer than I'd care to admit—the two of them kissing, and me, a dirty spy, frozen to the spot, unable to stop staring. Then Rylie pulled away and smacked Clay across the chest.

"You can't do that to me!" She sobbed. "I'm getting married. I'm getting married, and I *love* him. What do you think you're doing? You can't kiss me!"

"I love you," Clay said. He reached for her hand, but she shoved it away. "I love you," he repeated. "Rylie, I've always loved you. And I will always love you. Please don't marry him."

Rylie only cried harder, the tears pooling onto her chest. It all seemed to me like a bad soap opera, and yet I couldn't help but worry, thinking of the two little kids who had run after each other on my childhood street—now adults with no more clue what to do than they had back then. Rylie sobbed and sobbed, and when that wasn't enough, she put her hand over her mouth and screamed, muffling herself until her face turned red.

And then she saw me. Her eyes went wide and her hand fell to her side, her mouth left gaping. She sobbed harder. Clay turned around, and his expression crumpled.

"Please," Rylie said. "Please, Lucas, you can't tell anyone. Please. This didn't mean anything. Please don't tell Todney."

I shook my head; I wouldn't.

"You can't tell Chris either," Rylie said.

I looked at Clay, but he turned his attention to the floor, and his hands turned to fists at his side. "Yeah, okay. I won't tell anyone. I promise."

While Rylie hugged me, almost suffocating me in the many folds of her dress, Clay stood back, silenced: the perfect, embarrassingly destructive image of love.

Thirteen

APPARENTLY THE MOST logical thing to do after having a secret back-room affair was to go ahead and pursue lunch plans. When in trouble, eat, right? So, after threatening to gut Clay like a fish if he ran off and made them look suspicious in front of Hannah, Rylie finished up with the dresses, bagged them, and took everyone across the street to the town's only taqueria. All the while, she smiled like nothing in the world had happened.

"Oh, my zipper got stuck," she said as we walked. And, as we opened the restaurant doors and looked for a seat, "The zippers are so small on those things. I swear I couldn't breathe. I almost passed out. Luckily, Clay saved me before I fainted."

Luckily, the food came before her lies could get any worse.

You can say a lot of bad things about small-town folk, but that we don't appreciate food is not one of them. When your options consisted of one McDonald's, one Italian restaurant, and the food court at the Everything Store, you took advantage of what you could get, and we wolfed down those tacos like we'd been starving.

"I love this town," Frankie said with guacamole dripping down her cheek. Our whole group nodded vigorously. Forget money; it was food that could make people agree to anything.

Clay sat at the end of the table, as far from Rylie as possible, and didn't say a word while he ate. Despite Rylie's threats, I couldn't fathom why he was still there, why he hadn't gone running for the hills as I certainly would have if I'd been caught with my pants down—figuratively speaking, though just barely. *This is what love does to you*, I thought: a man desperately hanging around just to be close to the girl he loved, and for what? He was stuck fighting a war he couldn't win where even proximity hurt him. And while Clay's battle for love was against the affections of another man, if *I* fell in love, my other man would be the Reaper. And that wasn't a fight I could win.

Still chewing and packing another taco to go, Frankie rose from her chair and told the rest of the group goodbye. "I've got my play tonight."

"Break a leg" came from every end of the table, Rylie grinned and promised to be at the second showing the following night, and then Frankie was gone. I watched her leave, waiting until I saw my mother's car pull up outside before I turned back to the group.

"So where's the honeymoon going to be?" I asked Rylie; images of Chris dancing the tango with the black-hooded bringer of death circled my mind, and I struggled to pay attention.

Clay tensed all over again. I expected as much—Clay had all the emotional patience of a tangled telephone line these days—but what I didn't see coming was for Rylie to flinch back like I'd burned her.

"What? What's wrong?" I asked.

She shook her head. "Nothing. Nothing's wrong. We just had a lot of big plans. We were going to go to Italy, and then it was going to be Hawaii, and the Caribbean; we couldn't make up our minds. But it doesn't matter now. We can't go anywhere. Not with Chris so sick. Which is fine," she added quickly, her smile back in place.

Her crimson lipstick was faded, smeared slightly around the edges of her lips, and it took all my willpower not to check Clay for similar marks. Our friends would assume it had been smeared on her taco—no one would wonder; no one would question a thing.

"I think after the wedding we'll go back to North Carolina for a bit. Todney and Chris both want to see their parents."

I barely held back a sigh. Visiting would have been Chris's idea; I was sure of it. Todney, for all his goodwill and proper attitude, had never struck me as the type to go running back to Daddy when times got rough. But Chris, Chris who feared death, Chris who only had good stories to tell of his father, would surely want to go back, if only to plead for acceptance one last time. And for that, I would never understand him. My parents had supported me all my life, made sacrifices left and right to keep me safe, to keep me happy, and I kept running farther away. Chris faced hatred firsthand and asked for more.

"How long will you stay?" I'd have said it didn't matter to me either way, that I could handle time apart, that I was not the type to become dependent or miss someone so easily, but I was far too busy imagining Chris packing his bags.

"Maybe a few months."

"Maybe if things aren't working out, that's a sign," Clay said. "I mean, you're fighting pretty hard for this wedding, and fate doesn't seem to be getting on board."

"What's your point?" Rylie's smile remained, though barely, and by the look in her eyes, it was a hell of a lot closer to razor blades than rainbows.

But Clay never did know when to run. "It means maybe you're rushing into something."

"Clay, this really isn't the time—" Rylie began, but Clay cut her off.

"I think it's exactly the time. Maybe you have options. Other options. No, think about it. You're nineteen. And you've known Todney for what? Six months?"

"Clay, you're making a scene."

"How many months, Rylie?"

"Nine."

"Nine months." Clay laughed. He stood up and smacked his chair so hard against the table it fell backward and hit the floor instead. "You know, it seems like a lot of things people aren't prepared for happen in sets of nine months." He turned to Hannah. "I'm sorry, I really am. Your brother is a really nice guy, and it's nothing personal. But I'm sure you can understand where I'm coming from. My friend here—" He pointed to Rylie. "—is only nineteen. And her and Todney? They don't really know each other. And this wedding just seems a little crazy in the grand scheme of things."

Hannah blinked several times but said nothing.

For a man who had just told me that love came quick and not to question it, Clay sure had a lot of high opinions, and it seemed he was on a roll. "I'm just saying maybe Rylie isn't looking at the whole picture. It's a big world out there, and there's a lot of people in it. Some closer than you'd think."

"Clay, stop. That's enough!" Rylie's eyes were wet, but she did not rise from her seat. She pursed her barely crimson lips, and she glared, and she glared, and she glared until I thought surely she'd be able to shoot lasers right through Clay's very soul, but she never moved. "Get out," she hissed. "Get out."

For a moment, I thought Clay might protest; his mouth opened, his hands clenched at his sides, and then, suddenly, he nodded. Still looking quite near murderous and yet utterly defeated, he turned on his heels and left the restaurant. I stared between the swinging door and Rylie's wannabe stoic face, and then I ran after him.

I caught him halfway down the street. His cheeks were bright red, and the closer I got, the more I could see his arms shaking.

"Don't. Don't take care of me," he said as I reached for his shoulder. He tugged away from my grip, then, chest heaving, bent so his head was between his legs. "I don't need your help right now. Just stay with Rylie. I just...I just need some time, okay?"

"Clay..."

"No, really, I'm fine. I didn't... Someone had to say it, Lucas. I...I'll see you later. I'm just going to take a walk."

I'd heard a lot of things from Clayton Ortiz, Problem Starter Extraordinaire, over the years, but that he didn't need my help was rarely one of them. I *was* the help; I was the go-to guy, the always-got-your-back, tell-me-all-your-problems therapist of a friend, and it was a job I took grudgingly, but one I did well. I was not so easily fired.

"Do you want company?"

"No."

I started to argue, but at the same time, Clay started to walk. And that was it. His back turned to me, and he walked away. With his and Rylie's argument still screaming in the back of my brain and their kiss imprinted on my eyelids, I began to feel like I'd been dragged onto this roller coaster one too many times. I was too old for this, or maybe too young, but there was one thing I knew for sure: one more round and I'd lose it.

So I walked back to the taqueria, and just like that, I was off the hook; no problem to fix, no argument to settle, no disaster to calm. The problem, at least for now, had been swept under the rug, and I had not been dragged in just yet.

This day really was full of surprises.

Back in the restaurant, Rylie was entertaining Hannah with a story about Todney's proposal, but she looked up when I came in, and whatever smile had lit up her face a moment before disappeared in an instant.

"If he's sent you with a message, I really don't want to hear it right now." She stabbed her burrito with her fork and then pushed the plate away. "I'm really not so hungry anymore. Do you guys want to go to a movie or something?"

Glad for the change of topic, I shook my head. "I can't. I'm going to Frankie's play tonight." The excuse to leave really could not have come at a better time.

Apparently it wasn't the right answer, however, because Rylie burst into laughter.

Whatever the joke was, I wasn't in on it. "She does! She just told you." I said. "I promised I'd go."

"Frankie's had a school play every year for the last oh...four years?" Rylie said.

I nodded again, still not seeing her point.

"You've never gone once. Last year you said, and I quote, 'I'll get around to it if she makes it to Broadway.'" She sniggered. "You're not exactly the supportive brother type, Lucas. I've gone every year, and you've never once told me to save you a seat."

So maybe I'd missed a few plays. And maybe I'd come home drunk to find Frankie still in her costume on a few more occasions than I should have, but I was not a terrible brother, and I certainly wasn't as much of a joke as Rylie's laughter made me out to be.

"Well, I'm going tonight," I told her. "And I'm looking forward to it and everything." I retook my seat at the table and got to work on finishing my third taco.

"Yeah, okay, sure you are," Rylie said, still grinning.

Too tired to protest, and too lazy to be properly offended, I stuffed more taco crumbs into my mouth.

"You guys are a real fun bunch, aren't you?" Hannah said.

"I'm so sorry,'" Rylie said. "Again. I don't know how many times I can say it. I feel awful. Clay is...he means well. He just doesn't always know when to bite his tongue." Or, for that matter, whose mouth to keep it out of.

I licked the last bit of salsa from my lips and stood up. "That is what happens to people who fall in love. Disaster and bad choices. May fate be kinder to you." I checked the clock on the far wall; Frankie would still be in rehearsal, but it didn't leave me much time.

Rylie looked at me, stunned, while Hannah watched the table with the sort of impassivity that came only with the very uninterested, or the very confused. "I've got to go if I'm going to make it to Frankie's play on time. I've got to pick up some stuff first. I'll see you guys later."

With their dumbstruck faces staring after me, I left the restaurant. I was barely outside when my phone rang. I pulled it out just as I passed by the town florist.

"Don't forget the flowers," Chris said.

ONE HOUR AND one trip to the flower shop later, I stood outside the steps of my old high school. Admittedly, I still felt bad about my little outburst in the restaurant; Rylie hadn't technically done anything wrong except kiss Clay back, but, well, she didn't *have* to kiss back. She didn't have to ask me to lie, and she certainly didn't have to go around flaunting her "love" and marriage in front of everyone. I was still recounting everything I'd said and daydreaming of what I *should* have said, while my family gathered outside the school.

The twins ran circles around the courtyard, shooting invisible guns at each other until my mom grabbed them by their shirts and pointed them toward the theater door.

"In," she ordered, and they marched like soldiers.

My family got seats at the front of the room. ("We want her to see us from the stage and feel supported," my mother had explained. "It will give her confidence.") And while I tried to position the flowers in my lap and straighten my too-tight, never-worn button-down shirt, my mother made small talk with the Myers. They were the only family in town who had more kids than we did. The seven Myer boys, according to legend, had caused so much trouble in their combined ten years of schooling, they'd made three different teachers retire. I'm not saying that I was proud or anything, or even that I liked gossip, but it was sort of nice to think that one day they might just have a worse impact on this town than I had. Nathan's accident was going to take a whole lot of menace to beat.

The play didn't start until half an hour after we got there, and so, for thirty minutes, I entertained the twins with stories of goblins and a creature I'd made up in the fifth grade named Skelecrow—a half-skeleton, half-scarecrow hybrid mutt who only had one kidney and half a brain. The twins recoiled with every growl, every blood-curdling detail. But Sharon, who sat squished between myself and my mother, frowned with her little arms crossed over her chest.

"I don't like that story," she said. "Why do you always have to tell scary stories? I don't like scary stories. What about the skelecrow's heart? You forgot the best part!"

"I did?"

"Yes. You did." Sharon sat on her knees so she was just barely as tall as I was. "You missed the part where the mean Skelecrow meets the beautiful skeleton princess girl and they fall in love. The end." She beamed. Happy endings were surprisingly easy when you were eight.

"I don't like it," Daniel said. "I like the scary version better."

Sharon rolled her eyes. "That's because you're a boy."

"I like the story!" Anthony said. "And I'm a boy."

I ruffled his hair. "Good. Because it was a very good story." Anthony looked up at me with the sort of puppy dog eyes that could win awards, and for a moment, I couldn't quite believe he and Daniel were already twelve. It's a parent-ly thing to say, but there comes a time when you watch a kid grow up, and in your eyes, they just stop: they're forever five or eight or ten or whenever it was you stopped seeing the changes—whenever it was you stopped paying attention.

Looking at them now—at the twins, nearly teenagers; and Sharon, almost a full-blown princess—it occurred to me that all this time I'd been stuck, they'd been marching onward. And soon, I'd be left behind.

THE PLAY STARTED with the sort of flare only real theater could provide—an announcer's booming voice, a trumpet's blow, and the dramatic unveiling of the stage. It was a simple scene: one couch, one lamp, a bookshelf in the corner, and what looked like most of the school's library placed inside it. If the school was anything like I remembered, the budget set aside for the arts might as well have been zero, so the costumes were clearly handmade—scraps taken from Mom and Dad's closet—and there were no microphones, so the actors had to scream. And no one, not even the main act, was all that good. But here's the thing: when Frankie got up on stage, the play changed.

Frankie played the bitch. She was the bad guy, the girl with anger-management issues who swooped in and tried to break up the happy couple, and she was damn good. She never faltered on her lines, and when she bowed at the end of the show, she got the loudest applause. But even as I clapped, I just kept thinking they got it wrong: we spent so much time as kids being taught we should fear each other, that it's another person who destroys relationships and happiness. But no one ever thought to tell us that life itself is just as destructive. Fate swoops in, and just like that, you're gone.

LATER, MY PARENTS took us out for ice cream, and after we all crammed into a single booth in the far back, we got to talking about the future. My parents wanted to know if I'd given any thought to the idea of returning home to the community college for my next semester. Or rather, my mother wanted to know, and my father buried his face in his ice cream, far too content with his one weekly serving of allowed sugar to say a word.

"I mean," my mother said. "It does make sense. There's so much to take care of here."

And it did make sense, and there was an awful lot to take care of at home, and I'd thought a lot about it those past few months. I thought about it when I met Chris, and I thought about it when Clay almost ran away, and I thought about it *a lot* when I caught Clay and Rylie swapping spit. If anyone had to take care of this place and the people in it, it was me. And so I swirled my ice cream around the bowl and thought about it again—about living every day staring out my window at a bunch of ducks, about spending my weekends in Nathan's room, visiting Chris in North Carolina, and drinking too much. And though none of that was overwhelmingly appealing, I'd be lying if I said I hadn't thought about the good stuff too—about seeing my sisters and brothers more than once a year, about helping my mom before she caved in, about talking to my friends through more than just text and Christmas break. It had taken me over a year to see it, but living in a small town wasn't hell; it just wasn't all that much fun.

"I'll think about it," I told my mom, and for now that seemed good enough; she smiled and went back to her ice cream, and I thought I was off the hook.

Then Frankie scooted her chair closer to mine and folded her hands around her chin; her ice cream was long gone, but sitting this close, I could smell the strawberry sherbet. "Did you like the play?" she asked.

I nodded. "You're really good."

"Why'd you come?"

"I wanted to see you."

Frankie smiled. "You're different."

"Different?" I asked.

She nodded. "More like my brother."

I opened my mouth, confused and ready to ask more, but before I could, Sharon crawled into my lap with her own ice cream still sticking to her chin. She grabbed my T-shirt in her sticky little hands and looked up at me with those same unfair puppy dog eyes she could have only learned from her brothers. Manipulative bastards, the both of them.

"Don't go back to school," she said. "I like it when you're home." She reached up and pinched my cheeks; I made a face like a fish, and she did the same, giggling through the hole between her lips. "Stay home with me, and we can be fishies together. Forever."

It was a hard sell, but the offer had its merits. I'd never thought in a million years I'd be saying it—that staying here in Franklin Creek could ever even cross my radar of possibilities—but there was just something about living out the rest of my years as an innocent fish, swimming my days away, that was infinitely tempting.

Anyway, my immunity to puppy dog eyes had long since slipped away.

AFTER THE KIDS went to bed, I snuck over to Rylie's house, and Chris let me in through the back door. "She's not happy with you," he said. "She thinks you're siding with Clay." He slid one hand under my cheek and used a kiss to pull me into the house properly. I let him take me, and soon enough, I found my back pressed against the wall and his hands on my hips.

"I'm not on anyone's—" I paused to kiss him. "—side."

Chris pulled away. "No. You just told her that love was a bad idea."

The conversation seemed like a bad idea, so I cupped Chris's face in my hands and kissed him hard. He tasted like Gatorade and blueberries and something nutty that had to be, by its very definition, healthy—all part of the cancer-fighting machine, I supposed.

"Are you shutting me up?" he whispered against my lips, but there was a laugh in his voice now. His tongue fluttered across my bottom teeth, and I moaned, and then he pulled away again, and I forced myself not to chase him.

Beneath the single light of the kitchen, Chris was paler than normal—or at least he was paler than the shade of bloodless I'd come to associate with him these last few weeks. He was bald, head shaved clean, but his smile didn't miss a beat. I wanted him so desperately in that moment that it made the very act of breathing difficult. I wanted to touch him in ways that had nothing to do with sex or romance. I wanted to hold his hand and feel the pulse in his wrist. I wanted to feel the warmth of his cheek, and I wanted him to talk to me until I fell asleep to the sound of his voice. But mostly, I wanted him to know I needed him, to give him a reason to stay without actually having to need him at all. Because I knew then more than ever before that needing him would not end well for me, and it was not a risk I wanted or was willing to take.

AFTER, AS WE lay in bed for what I swore was the last time, and Chris hooked up his oxygen tank so our fucking didn't kill him, I stared up at the ceiling and silently designed my room in hell. I predicted something small, a six-foot by six-foot cell. Red drapes, if only because they were set on fire.

Chris rolled over so his chin pressed against my stomach. A little plastic tube rested under his nose. "Are you going to look this guilty every time? I'm sick. I'm not dead."

"Good people don't have sex with people who have cancer," I said.

"Great people don't prejudice who they have sex with based on disease." Chris rolled away. Even when he was mad at me, he still looked good, and I couldn't believe I actually kept coming back to that. He had cancer. He was bald. He was hooked up to a damn oxygen tank, for Heaven's sake, and still, I was staring at his bare chest. It didn't help that he was still naked, either, or that he refused to cover up with a blanket, or that when I kissed his neck, he caved and made a sound that should have been illegal.

"I hate you," he said.

"No, you don't."

"Well, I should."

"Yeah, you should."

He laughed and buried his face into my chest. All the air went rushing out of my lungs, and I stupidly hoped it was leaving to help Chris. He needed it more than I did, and maybe "steal my breath away" could actually come to some good.

"How was the play?" he asked. His Adam's apple bobbed against my skin.

"Frankie was amazing. She's going to make it to Broadway. You should have seen her. I mean, she must have practiced so hard to know all those lines. But I never saw her practicing. It was just like she was instantly good. And—" I paused, and then, "—I'm worried."

Chris looked up at me, and I took his attentive stare to mean *go ahead, bitch away, I'm listening*, so I kept talking.

"I'm worried that if I leave, I'll come back and have no idea who my brothers and sisters even are. I'm worried my mom can't handle them all. I'm worried my dad is going to die. I'm worried Rylie is going to leave Todney for Clay. And I'm worried she won't. And I'm worried you'll die, and I'm worried that when I go back to school, everything will fall apart here, and I'm worried I won't care." I said it all in one breath—one giant accident all tangled up in one, and for a moment, I couldn't look at Chris, didn't dare meet his eyes.

That is, until he met me there first. Moving up the bed, he grabbed my chin and turned my face so we were eye to eye.

"You care," he said. And that was it. No explanations, no elaborations. The man with all the words, condensing just to two. I waited for more, held my breath, and hoped he'd tell me why, tell me how, but he just smiled and kissed my cheek and whispered again, "You care."

"How do you know?"

"People who don't care don't really worry about not caring." Chris yawned, lay down again, and then took this deep breath that must have cost him a hell of a lot of strain on those cancer-filled lungs, before finally he said, "You don't have to pick, you know. You can go finish school, and you can come check on your family and your friends, and we can be together. People are always saying long distance doesn't work, but people have been doing it forever. It's not a bad thing to leave. If nobody ever left anything, we'd all still live with our parents, and no one would go anywhere. People move. It's human nature to migrate; we've been doing it forever, and we'll do it until we die out. The only difference between running away and moving forward is going somewhere with a purpose. So—" He yawned again. "—go back to school. Just make sure you're doing something while you're there. And don't forget everyone at home. Not if they matter."

I was too busy thinking about what he'd said to speak, and before long, the room fell into a silence that was broken only by Chris's ragged breathing as he fell asleep. The longer the silence stretched on, the more I got to thinking about those two ducks outside my bedroom window at the beginning of summer. When the time came, they'd fly away, migrate halfway across the country if they felt like it, if natured called. But for now, they were content just to swim together, never knowing when they'd be kicked out, or if the pool would be drained, just that for the time being—on a hot summer's day with their feathers curled together—it was enough.

Fourteen

10 Days Before

By the end of the week, Chris became unable to leave the house, and the doctors started "private" chemo, AKA a personal bag of poison to hang above his sofa. A year ago, I'd promised myself I would not spend my post–high school summers sitting around on some couch for three months, but there you have it. My ass created the sort of connection with those cushions that would have made the world's best couch potato jealous. With nothing helpful to do, I reclined back into the sofa, enjoying the way the fabric caved underneath me like a marshmallow, while the nurse positioned the IV into one of Chris's many abused veins.

Chris closed his eyes, his face pinched and in a tight-lipped expression I could only assume meant: *I am in terrible pain.* By the time the nurse finally got the IV in, he was cursing up a storm.

"It's like you're trying to kill me early," he said.

The nurse said nothing, which I thought was wise, and when she was finished, she wished Chris good health and a good day and then left to talk to Todney about the payments.

"He's going to go broke." Chris glared at his arm, at the couch, and then, with increasing fury, back at the little bag hanging above him. "And it's not even working."

"Do you have any money?" I asked.

Chris shook his head. "Lost my job at the grocery store."

He'd been a cashier. Having never finished college due to his long-time inability to walk into a classroom and his general cancer-ness, he was qualified for little else.

"They said it was because I was late and sloppy, but..." He shrugged, and I filled in the blanks easy enough. It wasn't legal, wasn't ethical, but they'd fired him because of the cancer—they knew it, he knew it, and I knew it, and still there was nothing to be done about it. Not without a court case and a hassle he had no money for, let alone the time. Life, I was quickly learning, rarely played by the rules.

I reached for Chris's hand, but he waved it away and curled into the farthest corner of the couch, silent, his gaze fixed on the opposite wall.

"Do you want to watch TV?" I asked.

No answer.

"Looks like Todney and Rylie have HBO. We could watch a movie if you want."

Nothing.

"*The Terminator* is on."

"The correct term," Chris said, his tone dripping in distain, "is terminal."

I STAYED ANOTHER hour though Schwarzenegger remained the only voice in the house. Before I left, Rylie stopped me in the front hall and gave my shoulders a short squeeze.

"I forgive you," she said, though I'd almost forgotten that she was mad at me or what it was that I'd done wrong in the first place. Then our conversation at the restaurant came floating back, and I nodded, solemn faced because I thought that would be the most appropriate response.

"I know you've had a hard time with relationships, and it's not your fault that you're cynical," she said. "I have to learn not to take it so personally."

There was an insult in there somewhere, but I was too tired and too relieved with her forgiveness to bother being offended. I didn't need another problem, another fight, and for what it was worth, it was all true. I *was* cynical. If lives were books, it would have been my subtitle.

"I'm working on it," I said. I looked back at Chris, who was lying on his side, either asleep or pretending to be, his face lit up by the glow of the television. My heart ached, and I thought: *I feel pain, so I care.*

As I said goodbye to Rylie and took Clay's car back to my house, I thought it over and over: *I care, I care, I care.*

MY PARENTS AND I returned to Rylie's house later that evening for their first official meet-the-boyfriend dinner. I'd like to say it went against tradition—that normally my mother would invite said boyfriend over and make a big elaborate dinner and we'd all talk and laugh all night in the comfort of my childhood home—but it was a tradition that had technically never seen the light of day due to the fact that Chris was my first actual long-term boyfriend, and certainly the only one since Nathan to have met my parents. Still, as we drove, my mother lamented no less than five times that she could not "cook a warm meal for the boy who stole my son's heart," and I wondered again why cooking meant so much to her when it seemed so arbitrary to me.

By the time we arrived, Rylie's parents were already in the kitchen, arguing over whose cooking was better while Rylie, Todney, and Chris sat at the kitchen table, holding in their laughter. Rylie's mother was a thin, dark-haired Mexican-American woman who wore her hair up in the same messy bun that Rylie always did. She threw her arms around me the second I walked in and peppered my cheek with kisses.

"*Mijo*, taste this." She grabbed a forkful of tamale and brought it to my lips. "Isn't that better than some plain old lasagna?"

"He hasn't even tasted the lasagna yet!" said Rylie's father. He was a rather plump, balding Italian-American man who had the vague look of handsomeness gone to waste over time, but when he smiled, his teeth were still shockingly white against his olive skin. The last name Graham, for the record, is neither Mexican nor Italian, but every time I'd asked Rylie where it came from, she'd always answered the same way: *"Don't mock the mutt. I'm America."* And that was that.

"Everyone has tried your lasagna," said Rylie's mother.

This was true. After nineteen years of backyard barbecues, Fourth of July parties, and birthday get-togethers, I could taste both Rylie's father's lasagna and her mother's tamales in my sleep. I think everyone has that one thing they can cook well—for me it was always just scrambled eggs, and for my mom green bean casserole—but Rylie's folks had perfected their specialties long ago, and they were both mouth-wateringly delicious.

My parents greeted Rylie's parents with handshakes and hugs all around, and then we took our seats at the table. I sat beside Chris who kissed me in greeting, and we held hands under the table while the Grahams served lasagna, tamales, and salad.

"This looks delicious," said my mother, and my father nodded his agreement through an already full mouth. For a while, I watched him eat, the way he damn near salivated for every bite, the way his double chin wobbled, the way he barely stopped between bites to breathe. And I watched my mother too—picking at her food, staring at my father out of the corner of her eye, her whispers of "slow down" and "you'll have another heart attack, is that what you want, to make me cry?"

But there would be no crying over food that night, not when the tamales melted in my mouth, and the lasagna was just on the right side of too saucy—that sort of rich, creamy flavor you knew couldn't be good for you, but was so good *to* you that you just didn't care. Silence fell as it always does in the company of good food and hungry mouths, and it wasn't until we started up our second helpings that my mother dared start up conversation.

"I love what you guys have done with the place." She smiled at Rylie and Todney across the table and then gestured around their still very new home. Anything that screamed "Rylie"—the love seat with the blue fabric patches, the picture frames made of recycled glass, and the lampshade made of seashells—was clearly garage sale bought, but the touches of Todney's wealth were littered all around. A stainless-steel refrigerator. A shiny new microwave. A black leather sofa.

"Todney is really the interior designer here," Rylie said and squeezed her fiancé's hand. "He has this whole picture of our home with red drapes and wood panels. It's very..." She turned to Todney, mouth twitching to keep from laughing. "What do you call it, honey?"

"Sophisticated cabin in the suburbs," Todney replied.

"And what do you do, Todney?" asked my father.

Todney set down his fork. "I'm in med school still. Studying to become a surgeon."

So the money wasn't his then. I suspected Dad, the homophobic preacher, and his wife weren't as out of the picture as Todney had made it seem; family money really did do wonders for a new marriage. Maybe it was an apology. Maybe just a bribe. Maybe it just wasn't so easy to leave your family behind. "It's a process, but I'm hoping it'll be worth it in the end. My mother is a surgeon already, so I've always known a lot about the medical field. She's been a big help when I've needed to study."

"If he hurries up, he can cut all the tumors out of my lungs." Chris grinned, but the joke was lost on the rest of the group.

My mother frowned and stared down at her food, and my father cleared his throat and said, "How are you doing, Chris?"

"I'm fine," he said. Lie number one. "Been feeling a lot better lately." Number two. "I'm just glad to be here tonight. It's really great to meet you. Lucas has told me so much about you." Number three. As far as I could remember, the most I'd said about my parents was that my mother had birthed me and my father had helped in the impregnating process.

Before I could stop myself, I blurted, "Chris was an Olympian." I don't know what came over me, why I suddenly had such an urge to impress my parents, but good old-fashioned word vomit came just in time to ruin a great meal.

My parents' faces lit up, but Chris's dropped. "Uh, yeah," he said, forcing a smile, and I wanted to slap myself for making him lie again. "I was a diver. Didn't get too much time or anything, but it was a great experience." He rubbed a hand over his bald head. "And I promise I was a hell of a looker before the chemo. So you don't have to worry about your son having bad taste or anything."

"You still look good," I said, and this time when Chris smiled, it at least looked real.

AFTER DINNER, RYLIE and her parents cleared the table, and while her father made us all bowls of ice cream with a million and one "necessary" toppings for dessert, her mother entertained us with a story about Rylie as a baby. I supposed it was more for Chris and Todney's sake than for my family's, as I could recall having heard the story a thousand times before, but it was still cute. Baby Rylie, still young and naïve and blameless, had located a Sharpie and drawn a masterpiece on her father's face that didn't come off for weeks.

"Thank God she didn't try and eat it!" said her mother.

Todney squeezed Rylie's hand, his eyes full of that same puppy dog love I'd seen the very first day we met. Fast-forward through the stress of a wedding and a dying best friend, and some things, it appeared, were still constant.

"She's always been too smart to make big mistakes," he said. Which was, admittedly, pretty funny when I'd caught her making out with another man just days ago, a man notorious for *his* mistakes, and supposedly the biggest mistake of her life. But who's paying attention to the details?

Before anyone could say anything else, Chris excused himself from the table and ran straight for the bathroom. We heard the door slam, but fortunately, the bathroom was too far away for anyone to hear anything else.

"The chemo," Todney explained. "I promise it was not your cooking, Mr. And Mrs. Graham. He can't really keep down anything these days."

Something Chris had said back at the beach all those weeks ago came sprinting into the back of my mind: *you get cancer, and suddenly you are cancer.* I wondered how many conversations about his health Chris had heard taking place behind his back; how many did he tolerate straight to his face? How often had *I* spoken to him of nothing but how he was feeling, of how he was doing? Being a statistic had to be exhausting.

"He's learning French," I said aloud. My parents, Rylie's parents, and the happy couple all looked over. My mother's expression said, clearly enough, that I was being inappropriate, that it was tactless to interrupt serious news, but it was too late to stop now, and frankly, I didn't care. "We both are. And we're getting pretty good. We can have full conversations if we only use short sentences."

"That's great, dear," my mother said, and I knew she was lying, but it didn't matter because it *was* great. Because when you got a cold, no one talked about if you'd bought tissues, how your cold medicine was working, or when you thought you'd be better. You kept talking about your soccer tournament next weekend and what you were having for dinner, because your sickness was just a part of your day and not an identity. Just another of many temporary character traits. And so maybe Chris's cancer was like that too. And maybe drinking too much was just one of Clay's unfortunate but temporary qualities, and a mistaken kiss was Rylie's, and Nathan was still asleep, and that *sucked*, but it was just a subplot of their lives and not the whole story. And maybe, just maybe, I was more than the kid whose sort-of-almost-ex-boyfriend was in a coma, who should have told him not to drive that night, who left a scar on this town that wouldn't be wiped out for years. Maybe I was just as capable of starting over as Chris was of being healed and Nathan was of waking up one day. Maybe my story wasn't over, and I was going to learn French, and I was going to go to Paris with Chris, and maybe happy was still possible.

WHEN THE LAST bowl emptied, the parents migrated to the living room to drink coffee and talk while us adult-kids watched a movie in Rylie and Todney's room. The husband-and-wife-to-be took the bed, and Chris and I made ourselves comfortable on the couch, once again solidifying my future potato lifestyle. The movie was your pretty basic romcom. Boy meets girl. Boy lies to girl. Girl breaks up with boy. Boy talks to friends. Girl talks to friends. Boy makes it up to girl. The plot was neither unique nor unexpected, but it was still vaguely enjoyable if only because the actors seemed to genuinely believe their lines.

"Do you guys do this often?" I asked around the time the boy started planning his comeback technique. Spoiler alert: it involved flowers, a declaration of love, and a passionate promise not to lie again. "Hang out in your guys' bedroom and watch bad movies?"

"Yes," Rylie said. "And shut up. This one is Todney's favorite."

Todney neither confirmed nor denied this fact, but leaned into Rylie's shoulder to continue watching.

I leaned back too, and then Chris ran his socked foot up my leg. "You ever think about how fundamentally strange footsie is? I mean, you're really just kicking someone and hoping that it's sexy when it generally never is."

"Where do you come up with this stuff?" I asked, trying not to laugh.

"You have a lot of time to think when you're dying," he replied.

"You're not dying." The doctors had never confirmed it. He was sick, but lots of people got sick without dying.

"Oh, but I am, Lucas. Oh, but I am." He rested his head in the crook of my neck and laced our hands together. His fingers were cold; compared to the natural warmth of my own, they felt like icicles melting into my skin. I forced myself not to flinch, but instead wrapped my arms around his body and pulled him closer. After a few minutes where he shivered against me and refused to watch the movie, I pulled his hand above our heads and splayed his fingers and my own until I could see through the spaces in between.

"Look," I said, nudging his face toward the ceiling. "Look at all the possibilities."

He gave a shaky, halfhearted sort of laugh. I pretended not to see the tears in his eyes, and I was sure he pretended not to see the ridiculousness of my under-thought plan because he actually squinted and looked through our fingers, though we both knew there was nothing to find.

"I see a dark ceiling," he said. "Is this a symbol of our blackened souls?"

"Yeah," I said. "Surprise. We're going to hell."

"I didn't even pack. You should have warned a guy. All I have are sweatpants, and obviously I'm going to need some shorts for this. You think there's a dress code? I mean, I'm going to want to wear some tank tops due to the eternal fire and all, but if hell is anything like the high school I went to, there's going to be a no tank top rule."

"Nah, we're going VIP. No dress code, no rules."

Chris laughed. "What do you think you have to do to be a VIP in hell? I don't really want to board with Hitler."

"Well, you don't have to worry about that for a while because you're staying here on Earth. With me." I kissed the top of his head, but rather than look at all comforted, he stiffened and looked away. While Chris always knew exactly what to say to me—what I needed to hear—I never could find the right words for him, and it seemed every time I tried, I just made things worse. Because while Chris understood the value of life—perhaps more than most—I would never understand what it was like to die. At least not until I was doing it myself.

I rubbed circles over his back as I had no idea what else to do, and I doubted I could do any more damage. "Don't you dare give up," I whispered, already hating the cliché hang-in-there-cat posters sound of my voice. "You did this once. You can do it again." Miracles happened. Sometimes the boy who lied won the girl over in the end. And sometimes the boy with cancer lived to beat it one more time.

On the TV screen, the couple kissed—a slow build, eyes meeting, lips trembling, hands reaching up to pull each other closer—and though the movie had only lasted an hour and a half, they promised their everlasting love into each other's mouths. The time between meet and love was notoriously short in romcoms, but I was starting to understand.

When you met the right person, you didn't learn to fall in love. You just fell.

MY PARENTS TOOK me home around the time the movie ended, and once we arrived back in our much smaller house, I sat them down at the kitchen table. It was the only place in our home where three people could all see eye to eye, and what with food and dining being the world's great equalizer and all, I thought it fitting. I clenched my fists to steady my nerves and forced myself to look them both in the eye one by one.

"I'm going back to school in the fall. In the city," I said.

My parents, who had already begun talking amongst themselves about how great the dinner was and how charming Chris was and how tragic and beautiful life was, went suddenly quiet.

Then my father nodded and said, "We thought so."

"You were so happy in the city," said my mother. "There was never really a doubt in our minds that you'd want to go back. We hoped..." She trailed off, looked at my father, around the house, and then finally back at me. Frankie must have already put the kids to bed, because our home was, for once, silent. "We want you to be happy, Lucas. But we miss you. And your brothers and sisters miss you."

"I know. That's why I'm going to go to school, but I'm going to visit at least once a month and spend the holidays here. There's a bus close to campus that can bring me right home. And it's not that expensive." I pulled up the information on my phone and passed it across the table. It was an overtold tale, the teenager venturing out to see the world with nothing but a bus ticket in his pocket and one question on his mind: how am I going to get back home? The road was a wasteland of endless metaphors and existential crises, but luckily the twenty-first century was well equipped with ways out. I'd just simply failed to look until now.

My parents studied the bus information for several minutes before passing my phone back to me. I pocketed it and ignored the soft vibration that meant an incoming call.

"So?" I asked.

My mother sighed, and my father nodded.

"You know the deal," my father said.

I did. "I pay half of what the loans won't cover."

"And?"

"And no drinking. And no drugs. And make responsible friends unlike I did at home," I repeated the old mantra for the thousandth time, but my mom shook her head.

"Your friends here aren't *so* bad." As much as my mother blamed my friendships for the mess with Nathan and how very drunk I'd been that night, I also knew she felt almost as obliged to like them as I did. She certainly had always adored Rylie and had always taken care of Clay. Maybe it was because her motherly instincts knew no bounds, but maybe it also meant we weren't all as evil as we'd made ourselves believe.

After wishing both my parents a good night, I walked to my room and listened to my latest voicemail from Chris: "Your parents were great. Now I know where you get that hidden charm. Do you think they'll come to my funeral? I don't need a big crowd or anything, but I want someone's parents to be there. Haven't asked mine yet. All right, I'll talk to you later. Good night."

I lay upside down on my bed, feet propped up on the pillows and head dangling over the edge. I held the phone in the air, staring at the Call Back button as though this would make an adequate answer appear on my tongue. When nothing happened except for mass amounts of blood rushing to my brain, I gave up and tossed my phone across the room. Maybe it was all the endless talking about death, or the constant reminders that there was no happy ending in my future, but I'd had enough. I didn't want to talk about Chris's funeral, and I certainly didn't want to watch him withering away every day, and the more I thought about it—about black suits and roses and a funeral march—the more this one vein in my forehead started to pound, and the more I felt like screaming.

It's human nature, I think, to fall in love with the living. Maybe it's biology, centuries-old mating cycles that attract us to healthy working lungs and colored cheeks because we think: this one's good, this one will pass on the good genes. I'm no biologist, and I'm sure I don't contain one philosophizing bone in my body, but I do know this: I was attracted to Chris because he talked fast. Because despite imperfections in his legs, he walked with determination. Because he spoke of life as though it didn't end. I had been attracted to Chris for everything he no longer was, and I had fallen for him when he became nothing. And for that, I hated myself. I hated my attachment. I hated feeling. I hated cancer. But above all, I hated the unfairness and unpredictability of human life, that you could win every battle just to lose the war in the end. This was what it meant to love.

I knocked the lamp off my desk, growled at nothing, and then reached out for my phone, which was still lit up and waiting on the floor. I meant to text Chris back but somehow ended up calling Clay instead. So I waited, my face still overheated and my heart beating too fast, through the personal dial tone music he had installed. When finally Clay answered, his voice was low and slurred, which might have been disconcerting had it not been so very familiar.

"I didn't do anything this time," he said. "I swear."

"I know," I said. "I did."

Clay groaned. "Did you kill someone? Because I'm way too drunk to help you bury the body."

"Really? That's your biggest concern?" Barely holding on as is, I didn't have the patience to wait for an answer, so I pressed on. "I didn't kill anyone. But that's the problem."

"You want to kill someone?"

"No. Death. Death is the problem."

Clay sighed heavily. There was a sound on the other end of the line, like he was putting something away or stacking bottles or juggling, and then he cleared his throat. When he spoke again, his voice was focused and far clearer.

"Is this about Nathan or Chris?"

"Both," I said. Because Chris was fresh and Nathan was a stale, throbbing wound, but both had left their mark. Both lives were on the line. Both were doubtful to make it through the year. And both had wanted so much more from me than I could ever give.

"Well, go ahead," Clay said.

Three little words to break the dam straight open. "There's no point," I said, and that was it, as far as I could manage without yelling. Next thing I knew, I was pacing the room, and I was screaming every word, not caring who in the house could hear me. Nothing mattered but the shaking sound of my own voice. "What's the point in falling in love if everyone I fall in love with dies? Where's the movie that tells you about that, huh? Where are the breakups? And the exes showing up to bring back old feelings? And the—and the cheating? Do you know what I'd give to have a real old-fashioned breakup because things just aren't working out? There are thousands of movies that tell you how to deal with a breakup, but where's the guide of what to do when everyone you date dies? I'd be better off alone, and I told you that! I told you all that, and no one believed me. You acted like I was crazy. Like I was selfish. But this? This is selfish, Clay! He's going to die, and it's going to be my fault. *He's going to die!*"

I grabbed a picture frame off my desk—a photo of Chris and I that Rylie had taken and framed because she knew neither of us ever would— and I threw it at the wall. The glass broke. For a moment, I remembered Clay and the Night of The Shattered Dishware, and I understood him more in that moment than I ever had before. Clay hated life because he was not loved, and I because I was, and though they should have been very different problems, I thought that perhaps they were exactly the same. *Love* was the problem; we couldn't live with it, and we couldn't live without it.

"It's not fair," I said, and I hated my own voice. I hated my own pleading. I hated that I could do nothing. *This is why parents always tell you life's not fair*, I thought. So when something happens they can't explain, they still have a reason for it. Now whenever we complain, we just sound pathetic. Life isn't fair, and so you soldier on while the "why" beats relentlessly at the back of your brain for all of eternity.

"I know," Clay said. "I know. It sucks. I know. I'm sorry, Lucas. Maybe he'll make it, you know? Maybe Nathan will wake up." Clay didn't believe a word—couldn't have—but that goes to say: when you asked to be comforted, you hear what you want to.

"Are you still leaving?" I asked.

"Of course not."

"Of course not?"

"My mom doesn't need me. She doesn't even know me. But you do. For the first time ever, Lucas Burke needs me, and I'm going to be here."

I chuckled. Sighing once more, I ran a tired hand over my face and looked around at the broken remnants of my room. There was a *shh* on the other side of the door, and I could only imagine how many of my siblings were standing there, ears pressed to the wood to hear the scandal of their big bro's massive meltdown.

"Maybe he won't die," I said. "Lots of people beat cancer."

"And wake up from comas," Clay said.

"And beat addiction."

"And win back the girl of their dreams."

"Look at us being hopeful," I said.

"Honestly?" Clay let out a long, wavering deep breath. "What else do we have?"

Fifteen

9 DAYS BEFORE

The following evening, I drove Clay's car back to his house. He was waiting outside and jumped up when I pulled into the driveway. As far as visually detected sanity goes, Clay looked good—no sunken eyes, no shaking hands—but his smile was tight when he took the keys. I leaned in close and smelled his breath.

"Mints?" I asked when I failed to pick up even the slightest whiff of alcohol.

Clay rolled his eyes. "I'm sober."

"Really strong mints?"

"Really sober." Clay hopped into the front seat and leaned back against the headrest. He sucked in a deep breath and then let it out all at once as he stared out over the dashboard. The sun was just beginning to set. Pink and orange streaks crisscrossed over the skyline, bathing the endless rows of houses in the distance with their glowing light.

Clay smiled and patted the passenger seat. "Let's chase the sun."

I climbed into the car, ready for another Clay-Sponsored Adventure, but it never came. We did not chase the sun. We embarked on no great adventure. We put on our seat belts, and we drove at a reasonable and law-abiding pace, silent, until we reached Rylie's house and I hopped into the back seat. She, Todney, and Chris clambered inside, Chris up front where he and his medical equipment could fit, and the rest of us squished in the back.

As she took her seat beside me, Rylie glanced at the back of Clay's head. He glared pointedly at the rearview mirror, and for a moment, a tense, rage-filled wave seemed to radiate through every inch of the car—thick and uncomfortable, like being outside on a humid day.

"I'm only doing this for Chris," Rylie whispered in my ear. "Do not make me talk to him. I swear, Lucas, I am not in the mood."

I nodded but didn't feel much like answering.

Chris heaved his oxygen tank through the door and placed it by his feet, and while we drove on, he took deep, wavering breaths and continuously adjusted his nosepiece. He was entirely bald now, no eyebrows, barely any lashes, and his lips were chapped. When he turned around, he blinded me with a smile, and I waved back.

Ten minutes later, we pulled up to the front steps of Clay's old community college. Summer classes were over for the day, and the building was closed—simple wooden doors locked tight within a tall brick building. Despite being rather small and very unwelcoming, the architecture was undoubtedly impressive. All tall pillars and steel fixtures and an impressive aura of knowledge all around, it reminded me more of a British castle than an American public school.

Rather than royalty, we found a tree in the back of the courtyard covered from top branch to root in used pieces of gum.

"It was like an initiation," Clay explained, crossing his arms over his chest and looking fondly at the abused little tree. "First and last day, you put a piece on. It's how you left your mark. You know, I never put my leaving piece on. Anyone got gum?"

Rylie reached into her purse, but Chris moved her hand away before she could retrieve a single piece. She looked at him questioningly, but Chris just shook his head and nodded at Clay.

Clay sighed wistfully and circled the tree again before speaking. "It really is a nice place. The first class I went to I had this professor with a beard down to his shoes. I swear. And we were all expecting him to be one of those future-hating, conservative old guys. Turns out he's this health-nut vegan who can't get off his iPhone for two minutes to actually teach the class. But finally he started talking and..." Clay shook his head, his lips pressed firmly together. "Smartest guy I've ever met. Genius. Guess he died a few weeks ago."

Todney's eyes narrowed, and he immediately opened his mouth, but Chris nudged him to be quiet. I was secretly thankful; an angry, ranting Todney didn't exactly spell out a good time, and I was scared for what he might say. But mostly I was scared for what he wouldn't. Talking circles around this mess Chris was in never did make it less painful.

"We can talk about death in front of me," Chris assured us. "It's okay. The words aren't going to send me straight into a coffin." He knocked one fist against his head. "Still going strong. So where's this secret passageway, huh?"

"Right." Clay blinked, finally breaking his staring contest with the tree, and then led us across the quad. We stopped at a chain-link fence behind the science building. "This is it. Right over the top is the pool."

"And you're sure it has water in it?" Rylie asked.

Clay nodded. "I'm sure."

"My neighbor has a pool," I offered. "We could always just climb the fence in my backyard."

"Not as much fun," Chris said. "Your neighbors will chase us out with a broom if we get caught there. If we get caught here, the owners will call the police."

"And why is police activity the objective here?" Todney asked.

"'Cause." Chris dumped his oxygen tank into his best friend's arms. He pushed one foot into the space between two links, then the other, and he began to climb, forcing Todney to hurry up after him, the oxygen tank held atop one shoulder. Clay followed behind.

Rylie scratched the back of her neck, and we both collectively winced at the crash of Chris's oxygen tank hitting the ground on the other side. I could only pray that everything he wore to save his life—the tubes and the medicines and the needles—had fared better.

"We are one hot mess," said Rylie, and then she climbed up too.

I laughed and followed.

The public pool was still closed—its grand opening the next weekend—but as that was the same day as the wedding, and no one knew how long Chris had left to be swimming, waiting wasn't really an option. The pool had already been filled, the floors shined, and posters were stapled along every wall, advertising all the new features of the remodel and hoping for private parties. Clay tore one down, made a paper plane, and chucked it across the length of the pool. It fell two feet short of the edge and sunk.

I'd never been the grossly poetic type, the kind to focus on a single second and force it to define my life, but in that moment, as the corners of the paper soaked through and the little plane went down, I could see nothing else. There was just the plane and me and this sinking sense of dread while my stomach followed the paper's descent all the way to the pool's bottom. I thought I could *hear* the crash of it, though it was impossible. I thought I could see its passengers writhing, though there were none. *Mayday, mayday, we're going down.* I sat down by the pool's edge, removed my shoes and socks, and put my feet in the water just above the plane's ruins. The sunset turned the blue water pink.

Chris dragged his oxygen tank across the yard and sat down by my side. "The sunsets are prettier in North Carolina."

"You want to go back?" I asked.

He shook his head. "No. That's it. The sunsets are prettier. The rest sort of sucked."

I laughed. Clay sat on my other side, while Todney and Rylie picked a place across from us, playing footsie. Rylie put her head on Todney's shoulder, and together, they watched the sunset.

"Romantic, aren't they?" Chris said. For a moment, he almost sounded genuine, but when I turned to look, the skin around his eyes crinkled, and he grinned. "Oh, come on, you cynic. It's sort of cute. Even with their binding contract and all."

I remembered that first day at the beach and his adamant speech about human decency.

Is that a promise?

You bet your ass it's a promise.

"Yeah," I conceded. "They're cute."

Rylie giggled at something Todney said, and Todney beamed, and Chris's shit-eating grin intensified.

"Love *really* is a beautiful thing," I mumbled before he could say a word. Chris snorted.

"Cynic, cynic, cynic," he said in singsong.

On my other side, Clay dropped his head into his hands. "I can't do this, Lucas."

I contemplated the options; whatever he couldn't do was almost definitely one of three things: being sober, watching Rylie happy with her fiancé, or perhaps developing a conscience that didn't approve of sneaking into closed public pools.

Luckily, Clay saved me the pressure of guessing by immediately groaning and whispering into my ear, "Do they have to look so damn happy about it? I could really use a drink right now. Do you think the liquor store is still—"

"No," I said.

"No?" he repeated.

"No."

Clay pursed his lips, but he nodded and looked back out over the pool without saying another word. His hands shook in his lap, and he paled. Between him and Chris, I, the San Franciscan from the cold gray north, almost looked tanned.

"You think you'll ever go back to school?" Chris asked Clay.

"He should," Rylie said. She looked up from her place on Todney's neck and the dark hickey she'd left behind to send a surprisingly genuine smile in Clay's direction. "You were always too smart to drop out."

"I might," Clay said.

Rylie's grin intensified. "See? Clay might stop being stupid. Wedding bells are in the air. Life is starting to work out."

"Congratulations," Chris said.

It was like someone had thrown ice into the pool, and even the lingering sunset—warm on our backs—couldn't stop everyone from freezing.

All smiles fell, and Rylie cleared her throat. "I'm sorry, I didn't mean—"

Chris cut her off with a snort and a wave of his hand. "Will you guys stop freaking out? I mean it, congratulations. Life goes on, even after the thrill of living is gone."

"John Mellencamp?" I asked.

"Always preferred John Cougar," Chris said.

When still no one smiled, Chris adjusted his oxygen tank with all the dignity a twenty-one-year-old using an oxygen tank could muster and said, "I can still make a miraculous recovery. I could be in the summer Olympics next year."

"There aren't summer Olympics next year," I said.

"Wow. You can't even give a dying man his fake hopes?" Chris shook his head. "Why don't you just yank out the tubes and let me die." He pulled out the nosepiece that supplied him with oxygen and took a few fake gasping breaths. Still, no one laughed. He sighed and pushed it back in. "That was a joke. You're all a bunch of killjoys, honestly. So if we can't joke about death, can we at least joke about the American education system? Clayton—" He cleared his throat and tried to sound dignified. "What is your decision? School or no school?" He smacked his lips together and then struck up the *Jeopardy* theme song.

Clay wrung his hands together. "I guess so. I'm going to move out, I think. Get a job and pay my way through college. Then I'll start my own business."

"Ambitious," Chris said. "I like it." He looked to the rest of us, his eyes alight with the sort of excitement that only came from the very inspired or the very mad; I never did know where to place him. Maybe the geniuses of this world are always a little mad. "Let's hear it then. Craziest childhood dream. You all know mine. Come on, it's only fair."

"I'll set the scene," Rylie offered. She opened her purse and pulled out a pack of cookies, which she passed around while she spoke. "Since we can't drink tonight—" She shot Clay a look that quickly dissolved into a smile. "—sugar is almost as good." She took a bite, chewed, and said with her mouth still full, "My lifetime dream was to win Cupcake Wars. These?" She held up her cookie. "Store bought."

Everyone laughed except for Todney, who, honestly, I'm not even sure knew *how* to laugh. He did grin, though, which for him probably added up to the same thing.

"I can beat that," he said. "I wanted to be the first Black president."

Chris shook his head solemnly. "Damn you, Obama." He shook his fist toward the heavens. "Stealing a young boy's dream like that."

Todney rolled his eyes. "Okay, so I actually wanted to be a king. And until I was ten, I didn't read anything that wasn't medieval. I was going to be a knight and then work my way up to the kingship position." He grinned. "Then came the dark time in my life when I learned that America did not, in fact, have kings. So I switched over to the presidency gig. Thought I could live with an oval office instead of a throne."

"I'm sure you would have been a great president," Rylie said. She kissed Todney's cheek. "What changed your mind, baby?"

"I joined the debate team in high school and learned I could not argue for my life. They'd have eaten me alive. I was terrible."

"He said 'um' like five hundred times in one debate," Chris said.

"You know what? Why don't you just tell my stories for me?" Todney said.

"Hey, don't get snappy. I only have so much time left to use my words. I'm not wasting any time."

"So *now* you're playing the dying card?" I asked.

Chris smiled with his tongue between his teeth. Even without hair, even with sunken eyes and not a drop of color in his face, it was one hell of a sight. "Why not? It's the only card I got left." Before the depressing statement could do more than wipe the smiles off our faces, he elbowed me in the ribs and demanded another story.

I complied. "I wanted to play in the MLB. I was going to beat Barry Bonds's record." I mimed hitting a baseball with my invisible bat. "But, you know, legally. No steroids."

"And show off your baseball butt?" Chris asked.

I laughed. "Well, that was the secret agenda."

"I have another one," Rylie said. She leaned into Todney, their fingers still tangled together—this knot of different-sized, different-colored digits that somehow still seemed to blend into one. "In ninth grade, we had to take human sexuality, remember? And I had Mrs. Peterson. One day she brought in this plate of cookies. She asked who wanted one, and we all raised our hands." She plucked a cookie out of the box and took a large bite. "Then she dropped them on the ground and rubbed them around in the dust on the floor." Rylie dropped the cookie into the water to demonstrate and then pulled out it, soggy and dripping, and held it up for all of us to see. "Asked who wanted to eat it. All the hands went down. Then she says 'these cookies represent a woman who has too much sex. No one wants to sleep with a woman who has been used up. Which is why you should save your virginity until you're married.'

"So I'm thinking this is bullshit, and I stand up and I grab a cookie off the tray, and it's gross, covered in dirt and dust because you know they don't clean the floors in that school, and I eat it all in one bite." Rylie ran her tongue over the sopping wet cookie and then popped the whole thing into her mouth. "I decided that day that I wanted to sleep with *everyone*," she said as she ate, crumbs dripping down the corners of her mouth. Todney's eyes went wide, but Rylie didn't seem to notice. "I was not going to give in to this complete fucking bullshit that a woman is defined by the number of male hands that have touched her while a man is praised for the number of female hands that have touched him. So I decided I was going to sleep around, maybe make it a profession, and I was going to get real rich, and have a lot of fun, and then I'd come back to that teacher and show her just how well I've done for myself sleeping around *just like a man*."

Rylie reached for another cookie. "And then I fell into two long-term relationships back to back, and my sleeping around days ended before they began." Todney reached out and squeezed her hand, but she immediately swatted it away. "That's not a compliment." She pointed her cookie at him. "That doesn't make me or our relationship more special or something. Whether I slept with two guys or thirty-two, it doesn't matter, right? *Right*?" She raised an eyebrow so dangerously high that I didn't blame Todney for wincing.

"Right...dear," he said. Rylie smiled and kissed him. I carefully avoided the urge to look at Clay.

After that, the conversation dwindled, and I sort of leaned into Chris while I kicked my feet through the water. He was cold to the touch, but luckily it was so hot outside that I didn't care; he felt like my own personal icepack, and I thought I could live with that forever if he could just live through the week.

"Do you have a will?" I asked.

Chris frowned and shook his head. "No, I don't have enough stuff to give away. You can have everything if you want. I have a couple notebooks. Some T-shirts. Oh! I have a watch. You can have my watch."

"That's morbid," Clay said.

"No," Chris said. "It's practical. You've got to talk about this stuff before you die, or none of it gets done. Though that'd be kind of cool. If everyone got like ten minutes or something to be a ghost and let everyone know their last wishes. In case you didn't know you were going to die."

"It'd be helpful," I agreed.

"Will you read a really cheesy poem at my funeral? I want it to be extremely mushy. Something that will make everyone cry."

I nodded.

"Good," Chris said.

"It'd be more fun to read a scary story or something, though," I said. "About ghosts and rotting corpses. Especially if it's an open casket."

Chris laughed until his eyes watered. He wiped them on the back of his hand. "Fuck, I love you," he said, still wheezing.

I smiled. Apparently it wasn't what Chris wanted, though—which I knew on some level but had hoped to ignore—because his smile dropped, and he looked away with the sort of ferocity that you only see in bad soap operas. Yet again, I'd failed to say it back. Yet again, I'd let him down. And as much as I wanted to remedy that—and I did, really— the words wouldn't form in my mouth. They were three too many, and I was a coward.

"Well, we came here to swim, didn't we?" Chris said, and just like that, he disconnected his oxygen tank, took off his shirt, and jumped into the pool.

Todney blinked, his expression caught somewhere between surprise and worry. "I knew he wanted to come here, but he hasn't been in water in three years. I didn't think he'd really do it."

Chris surfaced in the middle of the pool. His head popped along the surface, his arms splashing wildly to keep him afloat. Chris always looked good as far as I was concerned, but there's something to be said for a man in his element, and in the water, Chris looked at home. He belonged with water droplets tumbling down his nose and pooling above his lip. He belonged in a world of crashing arms and flailing legs, and a smile that seemed to stretch right off his face. He was a creature of the water.

"Come on, you chickens." He splashed Todney across his expensive leather shoes.

I held my breath, ready for the fallout, but Todney didn't so much as frown this time. He didn't even blink. He kicked off his shoes and jumped into the pool, his nice jacket and pants still on, now dripping, clinging to his body. As he surfaced, he howled like a caged animal freed for the first time.

"That feels good," he said.

Chris grinned. "It does, right?" He raised his fist, and Todney tapped it with his, which I hadn't seen anyone do since the seventh grade. It struck me then, fully, that Chris and Todney were real friends, and not the known-each-other-since-high-school kind, but the through-thick-and-thin kind, the kind Clay wanted and needed me to be.

While Rylie sat on the edge of the pool, her feet kicking, laughing at the boys in the water, Clay stayed isolated. He sat with his knees pulled up to his chest, scanning the yard, but didn't talk.

I tugged my attention away from Chris and elbowed Clay in the ribs. "You want to get in?"

He shook his head. "Not today."

EVENTUALLY I GOT in the pool too, and it didn't take long for the rest of the group to follow. An hour after the sun went down, we dried off with our own clothes and sat under the streetlights outside the compound to dry. Chris hadn't said a word to me since his unacknowledged "I love you" and was now sitting with Rylie, listening to her rants about sexist media. While I was certainly not pining, thinking "woe is me" as I tried to catch his eye or anything, I'll admit that I was concerned. I'd seen Chris bitter, seen him cursing the unfair existence of our vastly cruel universe, but I'd yet to see him angry.

I scooted my ass across the pavement until our shoulders were touching and waited for Rylie to finish her speech. She was discussing what she called "the policing of a woman's body" and how it was unfair for men to take off their shirts whenever they wanted, but that it was a crime for a woman to do so, and how, yes, not every body was perfect, but she'd seen enough hairy chests to last her a lifetime, so wasn't it men's turn to be made uncomfortable by imperfect breasts? No matter how fast she spoke—which was very—Chris nodded at all the right parts, mumbled *uh-huhs* and *that's-so-trues* and never once broke eye contact.

Then she caught my eye and slowly brought her point to a close. "I have to ask Todney about something. Be back." She kissed Chris's cheek and then went to sit in her fiancé's lap.

"Are you mad at me?" I asked.

Chris shook his head. "Nope."

"Okay." I didn't want any trouble. But Chris had taught me to open my mouth, and the seal I'd had on my words was broken now. They spilled. They spilled everywhere. "You said you didn't care if I ever said it back. You said you wouldn't pressure me, that it didn't matter. I'm not ready, and you said—"

"I know what I said!" Chris yelled. Our friends looked over and then quickly away again. Our years of drama weren't exactly the best of times, but they sure taught us when to feign ignorance. Chris lowered his voice. "I told you I'm not mad. So just drop it."

"But you're not happy."

"No. I'm not. You try unrequited love. It's not the best feeling in the world."

"I didn't say—"

"Yeah. You didn't say. That's the problem." Chris fiddled with the tube of his oxygen tank. His breaths came in thick, uneven gulps, and I thought that if this were a video game, each and every one would be costing him life points, draining his stamina bar until it was game over. I'd played a lot of video games in my time, but I had never played a game without a restart button before.

"I'm sorry." I reached out to touch his leg—the one with the fake knee—but I couldn't feel the metal through his cold skin. "You said you didn't care."

"Well, I lied. Just admit it. You can't love a dying man."

I had no problems admitting hard truths, and in fact, I often thought it was the very thing that made Chris like me to begin with. But I did have a problem with lying to a dying man, and an even bigger problem with being misunderstood. I wanted to tell him this—that it was not his illness that made the words so difficult, that I was not biased in favor of the healthy, but in favor of self-inflicted apathy—but I couldn't.

"You don't actually love me," I said instead. "You're just saying it because you think you're dying, and dying people say a lot of things they don't mean."

I think Chris tried to laugh; he choked, at least, and his brow line, still noticeably lacking brows, rose upward. "Did you seriously just say that?"

"It's true."

"It's not true!" Chris said. "Is it really that hard for you to believe someone can love you, Lucas? Because I do. And I'm sorry. I am. I'm sorry that freaks you out, and I'm sorry you don't think you're capable of love, but I love you anyway, you fucking bastard." He grabbed his oxygen tank and, using my arm as support, heaved himself to his feet, the tank tucked haphazardly under one arm. He straightened it and looked to Clay, our driver. "Can we go? Please."

Clay nodded, but slowly, and looked between Rylie and me with wide, desperate eyes.

"I'll walk home with Lucas," she said. "Go ahead."

I stood up. "Do you have to do this? We don't have to...it doesn't have to..."

"To what?" Chris asked. "Be complicated? Guess what, Lucas. Life is complicated. And love is *really* complicated. And you don't have to love me. I meant what I said. Love is not a commitment; it's a feeling. But I am a person, and I do not exist to make you feel better. I am not your book of wisdom. I can't fix everything for you. So stop looking at the dying to save your life, and do it yourself."

Clay pulled the car up to the pavement, and Todney, Chris, and the oxygen tank climbed inside. As they drove away, my heart thudded against the inside of my chest, tapping out a message in a code I did not understand.

Sixteen

8 Days Before

Twenty-four hours since I'd talked to Chris, I sat alone in Nathan's hospital room, waiting for my friends to arrive. Nathan looked the same as he always did, as he always would. He was still. His eyes were closed. His heart monitor beat a steady pattern, like a drummer playing in perfect sync.

"I don't know what to do," I said aloud, though I was sure no one—especially not Nathan—could hear me, and I was wishing that wasn't so familiar. I'd been saying the same thing for years; I didn't need the silence of a forever sleeping boy to remind me that summer was coming to a close, and I was still as lost and bitter as I'd been the day I first arrived back in this forsaken town.

Chris was supposed to change things, but people don't change other people. I was the master of my own destiny—at least that's what I'd been told by my kindergarten teacher, and when are they ever wrong? Unfortunately, destiny was widespread, and it contained about a thousand different paths. The master had a harder job than anyone had ever let on.

"Did I love you?" I asked Nathan.

He didn't answer, but his heart monitor did make what I'd consider a more positive beat than the one before.

"Did you love me?"

"It doesn't matter," I added after a while because it didn't, and I knew that Nathan's feelings for me were not the true answer to my question. If love was a feeling and not a commitment—not an agreement set by two people—then these were questions only I could answer.

I knew that, but it didn't make it any easier.

The door opened and Clay stepped inside. "Still enjoying the view of your own eyelids, huh, Nathan?" He pulled up a chair and settled down.

Sliding an arm around my shoulder, he leaned in close and whispered, "How are you doing? Okay? You talked to Chris?" His breath smelled vaguely boozy.

I shook my head.

"It'll be okay," Clay said. "You two will be just fine."

I nodded.

"I mean it. It's been a long time since I've seen you that happy. You crazy kids will work it out."

I nodded again, though I didn't entirely agree. The truth was, my happiness was just as complicated as the rest of it. Happiness was selfishness. Every time someone in the world partied, someone else, somewhere, was crying. Every time I fell in love, someone died. I'd tried to ignore it; I'd worn earplugs to drown out the world's crying, but I heard it now.

I couldn't stop hearing it.

I moved closer to the bed and ran my hand over Nathan's. The clip on his finger that monitored his pulse rubbed against my wrist.

"Remember the summer he got us all fake I.D.s?" Clay smiled at Nathan. "Every bar, I thought we were going to get caught. And it was the guy at the gas station that actually took them away." Clay laughed. "And Nathan took the fall for everything. He even came by and told my dad the whole thing was his idea, and he bullied me into it."

"Yeah." I thought it best not to mention that I'd gotten a new I.D. just months after, or that no one cared in the city. I knew my thoughts should be on Nathan, that this room—this tight, white, sterile room—was dedicated to mourning, to reliving our best times with our old friend, but my mind was still on Chris. I checked my phone—no new messages—then I checked it again.

"He's going to call," Clay said. "Or maybe you should just bite the bullet and do it yourself."

I shrugged. "I don't think he wants to talk to me."

"Of course he wants to talk to you. He's in *loovvvvve*." Clay pulled a deck of cards out of his pocket and split the deck, handing half to me. "War. Don't pretend anyone of you are too mature for this." He placed the empty card box upon Nathan's bed and cleared his throat. "I know a thing or two about love, in case you forgot. I'm sort of an expert on what it means to love, and what it's like to be unloved. You, Lucas, my friend, are not unloved. Far from it. Everybody has fights. Look at your parents.

They fight all the time, and they're still my all-time favorite people in the world."

We played cards in silence. Clay won the first round, and I the second, and when War lost its merit, we switched to Crazy Eights. It might have been an exciting game given some booze and the great outdoors, but in the quiet, it was just as boring as the last. We'd done it dozens of times before, and still we spent our time in Nathan's room as though he was napping—like if we spoke too much or shouted too loud, we'd wake him up, like that wasn't the goal in the first place. Maybe we were both just too scared that one wrong move would set his heart monitor off, that maybe it'd go flat for good.

Halfway through a rather mediocre round of Texas Hold 'Em, I reached again for Nathan's hand and showed him my cards. He reacted just as I expected: cold, icy silence. I sighed and put the cards down.

Just then, Nathan's fingers twitched. I barely noticed, too used to the action-that-meant-nothing to muster up any hope. And that's when the truly miraculous happened. Nathan's fingers didn't just twitch, they bent, and soon his hand was grabbing mine, squeezing—weak and feeble—but still squeezing all the same.

Clay gasped. "His eyes!" He pointed. "His eyes! They're open! *They're open!*"

Sure enough, Nathan's eyes *were* open and wide as silver dollars. He blinked once, then again, and then stared blankly at the opposite wall, saying nothing. I rushed to the side of his bed, squeezing his hand, my heart doing back flips against my rib cage. Clay ran out of the room, yelling for a doctor.

While I waited, I held Nathan's hand and forced myself to keep breathing. He was awake. At least, he was more awake than he'd been a minute ago, and certainly more awake than he'd been last year, and I'd take it. I'd take anything, any progress he could make, any good news the doctors could give.

Soon, a nurse rushed in and checked Nathan's vitals. Clay and I were kicked out of the room, and as the doctors ran their tests, the two of us paced the halls of the hospital.

"His eyes opened," Clay said, his voice high-pitched and dazed.

I nodded numbly. Nathan's brown eyes might as well have been tattooed on my brain for how vividly I kept replaying the sight of them; none of us had seen those eyes in a year.

"Do you think he could really...be awake?" asked Clay, and then, like the encyclopedia he was, "It's not likely. Most coma patients that wake up are only in a coma for a few weeks. I mean, there's been weird ones. The man who woke up after nineteen years, for one. But the chances, even if he did wake up, of his brain working..."

Luckily, Clay's depressing facts were cut off by the sight of Nathan's parents rushing into the waiting room. "We got the call," said his father. "Have you seen him?" His gaze stopped on me. His eyes were watering. He held his wife's hand in his; both pairs shook violently.

I nodded. "He opened his eyes. And he squeezed my hand. That's all we know." I wanted to say more, wanted to tell them something— anything—that would make their expression look just a little less pained. I thought of hugging them, and then I remembered just how rarely I'd seen Nathan's parents in the last year.

I had once been close to this town, friends with my friends' parents— friends with my own friends. I had known everyone back then, had been invited to dinner and family parties. Now, I was more like a stranger.

Nathan's father nodded and wiped his eyes with the back of his hand. His wife stared ahead at Nathan's door, waiting like I was—like we all were—for the doctor to step out and give us the news. If anything, this was progress, good news, but it didn't feel like it somehow. It felt like being teased.

It was several long minutes before the doctor stepped out. He scanned for Nathan's parents, and when their eyes locked, he smiled. "Mr. and Mrs. Marshall? I have great news. I believe your son is waking up. I'd love to discuss more of the details with you inside, if you wouldn't mind." He gestured to his office. Nodding and clinging to one another, a crying Mr. and Mrs. Marshall followed.

CLAY AND I were not family, and therefore we were not allowed to see Nathan as the details of his recovery were worked out. His parents later came to tell us it would be a long process, but that his brain activity was increasing, and the doctor expected good results.

So with the good news on our minds, we went outside and had a smoke behind the hospital, everyone too anxious to leave the grounds entirely.

"He's waking up," Clay said for the thousandth time. He leaned against the hospital wall, waving clouds of smoke away from his face every time he exhaled. "He's actually waking up."

"And you didn't think it would happen," I said.

"Neither did you," said Clay.

I stared down at my cigarette and remembered having my first smoke with Nathan. He'd bought a carton when we were thirteen—never told me how—and we'd tried them out on the elementary school playground after hours. Now, he hadn't smoked in a year. It had been more than three hundred sixty-five days since I'd heard his voice, since he'd laughed, since we'd spoken. It's funny, how quickly someone can disappear from your life; what's worse—or maybe better; I wasn't sure yet—is how quickly they come rushing back.

In a moment of excitement, of uncharacteristic optimism I had not known for years, I made up my mind and dialed Chris's number. The phone rang for a minute and then went to voicemail. I called again. This time, someone picked up, but the voice on the other end—a hoarse, sniffing voice—was not Chris's.

"Lucas?" said Todney.

"Yeah?"

"It happened, Lucas. It happened."

"I know," I said, not thinking about anything but Nathan's wide eyes. "It happened. He woke up. That's what I wanted to tell Chris. He woke up." I was surprised at the shaking of my own voice, and for a second, I wondered what it could mean, until I realized I was smiling. I was happy. Nathan was waking up, and Clay was going back to school, and Rylie was getting married, and all the bad things that had happened in my life were righting themselves. I was happy, and I thought my face would tear from smiling so wide. Chris would be happy to hear. He'd be proud. Maybe he and Nathan could be friends; I bet they'd get along.

Todney sniffed. "What? Wow, I...Lucas, that's great. But..." He choked out a sob. There was a shuffling sound, as though the phone was being passed, and then Rylie's voice took over.

"Lucas, it's about Chris. He was having a hard time breathing this morning, so we took him to the hospital and..." She took a deep breath. She was crying too; I could hear it in her voice. "And he didn't make it. Chris passed away a couple minutes ago."

I dropped the phone as everything inside me drifted. The grief was fast and all-consuming, sweeping over me like a wave, and in that moment, I knew exactly what it was like to drown.

THE HALLS OF the hospital were suddenly like a maze, more complicated than they'd ever been before, like they knew I was in a hurry and they had been set up just to deter my path. I was sweating. I'd been one hell of an athlete in high school, and I'm not too modest to admit it, but I hadn't played in years, and I was out of shape. It was weird, but the faster I ran, the more I kept thinking about these little things: like how fast I'd run the mile in tenth grade—four minutes, five seconds—and the color of Jeffery Munez, homecoming king's, tennis shoes—green. As I ran, I counted every rushed beat of my heart, counted my own pounding footsteps on the cold linoleum floor, counted every door I passed, every wailing widow, every shrieking family, and the cries of my friends as they followed in my wake.

They say hospitals are where you come to be saved, but I was beginning to think they were more a place where happiness came to die.

Chris's room was the third door to the left in the right-most hall on the seventh floor—an easy find with Rylie and Todney marking the spot. Todney had his arms wrapped around Rylie while she cried into his chest; his own face was stained with tears, and his shoulders shook.

I pushed past them and into the room.

Chris's eyes were closed. There were no machines connected to him anymore, and a nurse stood over his bed, pulling up the sheets.

"Stop!" I said before she could cover him. "Stop!"

The nurse—a portly woman with black hair tied up in a bun—raised her hands and backed out of the room. It took her six steps to get to the door. She had nine buttons on her shirt—one broken. Her shoelaces were pink. Part of me wished she'd stay, if only because memorizing the freckles on her face would have provided an easy distraction, somewhere to look that wasn't Chris's still form.

But she left—as I knew she would—and Chris and I were alone.

I could hear Rylie and Todney's joint sobbing from outside the room, the eeriest sound I'd ever known. I closed the door behind me and settled into the chair by Chris's bed. *If I had a nickel for every time I've sat next to a hospital bed this year.* I imagined—for the briefest of moments—Chris searching through his pockets and handing me every coin he had because that was the sort of thing Chris would do and the sort of person Chris was—or was it "had been"? I reached for his hand. It was cold. It had always been cold.

"You can't do this to me." I squeezed harder. I waited for him to squeeze back, but there was nothing. Nathan had opened his eyes today, and he'd had them closed for a year; Chris's had only been closed for a few minutes. Certainly he could manage the same miracle. So I kept squeezing, and I kept waiting, but no matter how tight I held on, Chris continued to disappoint.

"You can't do this to me, you bastard. Open your eyes. I'm not done. I'm not done." His hands were so stiff; there was no give, no comfort. Holding Chris's hand now was like holding the hand of a mannequin. Not just cold, but completely lifeless. Dead.

And in that moment—as the word struck—it didn't matter that I'd been warned, didn't matter that, for months, "death" had been written in the stars above Chris's head. All I knew then was that a person could hold your hand one day and be unable to the next. "Passed away" were just words. "Didn't make it" meant nothing. People didn't stop existing. They couldn't. And yet Chris wouldn't open his eyes, and he wouldn't hold my hand, and that was never something he had ever denied me before.

"I love you," I said. "I love you. Did you hear me? I love you! *I love you! I said it! Listen to me!* I love you." Tears tumbled down my nose and over my cheeks, leaving me with blurry eyes and that warm, sticky feeling that only makes sadness that much worse. I was crying, and I was screaming, and for the life of me—for the death of him—I could not stop. There were three teardrops on Chris's chest, five stripes on his hospital blanket, two freckles on his jaw.

"I love you. You wanted to hear it. Well, there it is. Listen. *I love you.*"

Seventeen

I'VE HEARD IT said that death is easier with a warning. You have time to see it coming. You have time to come to terms. For weeks, you imagine it: what the grief will feel like, how you'll handle it, how'll you'll survive. But here's the catch: you're always wrong. That's the one thing they don't tell you about terminal illness, that it's really not all that different from a sudden bus crash. Because sudden or expected, you can't understand death until it happens. Preparation is just a lie we use to get ready when getting ready is impossible.

When I was ten, I fell off the roof of my house trying to fly. I broke my leg in three places, and I'd thought then that there was no worse pain in the world than *that* pain. Even after the casts came off, physical therapy was torture; every step felt like knives being forced through the soles of my feet and up into my kneecaps. *This is as bad as it'll ever get,* I'd thought. But I was wrong.

This was worse; coming home from the hospital after watching the doctors take Chris's body to the morgue was much, much worse. *This* was real pain. Because my leg healed, and it worked today almost as good as new, but Chris would never come back.

The shattered picture of us still lay on my floor. As I stepped into my bedroom, I picked it up and pulled the photograph from the glass. Lying back on my bed, I stared at our smiling faces. I didn't spend a lot of time looking at my own reflection, but I knew, at least, what happy looked like, and Clay was right. I was happy in that picture. I was happy with Chris.

They say you don't know a good thing until it's gone, but I think I knew how I felt about Chris all along. Ignorance is different than denial, and I had been firmly in the latter; I knew that if I loved Chris, his leaving would hurt like hell.

Turned out it did anyway.

I don't know how long I lay there, but the shadows on my bed receded before the door opened and my mother walked in. Her hair was tied up in a messy bun, an apron slung haphazardly around her waist, and I wondered, with little interest, what meal she had just finished. She sat down on the corner of my bed and squeezed my knee.

"Did you know that when your father had his heart attack, they kept him in the hospital for two days?" she asked.

I shook my head.

"It was the most terrifying forty-eight hours of my life. And while I was sitting there in the waiting room, wondering if he'd be okay, I started thinking about the life we'd made together. About you kids." She smiled. Her eyes crinkled around the edges, full of unshed tears. "About our wedding. About this house. And I realized that I had built my life around this man. That who I was, who I am, is all tangled up in him. And I wanted so badly to regret it. I never wanted to get married. I bet you never knew that."

Again, I shook my head. My mother was many things, but a relationship-phobe had never been one of them. My parents, according to all appearances, were blissfully, disgustingly in love.

"No," I said. "I thought you loved being married."

"Oh, I do. Lucas, I do. But I've changed. When your father proposed for the first time, I said no." She pulled her knees against her chest and rested her chin against one. A goofy smile fell across her lips before faltering. "I liked him so much. But I was scared. I was scared of depending on someone. I was scared of letting someone get so close. I didn't know what that would do to me. But eventually, I caved. I loved your father so much that I said yes. But that day in the hospital, I just kept wondering why. Why did I let myself get here? If I'd just said no like I'd always wanted to, I wouldn't be crying alone in a hospital, wondering if my husband was going to live or die. But I couldn't regret it. Even if he'd died that day, I love my life, and I can't regret every piece of it that brought me here, even if it hurts sometimes. Love is hard, Lucas." She squeezed my knee a little tighter, and ruffled my hair with her other hand. "It's hard work, and it's not always happy, but it's worth it."

My mother pulled me into a hug so tight I temporarily lost the ability to breathe. She pressed my head into her chest, and I buried my face into the fabric of her dress as the tears began welling up in my eyes. I did not want to cry on my mother like a child, but if ever there was time to regress, I supposed it was now. I squeezed her arm and sobbed.

"I know it hurts, sweetheart," she said. "But the pain does not erase all the good. You are always going to have those happy memories. And then you're going to go out and make some more. I promise you."

Chris had said to me that people who cared didn't worry about not caring. He was right. I cared. As I cried into my mother's shoulder, nineteen years old and still a lost little boy, I knew two things for sure: I had learned to care, and caring had broken my heart.

7 DAYS BEFORE

Clay arrived the next morning with a bucket of chicken in one hand and a pack of sour straws in the other. He knocked on my bedroom door as though it was the entrance to my house, as though my mother had not already let him in to "comfort" me. I called for him to enter, and he stepped inside.

"Extra crispy." He set the chicken in my lap and then retreated back to the door where he'd left a rather large box I hadn't noticed before. I grabbed a piece of chicken and took a bite as I waited to see what else he'd brought, though I wasn't hungry and wasn't sure I'd ever be again. There's just something about mourning and appetite that simply don't go together.

The box, as it turned out, was a flat-screen TV, which Clay immediately began to set up. When it was programmed with the cable, he turned to a daytime soap and crawled onto my bed to watch.

After a while, he asked, "Do you think it's better or worse knowing he can't be with you because he doesn't have a choice and not because he doesn't want to be with you?"

"What?" I said.

"Chris. I mean..." He paused and reached for a sour straw. As he chewed it, he continued. "He died, right? So he can't be with you just by laws of nature. But he would want to. And I know that sucks. But do you think it's better than like...him dumping you? Because at least you know he'd want to be with you. It's sort of the ultimate 'it's not you, it's me.'"

I stared for a long time, long enough to watch the flecks of sour flavor goo gather at the corners of Clay's usually perfect high-class mouth and then shook my head.

"You're tactless," I said. "Thanks for the TV."

Clay nodded. "Andrea is going to dump Charles." When I simply continued staring, confused as all hell, he pointed at the television. "She's pregnant with Ian's baby, so she's going to dump Charles and marry Ian even though she loves Charles more."

I squinted at the TV. This Andrea girl was, admittedly, rather pretty even when she was crying with her fists crumpling the shirt of a man I could only assume was Charles. He had a large pimple on his nose, and his hair was a mess, and though I'd yet to see Ian, I figured she could do better.

"Why do you watch this?" I asked.

"Because it's the only thing that's honest."

"Are you kidding?"

"No. Look." Clay pointed as Andrea ran out of the house, crying. "They never pretend in these things that life is rainbows and butterflies, you know? Everyone gets hurt, and then they move on. It's 'shit happens' by the hour. Are they overdramatic? Of course they are. It's called catharsis. You watch it, and you realize—hey, my life's not that bad in comparison."

"What is this? Is this you subtly telling me to get over it?" I reached for another piece of chicken and ripped the bones out one by one. I didn't know how watching a bunch of sobbing attempts at good acting was catharsis, but a bit of violence always was. At least until I started thinking that maybe this chicken had a family too, that maybe someone loved her, and maybe she'd been taken too soon. I knew what Chris would have said—that chickens were just fulfilling their life's purpose, and when it was their time, it was their time—but I lost my appetite for meat all the same.

Clay shook his head. "No. I'm telling you they all cry. Every single one of them. Like all the time. And it helps. They cry, and they scream. And then everyone feels better."

"I'm not going to cry. I already did that. I didn't like it." I rolled up a sour straw and stuffed it into my mouth all at once. As far as sour goes, it was a bit of a letdown, and I almost wanted the extreme just to feel something—my eyes watering, my jaw clenching, anything but the emptiness I'd spent my whole life making sure I'd never feel.

"Scientifically speaking, crying is just a release of pent-up feelings. When you get a buildup of emotions, crying allows you to release it in a safe way that makes you feel better. And some scientists today believe it actually releases stress hormones and maybe even toxins, and I think—"

I slapped a hand over Clay's mouth before he could finish the sentence.

"I don't want to cry. Here." I stuffed the bucket of chicken into his lap. "Eat this. I don't want it anymore." I thought of the living chicken, its wings still on its body and not in a bucket, and then of the two ducks in the pool. "Do ducks mate for life?"

Clay shook his head. "No. Not usually."

I figured as much. As I finished off the sour straws, I leaned back into my bed and watched Andrea and Ian make out for a while. She didn't seem all that hung up over Charles, no matter what Clay had said to the contrary. I wished it was that easy, that you could walk away from the person you love and be perfectly happy ten seconds later. That the mourning, the longing, only lasted a scene. I'd heard people say that life was like a book, and when something bad happened, it was just one chapter in your story; but honestly, it was a pretty lacking metaphor. In any good book, one chapter leads to the next; each scene correlates with the one after. A plot drop like death affects everything.

We were silent until the end of the episode, then "How's Nathan?" I asked. "Have you seen him?"

"Yeah, I stopped by this morning," Clay said. "He's doing better. He's making eye contact with everyone in the room. Like he knows we're there. He's not talking yet, though. But they're really optimistic."

I nodded. I wanted to be angry at that, that Nathan's life had been restored just as Chris's had been taken, wanted to shake my fists at the universe for its vast unfairness, its pathetically poor timing. But mostly, I wanted to be happy that Nathan's life had been restored at all. And I was, sort of, in this deep, faraway part of myself that no longer felt connected to the me-that-was—the me on the bed with sour goo stuck between my fingers, waiting for a call from a boy who was dead and couldn't call and never would. Nathan deserved to wake up. And I wanted that, wanted to see his eyes open again, wanted to hear him say "hey, buddy" at least one more time. But I couldn't feel pain like this— this unbearable, all-consuming pain—and joy at the same time.

"That's good," I said finally. "I'll come see him. Soon." Soon was a vague enough concept, and I knew by Clay's expression—all sad and overly understanding—that he understood. Soon was after the funeral;

soon was so disconnected from me, from this room, that I couldn't possibly give it a when.

Clay patted my arm. "Everyone understands. And when he *can* understand, so will Nathan."

"I'm not sure I like this comforting you," I said.

"Would it help if I said I had a hidden agenda?"

I nodded.

Clay sat up straight and set the bucket of chicken on my desk. "I want you to come to AA with me. I thought...well, we all have things to fix now, right? I found a place, and I think it could help both of us. I've got...problems. That's the first step, right? Admitting it? I think. And it's supposed to be a safe place. You can talk."

"I'm not an alcoholic," I said.

Clay shrugged. "Does it matter? You're my guest. And everyone there is there to listen. So you can talk about what you're...feeling or whatever. I think it would be good for you too. And..." His voice dropped into a rushed whisper. "I don't want to go alone. There will be baked goods. A lot of them."

THE MEETING WAS in the main room of a church at the end of town. It was the one my parents went to—the gay-friendly one that didn't look at me like I had hellfire coming out of my ears. By the time we arrived, there was already a group of twenty or so men and women gathered around a table of cookies and donuts and coffee. Behind them, dozens of plastic chairs had been set up in a circle, and a man, who I assumed was the minister or the leader or whatever, was already sitting, his hands folded in his lap.

"Excuse me." Clay butted his way through the sugar-eager crowd. He threw his arms out to shield the baked goods. "We're going to need all of these. I'm sorry. It's an emergency."

The crowd backed off, though not without giving Clay about a dozen dirty looks. I gathered up the remnants of donuts and cookies into my arms and then sat down in the closest plastic chair. The donuts were sort of mediocre, but the cookies were store-bought in the best of ways, so I mowed them down while the chairman guy talked about the twelve steps and then the rules of AA.

Rule one: Keep confidentiality (which was a lot like "what happens in Vegas stays in Vegas," but with more emotions and less illegal weddings). Rule Two: Make "I" statements, not "you" or "we." Rule three: Stay in the here and now (whatever that means). Rule Four: Share feelings about your experience. Rule Five: No fixing or giving advice. And Rule Six: No asking questions or discussing while someone else is sharing.

After the rules had been established, the introductions began.

There was this woman named Meredith who had been sober for two years but kept coming to the meetings for "moral reassurance," and these two twins who couldn't speak without shaking, one who was an alcoholic and the other who, like me, was just here for support. Next to them was this old guy who said he started drinking after the war—he never said which one—and a man next to him who drank after his wife left him. This went on for some time—everyone standing, saying their name and "I'm an alcoholic," and then telling their story in a quick thirty-second pitch. When it came to Clay, he stood and cleared his throat.

"My name is Clayton Ortiz, and I'm an alcoholic...I guess. That's why we're all here, right? I started drinking when I was ten. After my mom left, my dad started...lashing out. And I guess he was easier to handle when I was drunk. And plus, I liked not being the smartest one in the room...no offense. I'm sort of a genius. Made it sort of hard to make friends." He sat down, but the second his butt hit the chair, he jumped back up. "Oh! And this is Lucas." He pointed at me. "His boyfriend just died. He needs food. He also needs alcohol, but he'll do that later."

"Hi, Clayton," said the group. And then, "Thank you, Clayton. Hi, Lucas."

I waved awkwardly. Swallowing the last of my cookie, I stood up, several donuts still balanced precariously in my arms. "I'm not an alcoholic, but I'm sad," I said before sitting back down.

The chairman—Robert, I think—gestured for me to stand back up. "Why are you sad, Lucas? Tell us more about what's going on in your life."

"Why? I'm not drinking."

"But you must have come here for a reason." Robert leaned back in his chair, his legs crossed over camouflage pants that had clearly seen better days, and waited for me to speak. He had the sort of bright blue eyes that when focused on you felt just like a police car's flashing lights. A warning.

I coughed and plucked a sprinkle off one of the donuts just to give my hands something to do. "I fell in love. And it was the one thing I never wanted to do. But I fell in love anyway, and it was really, really nice. And then he died. And I always knew he was going to die, so I kept trying not to love him. But I'm going to die someday too. We all are. And that's always bothered me. Because how are you supposed to do anything when you know it's just going to end? It's like trying to get homework done when you know you have a doctor's appointment in an hour. You can't focus. Because you know that as soon as you get started, you'll get interrupted. So what's the point? I lived my whole life like I've had an appointment."

It was overwhelmingly tempting to stuff a donut into my mouth just to shut myself up, and I knew I'd probably regret this later, but in that moment, with every eye on me—everyone *listening*—I wasn't scared to speak. I imagined Chris in the back of the room, the way he'd smile and tell me to keep going, and that gave me strength. I mean, I didn't think he was up in heaven, looking down on me or anything, as though he didn't have anything better to do in the afterlife than babysit, but it was a nice thought all the same.

"I have a lot of people in my life I don't deserve," I said. "A lot of people who have stuck with me when I haven't stuck with them. But this time, someone else did the leaving. And so I'm sad because that sucks. Because I miss him." I was crying then—stupid, sticky tears clinging to my cheeks, which should have been humiliating, except that Meredith cried telling her story too, and no one *looked* like they were judging me. "I don't cry a lot," I said just in case. "I don't talk this much either."

I sat down, and the room said all at once, "Thank you, Lucas." It wasn't as comforting as it was eerie, but at least they were trying.

There were more stories after that, and Clay ended up telling the room about his first suicide attempt—the one I'd been around for when we were thirteen—and then his second—which I hadn't been around for—and how drinking made him feel more alive. Meredith said she'd tried too, that she'd slit her wrists when she was twenty-one, but she didn't think about those things anymore. And I looked around at all these people who were perfectly alive and dreaming about death, and thought that if life was a game, it was pretty pointless to skip to the end. But then, not everyone liked playing.

THE MEETING ENDED with a prayer, and then Robert thanked everyone who had brought the baked goods and coffee, never mentioning that I ate them all, before he shared his tips for finding a sponsor. Clay approached this burly linebacker-looking guy who said helping people was his calling, and they discussed a potential sponsor/sponsee relationship while I waited in the car.

I just kept staring at my phone. I knew Chris wasn't going to call—that he couldn't call—but it was hard to reconcile. The twenty-first century, and everyone's just one button press away—but not Chris. Chris was in a whole other plane. Or maybe just in the morgue. I didn't know anymore.

Clay slid into the car a moment later. He smiled. It wasn't the fake, camera-ready smile I'd so often seen him wear, or even the charming one he thought would win over Rylie, but a real smile—relieved, I think.

"I meet Ben on Thursdays. And I can call him if I feel like drinking." He waved at the linebacker through the window.

He started the car. "You know, I think your mom knows. I found all these stop-drinking pamphlets in my backpack." Clay reached into the glove compartment and pulled out a handful of different folded papers, all with sayings like "You're Stronger Than You Think" and "Your Future Is Up To You" written on the front.

"My mom knows everything," I said.

"Do you think she's mad?"

"I think she's worried."

"Yeah, well," Clay said, "so am I."

As we drove back to my house, I stared out the window at all the little things I'd almost forgotten: the drug store with the inflated pumpkin outside no matter what holiday season it actually was; the nail salon that my mom used to drag me and my siblings to when we were too young to stay home alone; the park where I'd had my first kiss with a boy named Matt. I could have avoided a hell of a lot of pain if I'd never come back here. My mother's words drifted back to me: *but the pain does not erase all the good.*

"I'm sorry I wasn't there," I said, glancing at Clay. "When you were...down." I didn't want to say suicidal; it seemed too crass, even for me. "I should have checked in more. You were right. I was avoiding Nathan. So I avoided everyone else too."

Clay grinned toothily. "Did AA teach you to talk about your feelings?" His tone was as condescending as I'd ever heard it.

I rolled my eyes. "Forget it."

"No." Clay rested a hand atop my shoulder. "Thank you. You know, they say suicide is a call for attention, right? I think maybe I was trying to get yours."

CLAY DROPPED ME off outside my house, circled around the block to park, and then came inside. My mom had lunch on the table by then, and we stopped in the kitchen to eat. The twins were standing up on their seats, screaming about some video game Daniel had apparently cheated on and that Anthony felt he never got enough time to play. Frankie was on her phone as per usual but nodded at the two of us as we came in, and Sharon jumped straight out of her seat to hug us both. For such a little girl, she had one hell of a grip.

I hugged her back and then sat down at the table and thanked my mom for the meal. She nodded at me—this tight-lipped smile on her face, like she was scared I'd break if she said too much.

"Get down," she told the twins, and they did—surprisingly quickly— and then they too gave me the Look, and Frankie scooted her chair closer to mine. I shifted in my seat, suddenly feeling like I was on stage during a concert, but instead of waiting for me to play, this crowd was waiting for me to cry.

"I'm okay," I said, though it wasn't true. "How are...how are you guys?"

Daniel wasted no time in answering. He sat up as tall as possible in his chair, all eating forgotten, and began explaining the plot of his and Anthony's new video game. "And then you kill the zombie princes, and you win! I killed three more zombies than Anthony today."

"Did not!" Anthony stood up and crossed his arms over his chest. The uncontrollable cowlick he'd had since birth flopped over his face, making him look surlier than ever.

"Hey." Clay ushered him over and whispered something in Anthony's ear that I couldn't make out. Whatever it was, it had Anthony smiling by the time they pulled away. That was the strangest part about Clay—how quickly he shifted from selfish and confused, to saying the exact right thing at the exact right time.

After we finished eating, Sharon came and sat in my lap and told me a story about a princess who had an obsession with donuts and threw them at the Carrot King.

"Sounds nutritional," I said, and she laughed.

"Did that make you feel better?" she asked. "Mom said you're sad. And I don't want you to be sad."

"Yeah. It helped." I wondered how much a seven-year-old could know about sadness, what she would say if it was me who had died, or our parents, or one of her brothers. And then I thought: *it doesn't matter; at least she knows that sad is bad, at least she cares,* and that was more than I ever could have said for myself.

I ruffled her hair and then kissed her forehead. "You always help."

She beamed.

THAT NIGHT, I got a call from Todney explaining the details of the upcoming funeral. Given everything that was going on—the wedding especially—it would be a rush job done in only two days: his parents were paying; they would be in town the next day.

"Maybe we should cancel the wedding," Todney kept saying. I couldn't see him, but I could tell he was crying with every word; I wondered if he'd stopped crying since *it* had happened.

"It's tactless to have a wedding right now, isn't it?"

I thought of all the parties that were happening in the world, all the funerals, and of my mom and her wedding that almost didn't happen. "No. Probably not. The bad doesn't outweigh the good. Chris would be pissed if you canceled the wedding. He really wanted you two to get married."

Todney sighed. "He wanted a lot of things."

"Yeah," I said. "Number one was not to die."

After I hung up, I fell into bed and dreamed of caskets and black roses, and when I woke up in the middle of the night sweating, I pretended I could feel Chris's hand on my shoulder.

It was the last time I ever would.

Eighteen

5 DAYS BEFORE

The funeral was held in the same church where we'd attended AA, but there were no cookies this time, just a casket and a lot of people crying. Okay, so, "a lot" was sort of an exaggeration, since it was barely over twenty, but even a *few* people crying is overwhelming. There was, of course, Todney, Rylie, and Clay; and also my parents, Rylie's parents, and a couple people from the grocery store where Chris had barely worked. He wasn't from this town like we were, and I thought it sort of strange that he'd be buried here, but then, at least he was starting his eternity—if there was such a thing—with friends.

It was an open casket. The second I walked into the church, I could see people lining up in front of it, saying their last goodbyes. I took my time, though, and stalled in the entryway, using Sharon, who was holding tight to my hand, as a barrier between me and the last time I'd see him. Todney was sobbing. Rylie had her arms wrapped around him, whispering in his ear while she patted his back. There was nothing she could say to make this better, nothing anyone could say, but funerals are the time when everyone tries.

I'd never seen Todney's parents before, but I could only assume that the straight-backed, well-dressed couple beside them must have been the original Mr. and Mrs. Wright. They weren't crying, and I couldn't have told you if the blank-faced looks they wore were even sad, but they'd come, and maybe that meant more than anything else ever could. Or maybe they were just being polite.

Sharon let go of my hand when Frankie approached. Yelling for our mom, Sharon rushed off and clung to her leg instead.

"I yelled at her this morning," Frankie explained, shaking her head. She wore a loose black dress, her hair tied up in the bun, and when she looked at me, it hardly looked condescending. Miracles, I suppose, did happen after all. "I guess I've been in a bad mood."

"We're all in a bad mood," I said. "And she's scared. She's never been to a funeral." Neither had I for that matter. I'd once thought I'd attend Nathan's funeral, that my friends and I would cry together—like we did everything together—and throw dirt as he was lowered into the ground. Because people in comas didn't usually wake up after this long.

I felt like I was living in constant limbo, too sad to speak one moment and almost happy the next, and for the life of me, I couldn't piece my thoughts together. I was sad. I was glad. I was empty, and I was staring across a mostly empty room at a box that held my dead boyfriend.

"There's a space for you up front." Frankie's hand came to rest on my shoulder. "If you want to...see him first, we'll save it for you." She hesitated before kissing my cheek. For a moment, I could see us—me six, her three, running circles around each other in the living room. She wasn't angry yet, and I wasn't sad, and neither of us were in black.

I smiled and thanked her. I knew she was just being nice, but I couldn't help but think that whether or not they saved the seat for me, it didn't matter; this church was deserted. There were seats everywhere. Funny the things you worry about when you'd rather be crying.

After Frankie left, I trudged up to the casket. Back in seventh grade, I'd read the real story of the little mermaid, how while she had feet, each step felt like knives, and for a moment, I understood exactly what that was like. The closer I got to Chris, the farther he felt from me. Because once I saw his body, that was the end; no more pretending this was all a bad dream, no more hoping he'd miraculously wake up. My heart backflipped and somersaulted through my chest—my own little Olympian—and I bit my lip to keep from crying.

Never, in nineteen years, had that pressure behind my eyes been so strong, my hands so shaky, my legs so weak. I was falling out of a tree. I was building a cross for my dead dog and my fish and my hamster. I was staring at Nathan's overturned car. Grief did not pick and choose.

They'd put more color in Chris's face somehow, but he still didn't have any hair, and he still looked tired, which I supposed was good, like he was just sleeping forever. I was dressed in a black suit—something I'd found in the back of my closet from when I'd still gone to church—but Chris's was blue. Like the water. Or maybe all black had just been too cliché. I'd never bothered to ask him what he wanted to wear at his funeral, and so I could never be sure if he'd picked it out himself or if Todney had just felt it the best bet. After all, Chris no longer had a mother to dress him—at least, not one who had showed up.

I reached out to touch his face. It was warmer now—heated by the closeness of the casket and the bright lights of the room—than it had ever been while he was alive. "I love you," I whispered. "I'm sorry I never said it while you could hear me." Tucking his tie properly into his suit—which, granted, it already was, but I needed to do something with my hands—I patted his chest once and then took a step back.

I kept waiting to think he looked beautiful or angelic, but he just looked dead. He was a shell of the person Chris had been. He still had his hands and his nose, and that freckle on the right side of his ear, but there was no more Chris. After all, a Chris not talking really wasn't a Chris to begin with. He still had his mouth, but it didn't work, and that, more than anything, solidified the truth for me: Chris was gone.

To drown feels like this: your lungs collapse, your brain fizzles, and the feeling in your fingertips, your toes, your arms—the feeling that once connected you to the world—disappears, and you're left floating into the blackness.

BACK AT THE front of the church—which really wasn't all that far from the back of the church—the pastor settled behind the podium and called all two dozen of us to order. I hurried across the room and took a seat between Clay and my sister. The pastor read first from the Bible. It was a pretty overused passage about Heaven, if you ask me, which didn't do much to make Chris's funeral unique—just another funeral with another dead guy inside another coffin. It was not the horror story Chris had wanted, that was for sure. But it was beautiful, and by the end, even Frankie was crying.

I had no disillusions that I'd make it through the day without doing the same, but I was saving my tears. Chris was still above ground, which meant he was still a part of our world, and I could handle that: everyone gathered to talk about how great he was while he watched from somewhere in the room. Six feet under was a whole different story.

Once the pastor started reading a poem, Clay and Frankie reached for my hands simultaneously and gave them both a little squeeze. I met their eyes one at a time and mouthed my thanks, though thankful was the last thing I was feeling. The room was unbearably stuffy, and mostly, I just wanted out.

"Now Chris's closest friend, Todney, would like to say a few words," the pastor said.

Todney clambered up to the podium, his shoulders stiff. I noticed he wore a bit of scruff today, that his suit was less than perfectly ironed, that his smile was crooked. I liked him better this way, more imperfect like the rest of us.

"Chris and I grew up together," he said. "He was always like my brother. I mean, the resemblance is a little hard to see..." Everyone laughed, and Todney cracked a smile. "But he was always there for me, and I tried my best to be there for him. They always say guys don't make the same sort of friends girls do. That they don't let themselves get as close. Because we guys don't share our feelings or talk about things. And I guess they're right in some ways. We never sat around, talking about how each conversation made us feel, but I wish we did. I wish I knew more about what he was feeling in the end, what he was thinking. It was so easy to tell when we were kids."

He told a story then about him and Chris riding their bikes through town and Chris falling off; Todney had made a Band-Aid out of a leaf and patched him up, and he said it was then that he knew he was always supposed to be there for Chris. But that he'd failed this time. That hopefully the Big Guy upstairs was there for him now.

"And now to hear from Chris's dear friend, Lucas," said the pastor next.

Clay and Frankie squeezed my hand again, and I managed to disentangle myself in time to jog up to the stage. I placed both my elbows against the podium and looked out at what I'd hoped was a sea of people, but was more like a single wave. My stomach plummeted.

"I didn't prepare anything," I admitted, and a few people smiled. "I don't think Chris was too into prepared speeches. He talked so much, there was no way he was keeping that all in his head waiting for the right time. He said words were just waiting to be used, and I think he would have thought it was a waste of those words to keep them waiting...and now I'm talking more about words than I am about Chris." I cleared my throat. I glanced at the casket, then at the front row where my friends were staring, watery-eyed, and then at the back of the room. There was a stained-glass picture of Jesus on the wall, and he was almost smiling. I thought, just maybe, that was a good sign.

"Chris was a great chapter in my life. He taught me that you can't press pause, that everything moves forward, and that I have a voice. He meant a lot to me, and things like that aren't easy to talk about. But I'll just say this. I..." I bit my lip, met Clay's eyes, Todney's, and then my mother's. "I loved him." I managed a smile before stepping back from the podium and hurrying to my seat.

No one else spoke after me, except the pastor who read another poem and then the choir sang this sad song about death and Heaven, and I sort of swayed in time to the tune, my hands folded in my lap. When the song ended, one of the choir members pulled down a projector and they played a video Todney had put together.

In the first clip, Chris was in diapers, staring at the camera. His eyes were too big for his face back then, and he blinked several times before grasping the camera lens in one of his tiny baby hands. Another sad song started up, a background to the many pictures of Chris that had been taken over the years: Chris smiling, Chris flipping off the camera—everyone laughed at that—Chris in a Speedo and a swim cap, waiting at one of his diving competitions, Chris in the hospital. There was another video clip of him diving and a crowd cheering, and then of a gold metal being placed around his neck. This led into a video of him in the hospital, saying, "Am I bionic now?" as he stared down at his wrapped leg. And then, in an Arnold Schwarzenegger voice, "I will be back."

As the video dissolved into blackness, everyone clapped.

Frankie, in a rare moment of sisterly affection, rested her head against my shoulder and sniffed. "Do you think he'll really be back? I mean, do you think people get reincarnated or anything?"

I shook my head. With one hand, I played with her hair, the thick strands getting caught between my fingers; she had my father's hair. I hoped she would never have his health.

"I don't know. Probably not. I think everyone only gets one chance."

"Like love?" Frankie looked over her shoulder at our parents—arms folded together, crying in unison. If ever we were to attend their funeral, it would be a joint affair; I didn't think they'd survive alone.

I shook my head, thinking still of my parents, of Clay and Rylie, of Nathan resting wide-eyed and awake in his hospital bed.

"Maybe. Maybe not."

WHEN THE SERVICE ended, the funeral director closed and sealed Chris's casket before I and several of the other boys carried it to the graveyard. I was honestly surprised by how heavy he was, like I thought the dead might just float above us, or because there was no life left in his body, there would be nothing left to hold. But as much as Chris weighed on my mind, he weighed on my shoulder too.

It was still so early in the day that the morning dew clung to every blade of grass and dripped down the side of every tombstone. Across the way, a man knelt before a grave, flowers in hand. And then we arrived: a hole, six feet down, and a clump of dirt. Chris's final resting place.

Everyone who wasn't holding the casket had followed behind, and as we lay Chris down, they gathered in a circle around the hole. The priest gave another speech, this time about love and the acceptance of death and moving on, and then they lowered him into the earth, and each one of us, one little clump at a time, threw a handful of dirt into the grave and said our last goodbyes.

I don't know who invented the ritual, but it was a strange thing to see: everyone throwing dirt around like it was in some way respectful to do so. The whole funeral process is a bit of contradiction if you ask me: you pump a man full of chemicals so he'll never truly decay and then you bury him underground as though you're giving him back to the earth. I doubted Chris would have appreciated it much, having dirt thrown on him in his last earthly moments. A Viking funeral would have been more like it, thrown out into the water and burned, his ashes forever part of the sea. I thought he would have liked that, but he wasn't around to like anything anymore, and this funeral was for Todney, for Rylie, and for me.

I tried to remind myself that as I gathered my handful of dirt, that I was not saying goodbye to him for him, that he couldn't hear me anymore, and that with this last act, I was saying goodbye for me. Chris's part of the world was over; mine wasn't. And maybe that sort of thing would have worked a couple months ago, but as it was, I just kept replaying the way his lips felt on mine.

"You couldn't have waited just a couple more months," I mumbled. "I'm bound to get myself killed here sooner or later. Maybe I would have been the one in a car crash this time. Or picked a fight I couldn't win. Couldn't you have waited long enough so I wouldn't have to miss you?"

He didn't answer. Luckily, I was used to the silence.

AFTER ALL THE dirt throwing was over, we gathered at this little pasta place down the street from the graveyard. Most of the crowd—the crowd being our parents—went home, but Todney, Rylie, Clay, Frankie, and I settled into the biggest booth they had and ordered half the menu.

"I just need fried food." Rylie tapped her nails against the tabletop, her eyes scanning each person around her and then the waiter across the room who had only just left with our order. "Could they be any slower?"

Todney grabbed her hand and kissed at her knuckles. "Baby, it's going to be okay."

Clay made quite the show of engaging Frankie in conversation at that exact moment. Something about tri-tip and barbecues; I was too busy staring at my glass of water to really pay attention. We were a big group, too many voices and bodies squished together to handle, but the table felt empty without Chris. The loudest voice of all of us—the newest at that—had been silenced, and it left its mark.

"We should cancel the wedding," Rylie said. When I looked up, she was staring at Todney; her hands held his in an iron grip. "It's too soon. He's barely in the ground, and we're about to throw a party?"

"He would have liked it," I said. "Chris wanted you two to get married. He told me. He said he was actually happy it was happening. And you're his best friend." I looked to Todney. "He would want you to be happy, and if marrying Rylie is going to make you happy, you'd be stupid to stop that."

Clay went silent halfway through his lecture to Frankie. "I've got to go home." He slid out of the booth—making Frankie get up to let him out—and left the restaurant without another word.

I should have expected it, but I wasn't going to filter myself to cater to his made-up love story. I watched him go, feeling that familiar lump of unwanted guilt fester in my stomach, and then looked to the once happy couple across from me.

"You guys should do it. He would want you to do it. And I want you to do it. So just do it."

Rylie laughed. She had that look in her eyes too—the faraway sort of look that I knew wanted to watch Clay walk away but couldn't.

She let go of Todney's hand, heaved a deep breath, and then poked her fiancé's nose. "What do you think? Should we go ahead and do it?"

Just like that, the puppy-dog-love smile was back on Todney's face. "Yeah, Lucas is right. Chris would have wanted it."

Frankie and I clapped and cheered until the couple kissed. Our food came not long after—piles of mozzarella sticks, mini–corn dogs, fries, and bottomless milkshakes. I think even the waiter knew that someone had died or that someone wanted to die because his expression was nothing less than concerned as he set down the last plate of fried food: chicken nuggets with a healthy side of mashed potatoes.

I was already halfway through my first helping of all-of-the-above when Todney cleared his throat. "Lucas."

I nodded, mouth full.

"If we're going to do this, then I'm going to need a new best man. And I can't think of anyone more qualified than you."

I choked. Honestly, I hadn't seen that coming. I'd been friends with Clay my whole life, and I hadn't even expected to be *his* best man—and not because I was unsure whether he'd ever get married.

"Uh…" Swallowing, I set down my fork and stared across the table. "Are you sure?" All of the job part of being the best man was over: picking out the tux, going along for all the fittings, planning the bachelor party—I'd heard little more than "it was fun," which really meant, I was sure, "we blacked out." All that was left now was to stand next to Todney at the altar. An easy job, but still. "I'm not exactly…"

"You're perfect," Todney finished before I could. "If it can't be Chris, it should be someone who can uphold his memory. And I think you're perfect for that. He'd want it to be you. Say yes? Please?"

I couldn't say no.

LUNCH ENDED WITH slightly less tears than the funeral, and after everyone hugged, because hugging was, apparently, something grieving people did, we went our separate ways. For me, this meant to the hospital and up to Nathan's floor. His parents were sitting beside his bed when I arrived, telling him stories and catching his spoon every time he dropped it on his way to a bite of Jell-O. He didn't look up when I entered, but his parents did, their smiles half-cocked and their eyes wet; I think they were always wet. There are emotional people in this world, and then there are parents.

"Lucas," they said in unison, and Nathan's dad jumped up and hugged me. I accepted it, stiffly, and sort of wrapped my arms around him while I looked over his shoulder at Nathan's very awake form. His hair had been combed, and he blinked down at his Jell-O, too dazed to be fully with us, but certainly not sleeping anymore. I waved at his mom before I took the extra seat next to his bed.

"Hey, Nathan," I said. He didn't answer. I was used to that. "It's been a while." Still nothing. A year full of silence, and a couple days wouldn't change that. "How are you feeling?"

His mom sniffed from the other side of the bed. She held his hand in one of hers, too tight for it to be comfortable for either of them, like if she let go, he might fall asleep again.

"Has he said anything?" I asked her.

She shook her head. "Not yet. But he knows you're here. Look." She nodded at Nathan, who, sure enough, was looking at me, blinking. "He's aware of what's going on, and he's only just mumbled a bit, but we're getting there. The doctors are optimistic."

When Nathan dropped the Jell-O spoon, I reached for his newly freed hand and ran my thumb over the back of it. He flinched slightly, which I took as a good sign; a week ago he would have just kept on sleeping. I thought of all the times I'd held his hand, and it struck me that 90 percent of them were while he was unconscious. Feeling a bit like the prince in Snow White, I pulled my hand away, but shot him a smile just in case.

"It's good to see you awake," I said. "I really missed you."

Nathan blinked again. His dark brown eyes were open and seeing me, and if that wasn't a miracle, I didn't know what was. I grinned, and for a moment, I wasn't thinking about how still Chris had been in his casket or how much I missed his voice. For just one fleeting moment, I was almost happy again.

"I don't know if you can hear me, but if you can, I have so much to tell you."

"We'll give you two a minute." His mom kissed the top of my head, and his father smiled from the doorway. The two left, talking and crying together all the way out the hall.

I watched them go, and once their voices disappeared, I reached for Nathan's hand again. "A *lot*," I said. "You won't believe how much you missed. A year is a hell of a long time to be asleep."

Nathan blinked. His eyes widened, and then he squeezed my hand. My heart started pounding, and I didn't dare move just in case anything I did upset him or scared him off; I didn't know what he'd been up to with his parents, but as far as I knew, this was progress. This was *big* progress.

"You know me," I said. "I'm not very good at this mushy stuff. But I'm here."

Nathan smiled. "Hi," he said. Yeah, definitely progress.

I smiled back. "Hi."

Nineteen

THE WEDDING

A wedding, I believe, is the sort of affair that should be beautiful but generally ends up chaotic instead. Rylie's was no exception. The tables in the banquet hall were perfectly designed. The napkins were folded in what the wedding planner kept saying were "beautiful swans." And the centerpieces glowed—literally. From all appearances, it looked like the start of a beautiful day, but it was not enough to keep Rylie from dry heaving into a paper bag, bent over a fan just to gasp for air.

I heard her gagging as I crossed from the men's room down to the kitchen. The women's room—where the bride and bridesmaids were meant to get dressed and do their hair and makeup, and whatever else it is women do on special occasions—was halfway down the hall and propped open. Women shuffled around Rylie, whispering platitudes to her and yelling at one another; Rylie's mother did most of the crying before she rushed off, past me and into the bathroom. The men's room had been little better—Todney muttering his vows over and over into a mirror, and, when his father arrived to see him, collapsing into his arms—but no one was crying in there. No one was even talking. Todney's father had the look of a man who had never hugged in his life, a stiff face and an instinct toward handshakes at the most, but when I'd left, they'd stood side by side, and I had to think that was enough.

"We shouldn't be doing this." Rylie gasped and tucked her hair behind her ear. "I'm fine. I'm fine." Ushering away her bridesmaids, she looked up just in time to see me hovering in the corner and gestured for me to come into the room. I sighed but gave in to my friendly duty.

Frankie stood against the far wall, pale-faced even behind her makeup. Her dress was on, her hair was done, but her eyes were the size of her dress's bow—big and overwhelming.

"Do you think Chris would be angry?" Rylie asked as I entered. "He helped pick out my dress. He never got to see it finished. We shouldn't be doing this."

I'd hoped to go a day without hearing Chris's name if only to give myself a glimpse of a future without it, but life, as I was quickly learning, rarely goes according to plan.

I shook my head. "He'd be happy for you. He's probably watching and excited right now." Whether or not it was true didn't matter—it was only for her comfort—but it still felt dirty on my tongue. It's a selfish notion, that even after people die they're hovering around us, ghosts looking out for us, as though they don't have better things to do. We, the living, are suddenly the center of their universe.

I hoped Chris wasn't around anymore, and I hoped that if heaven had pools, they were big, and he was in them—far away from me and the sad little bores of human life.

I didn't know if I believed in Heaven, but I wanted to.

Rylie moved to the center of the room where her dress was hanging. She took it off the rack and held it up in front of her body.

"This is it," she whispered. "All this time planning, and this is it. I feel like I'm five and it's Christmas Eve. You're planning and waiting, and then it comes, and it's over, and it's...weird." She laughed and then fanned her eyes as they began to fill with tears. "No, I already put my mascara on!"

"You look beautiful," I said, and she did. Her hair was tied up in a bun, braids weaving in and out of it, and her makeup was perfect. The perfect look for the perfect day.

Her mother walked back into the room then, and they exchanged a few greetings in Spanish before the first tears finally fell from Rylie's eyes. "Am I a terrible person?" She dabbed at her cheeks with a tissue.

Her mother shook her head. "Of course not, sweetheart. Everyone deserves to be happy. And today is your special day. You've been waiting so long for this."

Rylie cried even harder.

AFTER I WAS dressed—suit, tie, and newly shined shoes to top it off—I stopped in the bathroom to have a one-on-one with my reflection. The stylist in the men's room had slicked back my hair, and I was wearing some sort of lip-something that was supposed to make me look better in pictures. I was me, but me shined up like an old coin—recognizable but strange—and I imagined Chris laughing at the sight. I wanted to kiss him, to get some of this lip stuff off me and onto him, but mostly I wished he was standing up at the altar and I wasn't.

When you lose a part of yourself, it leaves a scar; when you lose someone else, they leave a hole.

"Get it together," I told my reflection. "Rylie's counting on you. And Todney. And Chris."

I'd run cities away to make sure no one was ever counting on me; I had never wanted to be anyone's anything, never wanted to be depended on, but it was impossible, and I knew that now. We're dependent creatures, humankind, and I was no different. Rylie might need me now, might need us all now, but I'd needed her too. I had needed Rylie to remind me how to fight for what you wanted; I had needed Clay to lean on; I had needed Chris to remind me of all the things I'd forced myself to forget. And maybe the me in the mirror didn't look like the me I knew, but I finally felt like him: better than what I remembered.

I stepped out of the bathroom ten minutes before the ceremony was set to start. All of the groomsmen were expected to wait at the altar, and I was halfway to the stairs when the sound of Clay's voice stopped me in my tracks. For obvious—and in my opinion, understandable—reasons, Clay had not been invited to the wedding. Exes so rarely are. But I had known that voice since I was in diapers; Clay was here.

I tiptoed down the hall and stopped outside the women's room, which should have been abandoned; all the bridesmaids were to wait downstairs with us men. Clay spoke to someone in a hushed whisper. It wasn't difficult to guess who.

"We'll run away together. Just don't go up there. You don't have to do this. We can make this work. Just tell him you don't want to do this."

I loved Clay—I really did, and to this day, he remains the best friend I've ever had—but there are few things in the world I find stupider than men trying to steal women away on their wedding day. There are a lot of good reasons to get married and even more bad ones, but chances are, if there's less than a half hour until you walk down the aisle, you're probably fairly confident about what you're doing, cold feet or not. Every time Rylie had picked out napkins, chosen songs for her wedding playlist, or sampled a wedding cake, she'd had the time to pick between Todney and Clay, and, well, it was Todney wearing the tux.

But I didn't hear anyone arguing.

"I love you," Clay said.

I crept closer to the door, careful to stay out of view but was able to give myself just a fraction of a glimpse.

Rylie's eyes focused on the ground; Clay hovered over her. He took a step forward, so there was barely any space between them at all. "I love you. If you love me at all anymore, please, don't do this, Rylie."

She let out a sob just as the church bells began to ring. It was time.

I rushed down to the main room of the church and up to the altar. Todney smiled as I stood next to him. His brow was sweating quite a lot, and his hands shook through the pockets of his dress pants.

"Did you see her?" he whispered. "Does she look happy?"

I nodded, thinking, *what I could see of her around Clay's back looked nice.*

In front of us sat a sea of people, dressed in their best but smiling and talking to one another—such a sharp contrast to the funeral, my last big public event. From black clothes to those in every shade of the rainbow imaginable, from sobbing to crying, and the only tears here were from Rylie and Todney's mothers, and even these, I expected, were tears of joy. An avalanche of emotions rushed through me all at once—the unfairness that Chris couldn't be here, the confusion over life's intermingling good and bad, that unbearable grief that always seemed to sit at the back of my gut—and all at the same time, this overwhelming joy and hope that Rylie would walk down that aisle after all. And the fear that she wouldn't.

It was a confusing thing, rooting against my best friend, and the line between loyalty and right is thin, I'm sure, but I still held out hope for Todney. Because as certain as I was that Chris had made me happy, I was sure that Rylie could never do the same for Clay. A heart already taken is not one worth latching onto, and I'd seen the way Rylie looked at Todney in a way she had *never* looked at Clay. Maybe the heart really was blind, and maybe Clay was too in love to see it the way I did, but I *knew*. And I was terrified.

Maybe there was a reason the God of the Old Testament was so adamant against knowledge. It kind of sucked.

My sister was the last to come down the aisle—after Todney's sister and a few of Rylie's high school acquaintances. She looked beautiful—older than I'd ever realized, more confident than I'd ever given her credit for. With her chin up, her shoulders back, and her dress just brushing against the floor, she walked the length of the room and came to stand across from me: the maid of honor with her business face on. At sixteen years old, she looked older than I knew I'd ever be.

The music—the bridal music for which I'd never known the name of and still didn't care to—then filled the room, and everyone rose to their feet. I'd thought weddings in the real world would somehow be different than what you see on TV, but as it turns out, it's exactly the same: the mother of the bride sobs in the front row, the father sheds a few tears because of stuffy American gender expectations, the bride looks beautiful, and the camera goes off a good thousand times. And Rylie walked and walked and walked down the aisle, and I wanted to be awed and stunned and filled with joy at how beautiful she looked, but Rylie always looked beautiful; now she just looked beautiful in white.

There was no Clay latched onto her hip, at least, and as she reached the altar, she joined hands with Todney and beamed this genuine, face-splitting, lovestruck grin. An Oscar winner if it was a lie.

Everyone sat down, and the priest cleared his throat as he propped open his Bible. He scanned the crowd far too slowly, lingering on a few people here and there as though sniffing out the sinners from the righteous.

"Dearly beloved," he said, equally as slow, "We are gathered here today, in the sight of God and in the presence of these witnesses, to join together this man and this woman in holy matrimony."

This went on for a while—the general speech mixed with passages from the Bible and different poems Rylie and Todney had selected—your basic Shakespearean sonnets mixed in with a little Doctor Seuss: that we were all a little weird, and that love was just about finding someone whose weird was compatible with yours.

Then the priest said, "If any here can show just cause why they may not lawfully be joined together, let them speak now, or else hereafter forever hold their peace."

And then everything exploded.

Clay jumped up from the back row of seats where I could only assume he'd been hiding, and threw his hands over his head, yelling "I object!"

while he rushed down the aisle. He was dressed in a ratty old pair of jeans and a T-shirt, and even from all the way up at the altar, I recognized the all-too-familiar red gloss of his drunken eyes.

For one terrible second, I thought Rylie would run to him, rush down from the altar and throw herself—gown and all—into his arms. Todney would be alone. All the money, all the time, all the promises that had led up to this day would be a waste.

And Rylie *did* step off the altar, and she *did* run to Clay, but when she reached him, it was not to kiss or embrace him, but to grab him by his collar and drag him from the church.

In a movie, I think it would have been funny; in real life, it was nerve-racking.

We—we being the guests and the horrified-looking bridesmaids and Rylie's father ranting in Italian—were left in a strange sort of limbo, no one talking, everyone staring at everyone else, and everyone who thought anything like me straining to hear what was happening outside. I caught snippets that sounded something like "can't" and "shouldn't" and "thinking" but not nearly enough to string together a proper sentence. And then Rylie came back, fixing her hair with one hand, holding her train with the other, and rushed up the aisle.

She stopped in front of Todney and cleared her throat. "Where were we?"

RYLIE GRAHAM AND Todney Wright were married on a sunny August afternoon in a church just two hours outside of my hometown. When they kissed, it was with a perfect mix of class and romance, and as they walked down the aisle hand-in-hand, now Mr. and Mrs. Wright, everyone rose to their feet and clapped louder than anything I'd ever heard. Apart from a tiny hiccup named Clay Ortiz, it was a perfect day and a perfect wedding for a perfect couple.

The reception was not nearly as respectable.

Despite the fact that Rylie's parents were just across the room, despite the fact that Rylie and most of her bridesmaids were not yet twenty-one, the open bar received more traffic that night from the bride than anyone else. I.D.s, it suffices to say, were not checked.

As I ordered a Sprite—*just* a Sprite—I noticed Clay standing on the beach, still in sight of the venue. Images of him jumping into the ocean, of Chris sitting alone on the shore, of his false knee nudging my own before I could ever call him mine, stumbled around my very sober mind. Drink in hand, I left the ballroom and marched to the shore.

"Hey," I greeted as I sauntered up beside my best friend—a title that was lacking as of late.

Clay glanced over his shoulder and smiled halfheartedly. It seemed he was out of practice. "Hey. Shouldn't you be in there?" He pointed a thumb toward the dance floor where music, lights, and laughter spilled out and then were captured by the wind.

I shrugged. "I should. I'm working on my inner rebel." I stripped off my suit jacket and set it over a bush before taking a seat in the sand. Clay followed, plopping down straight onto his jean-covered ass, and let out a long, breathy sigh.

Ahead of us, the sun was just beginning to set beyond the horizon, strips of orange and pink and yellow streaking across the ocean water, lighting up the world from the sand to the horizon. The air was cool, but not cold, and everything—the birds, the crickets, the crabs climbing up the shore—was oddly still. It really was a beautiful night, which struck me as too good to be true, that this supposedly perfect day of Rylie and Todney's life was supported even by the weather. Nothing, not even the man upstairs, wanted to interrupt. Perhaps it was all the good karma they'd earned from the tragedies of the summer, or maybe they were just better people than Clay and I would ever be.

"She said she was my prize," Clay said. "That I needed something to fix my life. Something to aim for...or something. And that I'd picked her." He plucked at the edges of his jeans, his once perfectly manicured fingernails catching on the loose threads. "She said I needed to clean up and figure out my life, but not because I thought I'd win her in the end. She said she wants to be someone's partner, not their reward." His lips pressed together—chapped and bleeding in one corner—while his hair clung to his forehead, not its usual clean, styled self. This was Clay in pieces.

I reached out for his shoulder and squeezed. "Is it true?"

He nodded. "I think so. I thought..." He pushed back his hair, smiled a bit, then let it all fall away as he sighed once more. Clay revealed, Clay vulnerable, was a truly mesmerizing sight, and I didn't dare blink, didn't dare breathe just in case I'd never see it again. Twice that summer, I'd seen the mannequin move, and I feared the moment he'd go still again.

"I was happy when I was with her. I just thought... I thought I could be happy again."

"I think we're in charge of our own happiness," I said, which was something Chris had taught me, that I couldn't depend on him to make me happy any more than a wedding could depend on the sky to give it good weather; some things just worked out, and some didn't. Sometimes the boy of your dreams died after just a short few months, and sometimes the sun shone all day just when you needed it; life was a gamble. "Maybe life isn't about finding someone. I mean, I know that's what all the songs are about and the movies are about. Everything is romance. But maybe it's bullshit. Maybe we just need us."

Clay kicked a clump of sand with his tennis shoe, sending a seashell flying off into the distance. The sun had set by then, replaced by a full moon that was almost just as bright. Tonight would be the sort of night Rylie and Todney would tell to their grandkids and their great-grandkids, and everyone would guess that they had made it up.

"I'm not that good at being by myself," Clay said.

"Me either," I said, thinking of all the boys I'd watched come into my bed at night and leave in the morning. I'd never liked being in company—had always pushed people away if they stayed too long—but I hated being alone even more. "Nothing lasts," I said after a while. I picked up a handful of sand and watched all the little grains slip through my fingers. "I think maybe that's the way it's supposed to be. That you get these great things only while they're great, and then you move on. You and Rylie had your time, and now it's over. And maybe Chris and I could have had a longer time, but maybe it would have ended too. We could have had a bad breakup or something. I'm never going to know."

"Love rushed isn't love at all," Clay said. "I read that somewhere once. It's like the Rose and Jack effect or something."

"Titanic?"

Clay nodded. "Like how they thought they were so in love because they had a wild couple of days and died in the middle of it. It ups the stakes. Like being rushed makes you fall harder or something. I don't think it's true, though. I think he really loved you." He looked over, his eyes still glossy, his hands still shaking. "And I think you really loved him."

"I think you're right."

"You know..." Clay said after a while. "You know it's not your fault, right? What happened with Nathan? What happened to Chris?"

"I know," I said. And I did.

"Some fucked-up stuff has happened in this town, but it's a good place. I know you think it's cursed or something, but it's still home."

"I know."

"Next time you leave, try to come back, okay?"

"I will."

We sat in silence then, staring out at the waves receding and rushing back in, over and over, and I thought of what an easy metaphor it was: the flow of life, the good and the bad. But maybe, just maybe, my English teachers were wrong, and metaphors were bullshit, and maybe life just was. No secret meanings, no deeper lessons. Good things happen, and then bad things happen, and everything evens out in the end because those are the laws of nature, and everything—even the world itself—is a being of habit.

"I have to go back," I said. "I'm sort of the best man. I think I have to give a speech."

Clay laughed. "Probably. It's a pretty big part of the job description. Any idea what you're going to say?"

"Something about everlasting love and dedication?"

"Figures." Clay lay back, instantly filling his hair with sand. "You still going to be my best man?"

"You ever going to get married?"

"I'll try."

I flicked a bit of sand onto his shirt and then stood up, grabbing my suit jacket and laying it over him like a blanket. "Don't drink, okay? Please. Just go home. Please."

He nodded. His eyelids flickered, too heavy for his face, and then he gave me the thumbs-up while he closed his eyes and exhaled into the wind. "Have fun. Dance with her for me, will you?"

I said I would, and then, waving, walked back to the wedding venue.

No one missed me, of course—there was too much booze and music for that—but as I moved to my dinner table, Todney rushed over and wrapped a drunken arm around my shoulder. I half wondered if he was really drunk, or just drunk on love, and if there really was a difference at all.

I smiled and looked up at him, suddenly wishing I was a bit taller. "You having fun?"

He nodded. "It's speech time. You ready?"

I nodded. I cracked my knuckles and my neck and headed to the front of the room. Beyond me, Frankie and Sharon danced together out of tune, laughing and waving at my parents' table; behind them, Rylie swayed on the dance floor with one of her aunts, giggling as her hair came undone.

I cleared my throat. I was a whole bundle of negative personality traits, I know, but a loser was not one of them, and if the game was speech-giving, then I was prepared to play it to the death.

Frankie went first, giving her maid of honor speech with teary eyes and open arms. She spoke of meeting Rylie the first night I invited her over for dinner, of always being the "little sister" and having to fight her way toward friendship, how it was worth it in the end. She spoke of prom, of Rylie coming over to do her hair and provide "words of wisdom," of late nights talking on the phone, and of how glad she was that Rylie had found Todney—the only other person in the world she could imagine taking care of the older sister she never had.

Rylie was crying by then, and even Todney—drunk as he was—had tears in his eyes. I couldn't imagine why when weddings were the happiest of social gatherings, a celebration of life and love and all the things in the world that are supposed to make people *smile*, not cry. Frankie was not saying goodbye to her sister—to *my* friend—not burying her six feet underground or scattering her ashes. And though I knew that the tears were ones of joy, I couldn't understand that either. We didn't bleed when we weren't hurt.

My parents clapped the loudest after Frankie's speech, and she returned to her seat beside them while the rest of the room cheered wildly and Rylie beamed—the queen of the party.

When it came to my turn, I stood in front of my chair and raised my glass—filled with sparkling apple cider, because at least for now, the twenty-one-and-overs were watching. I smiled and tried not to focus on any of the faces, just on the scene as a whole: the glittering chandelier, the flowers on every table, that one empty seat at the back of the room where Chris should have sat, and for the briefest of moments, I saw him grinning back at me.

"A good friend once told me that humans are too emotionally evolved to need binding contracts to motivate love," I said. "Weddings, according to him, were the extra—the celebration and not the promise. Because you don't need a license or a legal contract to tell you that you're in love and to stay that way. Our hearts do that for us.

"I'm not very good at speeches, and I'm really not so good at love either, but I do know this: when Rylie and Todney are in the same room, that contract is with them, and I think it always has been. They're not going to be together for the rest of their lives because this wedding was beautiful—which it was—or because Rylie had the best dress—which she did. But because when they said 'I love you' to each other, everyone who heard it knew they meant every syllable." I glanced at my parents, center stage and holding hands—my father crying, my mother grinning—and at Rylie's parents, who hadn't stopped crying for hours now. The room was filled with couples: grandparents who had made the fifty-year mark, and cousins who were having their first child, and Rylie's friend from camp who had brought her Canadian boyfriend as her plus one.

If ever love was in the air, it was now, but I thought the metaphor was lacking somewhat: if I'd learned anything, it was that love was not a particle that drifted in like a virus, ready to be caught at any time. Love was personal, a thing that grew inside you if you let it. And I might not have had a plus-one by my side now, might not have had a hand to hold, but damn it all if I hadn't let love come anyway.

"I've had the lucky chance to be friends with both the bride and groom, and though I've known Rylie a little longer, Todney was never a hard guy to figure out. He's brave, he's loyal, and if he's half as good a friend to Rylie as he was to Chris..." At his name, a few people smiled, but not nearly as many as I would have liked. "Then he's going to be an incredible husband. I've never been happier for anyone. To Mr. and Mrs. Wright!"

I raised my glass higher, matching the cheers around the room, and then I drank down my cider in one gulp, thinking that if speeches were a game, then I might not have won, but at least Chris would have liked it.

Twenty

WE DUCKED OUT of the reception early. I was starting to think that we were incapable of seeing anything through—always ditching school, always leaving the party early. There had to be something wrong with the bride and groom running out on their own wedding, but there were more important things to be done where we were going.

Ten miles gone, all huddled together in the honeymoon limo with our nice clothes still on, Rylie said, "So let's do this again next year?"

"Who you marrying next year?" I asked.

"I don't know," she said. "Life?"

"Please don't ever be a poet," Frankie said, and Rylie kicked her, laughing.

She laid her head back against Todney's shoulder and said, "I'm serious. Today was perfect. And we were all together. Even Lucas." She reached out for my hand.

I took it but not without rolling my eyes first. "Thanks."

"Next year you can get married." Rylie pointed at Frankie, and I tried not to choke on my own tongue. "Okay maybe in a couple years," Rylie amended.

While they talked, fantasizing about what the next wedding would be like and who they'd invite, I drifted off to sleep and dreamed I was being chased by a duck with a bear's head. I'd learned in one of my G.E. classes—an unfortunate requirement, if you ask me—that dreams can be interpreted to understand your psychological state or whatever, but I was pretty sure this one was just a case of poor imagination.

I woke up covering my head and yelling, "Don't eat me!" while everyone in the car laughed.

"Get up, nerd," said Frankie; she pinched my ankle through my dress pants. "We're here."

NATHAN WAS SITTING up in bed, his hair recently combed, his shirt changed, and his eyes blank. His gaze roamed around the room, focusing on each of us for a split second before drifting away again. There was no recognition in his gaze, no familiarity, but the doctors kept saying that would change. I don't know the statistics or anything, but I'd guess that doctors are right about 80 percent of the time, and so we had a pretty good chance.

I pulled up a chair, sat down next to his bed, and propped up my feet on the metal bar that was meant to lift or drop the whole thing.

"Hey, buddy," I said, and though Nathan didn't say anything, didn't even look my way, I could tell he had heard by the way he blinked. You took what you could get in life, and all we had now were twitches.

Rylie, out of her gown now and dressed in a beautiful and completely too long blue dress, kicked off her heels and curled up on the edge of Nathan's bed.

"I'm married now." She showed him the ring. She told him about the ceremony, about how their first song had been a Beatles tune, and how she'd gotten cake in her eye when Todney had smashed it into her face. She showed Nathan all the pictures she'd taken on her phone—because it took too long to see if the photographer was worth his cost, she said— and then she gave him a foot massage, which she said was good for his circulation.

I don't know a lot about medicine or really science at all, but I know there's a big difference between asleep and awake, and Nathan was lost somewhere in between. He watched Rylie speak, blinked occasionally, and when she was all done, he said simply, "hi"—the only word I'd heard from him in over a year. It wasn't much to speak of, but it was crazy just how reassuring that one little word really was. Because dead people didn't say hi. I would know.

I'd like to have said that Nathan fully woke up then, that in the spirit of matrimony and all the good things that day had brought, he smiled at us and we had a good talk about everything he'd missed. But he didn't. For an hour and a half, he stared at us with the blank-eyed look of a lost child, and when we left, the doctor smiled and asked us if we'd noticed all the great progress he was making. I said yes, if only because it made it easier to convince myself.

On the way out of the room, Nathan said, "Bye."

IT WAS HOTTER in town than at the reception, and once outside the walls of the hospital, we shed our dress coats and used them as single-serving picnic blankets for sitting in the park. Todney brought out a few plates of cake from the back of the car and passed them around with the expensive silverware we'd stolen from the venue. We all dug in, and for a while, the world was quiet.

By the time Todney spoke, I had already finished half my slice—strawberry cake with purple frosting of the unknown variety.

"Are you going to leave when the summer's over?" he asked.

Summer was over in ten days. Half my room was already packed. I nodded. "Yeah. School starts. I've gotta."

Rylie groaned. "So it's back to radio silence from Lucas Burke."

For a small moment, a moment where the lump in my throat that Chris had left seemed too big to swallow and Nathan's silence was deafening, I thought about agreeing. God knows it would have been easier. But there were bruises on my soles from running so long, and this was the finish line.

I shook my head. "You'll hear from me. But be careful what you wish for."

Rylie beamed. "I am more than prepared for the consequences." Her dress got caught in the breeze and folded up around her thighs; she giggled as she pulled it down. "I've never been this happy. Ever. I hope Heaven is like this. That Chris is happy all the time. What do you think it's like? Do you think he's swimming? In a big heaven-sized pool?" She rolled over so she was lying on her stomach, her chin rested against Todney's thigh. "Or he's just dead," she said. "He's probably just dead."

"That's not very Catholic of you," said Frankie. "Shouldn't we be praying for him to reach the next level of the afterlife or something?"

Rylie rolled her eyes. "I'm not Mormon."

"I don't think that's Mormon either." Todney finished his last bite of cake before collecting all our plates into one neat pile, the forks crossed over the top. He placed a rock on top to hold it all down against the wind, as though a bit of litter might actually make a difference in our crapsicle of a town. I'm all for saving the world, but some things are just pointless.

Rylie reached for her purse and pulled out a bottle of vodka. "Snagged it from the open bar," she said. She took a sip and then passed it Todney.

When it came my way, I took a rather generous gulp. I hissed as it burned the back of my throat. It tasted like whipped cream on fire.

A part of me—the part that would be forever trying not to cry, not to think of Chris—will always feel guilty for it, but lying out in the park with my friends that night was one of the best nights of my life. The moon was just right to light up the sky, the breeze felt great on the back of my neck, but all at the same time, I was acutely aware that my year of mourning wasn't up—not by a long shot, not even close. My life was all tangled up in the good and the bad, but maybe that was normal. Maybe that's just what life was.

When the sun started to rise above the run-down smoke shop across the street, we stumbled to our feet and hugged like it would be years before we saw each other. And maybe it would be. Rylie and Todney would prepare for their honeymoon, would leave, and Frankie would go back to school just like me. Maybe we'd keep in touch, maybe next summer would be better. Maybe, maybe, maybe.

"I'm really glad it was you," Todney said to me before he left. I didn't know what that meant, but I nodded anyway, trying to remember what it was like to be the lucky one.

7 DAYS AFTER

The next week—and the last—of my summer vacation was a quiet one: no Clay plotting his lover's takeover, no Rylie calling to ask about table settings, no Chris knocking on my door just to talk. Two days before I was set to leave for the city, Clay came over to watch a movie. But because Sharon had never really cared for our plans, he ended up sitting at the table playing "interrogation" with her instead, while across the room, my parents sat engaged in a life or death round of Scrabble. Frankie sat at the foot of the couch, a book in one hand, her phone in the other. My mom's latest dessert surprise baked in the kitchen and filled the whole house with the smell of cinnamon.

As far as family nights go, it wasn't too shabby. I sat in the chair closest to the kitchen, a pad of paper propped up on my knee and a pen between my teeth. I'd written a lot of essays in my life, too many half-assed blurbs about the American Revolution and how to properly eat a meal in ancient Greece, but in my whole nineteen years of life, this list was by far the hardest.

I was only on number two when Sharon declared a tea break to go "potty," and on her way back, crawled into my lap.

"What are you writing?" she asked.

I thought of all the euphemisms I'd ever been taught in my life and settled with, "Things I want to do soon," rather than "Things I Want To Do Before I Die." "It's called a Bucket List," I explained. "It's to remind you of all your goals and stuff. So you live a really full life. My friend Chris had one, and he didn't get to finish it, so I thought I'd do it for him."

"Why didn't he finish it?" she asked.

"He got busy." Dying. Or passed away, I reminded myself. Was in a better place now. Was sitting with God. Blah, blah, blah. All the prettiest names in the world never did seem to make it any easier. But kids didn't know that, not yet. One day, Sharon would grow up and learn that there were as many bad things in the world as there were good. But it was a hard enough job for an adult to accomplish, let alone a seven-year-old.

"What's on your list?" she asked.

I read it off from the beginning. Number one: learn to speak French (at least half-assed fluently, though I left that particular bit out while reading aloud); number two: come home more often.

"Number three, watch movies with Sharon!" my sister squealed, and I wrote it down underneath.

"Number four," said Clay. "Make a bed in your dorm room this time so I can come visit. I'm not sleeping on the ground." He sat down on the arm of my chair and winked. I rolled my eyes but added it to the list all the same. I could see it already: Clay and me in the big city, trying to find anywhere that sold nonalcoholic beer, Clay hitting on every woman he could find, and maybe if I ever got the nerve again, me on every guy. It had been a long time since we'd been each other's co-wingmen.

"Number five, get better at video games," Anthony said as he appeared on my left-hand side. He jogged past and plugged our nearly ten-year-old video game console into the television. I made number six to buy my family a new one the first chance I got—granted I ever got a job.

At that moment, my mom screamed from the kitchen, "I win! I win! That is not a word, Tim, don't you dare try to cheat!" then turned to stare at us kids, a wicked grin taking over her face. "If you want that list complete, I'd put beat your mother at Scrabble, though I doubt it will ever happen."

Clay burst into laughter. "Your mom is still my favorite. No offense."

WE ATE APPLE tarts in the living room, all gathered around the TV to watch Anthony rescue the princess from the terrible castle. The game was vaguely sexist with a poorly dressed woman yelling for help while her brave and overly muscled savior rode up the steps on a white horse, but we had fun sending the knight in all the wrong directions.

I was on my second tart when my cell phone rang. "Hey, I'm outside. You got a minute?" asked Rylie. "I have a box of Chris's old things I thought you might like."

I was outside before I could even think to answer.

Rylie and Todney were both dressed in their sweatpants and T-shirts, a butt-load of suitcases and purses stuffed into the backseat of the car. While Todney waited in the front seat, Rylie leaned against the passenger side, a smile on her lips and a small microwave-sized box in her hands.

"When we were packing for the honeymoon, we found these. He didn't leave much but..." She shrugged and handed over the box. "Here."

I hugged her with the box pressed between us like an awkward, angular pregnant stomach. She laughed, a watery note to her voice, and then kissed my cheek and slid back into the car.

"We've got a flight to catch," she said. She blew kisses out the window, squeezed Todney's hand and then, as they drove away, watched me become a dot in her rearview mirror, that smile never leaving her crimson lips.

Back inside, Clay was busy making up princess names with my siblings, so no one noticed when I slipped up to my room, box in hand. It was a pretty crappy old thing, truth be told, like Todney and Rylie had pulled it from the bottom of the dirtiest junkyard—ripped on most sides with different taped signs advertising what had once been inside: wineglasses, Christmas stockings, clothes. And now: Chris. But despite its outward appearance, it really did feel a lot like Christmas morning, like this *was* the stocking, and I was seconds away from learning every important thing I hadn't known I didn't know.

The box was only half-full, and I felt it—not in the weight, but in the heart-wrenching moment when I pulled up the cardboard and found just a handful of objects. Two diving metals, a couple of books, a "How To Speak French" CD, a handful of pictures, and a folded-up scrap of paper. I grabbed the pictures. The first was of Chris and a man I could only assume was his father because they shared the same bright eyes and too-wide smile. They looked happy, if only because a picture records such a small indefinable part of life. For all I knew, they were arguing a moment before; for all I knew, his father was still as horrible and cruel as I'd always imagined him to be. Or maybe he'd been kind once upon a time. I'd never know, and somehow I found that it didn't matter; Chris was still gone, and his father still hadn't shown up to say goodbye. I wasn't even sure if he knew his son had passed.

I pushed the picture away and grabbed the next one—a portrait of Chris and me. The one Rylie had taken for us. The same one I had a copy of tucked under my bed along with the shattered glass of a frame I'd broken. The edges were worn and ripped, like maybe they'd been held too many times, and something burst in my chest that was halfway toward relief. I pocketed the picture and scanned through the rest— Chris and a friend I'd never seen before, never even heard him talk about, standing with their arms around each other, cheering after a swim meet; Chris and Todney smiling in the hospital; Chris kissing the cheek of a woman who must have been his mother.

After piling the pictures onto my desk, I reached for the note and unfolded it slowly, careful not to rip or wrinkle anywhere that wasn't already ripped or wrinkled; as it was, the paper appeared to have been set through a wash cycle on high. At the top, written in Chris's messy, endlessly curving handwriting were the words: Bucket List. The numbers were listed in reverse.

15. ~~perfect an arm-stand dive.~~

14. ~~dress all of mrs. richards' garden gnomes in american doll dresses~~

13. ~~steal a yield sign~~

12. jump off pier 39

11. hike mount fiji

10. streak at a raider's game!!!

9. ~~streak~~

8. ~~see that weird big ball of yarn on the highway~~

7. talk to dad

6. go to france

5. spend the night in alcatraz

4. see Todney get married

3. ~~cook an egg on the blacktop~~

2. ~~get Lucas to talk~~

1. ~~not die so Lucas doesn't have to be alone~~ Lucas will be fine. just make sure he believes it

The last line was marked with eraser shavings and smudges, so faded now that I was sure it had been written and rewritten a dozen times. I'd never thought a lot about how I'd be remembered, had never stayed awake wondering who would really miss me when I was gone, but the significance of being mentioned in Chris's Bucket List was not lost on me. Of all the wide expanses of all the crazy ideas in the world, I had made it on the list. The thirteen great wonders of Chris' life, and then two of little ol' me.

Downstairs, the house was filled with the sound of my siblings laughing, Clay yelling something about cheating, and my parents bickering about the tarts. My home filled with so much life that it made my chest ache, something I didn't even know I was capable of a few weeks ago. I still didn't know if feeling was good or bad, and I was sure I'd never find out, but of this I was sure: not a single cell in my body regretted it. And I had Chris to thank for that.

It was clear to me now that he was not meant to save my life, that he was not here to give me purpose or to teach a lesson, but that he had reminded me what it was like to be happy, and at the end of the day, that was something. Maybe that was everything.

I folded up the list and set it on my desk beside the pictures; I set my own list next to it. Maybe one day, if life allowed, I'd finish them both. If life had taught me anything, it was that it didn't play by the rules. The chances of me finishing everything in life that I set out to were close to none, but maybe that was okay. Maybe the point wasn't to finish. Maybe it was just to start.

I picked up a pen and grabbed my list again, quickly scribbling down a new first to-do item.

Number one now read: *Finish this list.*

About the Author

A.N. Casey graduated from the University of San Francisco in 2016 with a Bachelor's in Creative Writing. His short stories and essays have been published in the Indiana Review, Steam Ticket Literary Magazine, and Writing for a Real World. He can be found on twitter at @an_casey or at his blog www.ancwritingresources.tumblr.com

Also Available from NineStar Press

www.ninestarpress.com